Map of the prehistoric lands west of the Mississippi River in the 1500s.

The Dream

I was at peace, wandering a great valley with orchards, fields of corn and beans, and herds of elk and buffalo. Over the ridge, the sky grew dark. Uneasiness filled me as I climbed. I found lodges burned and crumbling, bodies of mothers and their children, men with their wives, and animals of all kinds. In every direction, fire smoldered and flesh rotted.

Calling for my grandfather, I ran through the village to the top of the temple mound. I could see the land on all sides. The orchard, the fields, the herds were all gone. Despair weakened my legs. Anguish weighted me to the ground. Feeling the pain of the land and its people, I closed my eyes, hid my face, and wept.

My cries echoed back with the sounds of danger. A brown bear charged toward me. In a moment, I regained my strength. Panic pushed me to my feet. Fear ran me to the edge of the mound.

I felt her breath. She bit at my heels as if it were a game. And when I slowed, she struck me with one blow that ripped away my arm. The giant beast held my arm above her head and said, "I, Brown Mother Bear, wish to know what you will give for this."

I had nothing, less than nothing. I stood without my arm, naked before the Great Brown Bear. "I am just a child and have nothing to give."

She roared, "Not true. You are an old woman, and you have much wisdom. Give your stories to the ones who have not heard. Become the storyteller your people need."

"What stories will I tell?" I asked.

She lifted her head and moaned out a crying song. Then she dropped to all fours and pressed her nose to my face. "Give to your people, or they will lose more than an arm."

Great Brown Mother Bear reared up once more. So tall, she blocked the sun, the moon, and the stars until all around me appeared black, black as eyes shut.

Manaha, Mother-of-None

Dedicated to:

Sandra Taylor Smith: *my inspiration, my joy, my wife, and my friend.*

Laura Lou Wilson, *my foundation.*

In Memory of:

Lewis Earl Smith, *my persistence and patience.*

My sincerest appreciation is offered to all who read, commented, and encouraged; especially, the creative community of talented and good-hearted writers at Backspace, including J. H. Bográn, who assisted with the Spanish translations. The inspiration, wisdom, and kindness of Bonnie Turner, Karen Dionne, and Christopher Graham played an important role in the final phase of this publication.

A special thanks go to Judith Henry Wall and to three dedicated editors, Holly Hollan, Arlene Uslander, and Arlene Robinson for their insight and contributions. Throughout the writing of this novel, the music of John Two-Hawks provided a subliminal sub text.

Cover Design by <u>Littera Book Designs</u>

Storykeeper

By

Daniel A. Smith

MMXII
ISBN-13: 978-1466212978
ISBN-10: 1466212977

Table of Contents

June 18, 1541, the first recorded Europeans crossed the Mississippi River into the densely populated land of Nine-Rivers Valley. Generations of sad winters have passed. It is now early summer in the southern foothills of the Ozark Mountains.

Storykeeper

Chapter 1

With every dream, she knew it was coming, but this time that made little difference. Manaha ran as fast as she had ever run. The ground shook as the lumbering rage closed in. A low growl swelled to a thundering roar, echoing on all sides.

Hot breath burned the back of her legs. She pushed herself harder. Jagged teeth tore across her heel. She pulled away, but only for a moment. Claws like knives sliced her shoulder and spun her around. One swipe and the giant beast ripped away her arm.

Manaha shuddered awake. The sounds around her were all familiar: the hiss of a pitch-pine fire, the soft song of others sleeping, and the call of night's creatures outside the village-lodge. Wet with sweat, she threw back the bedcover and tried to sit up. She had grown accustomed to waking with stiffness. This was more—her arm would not move. Cradling it like a baby, she

hobbled to the small fire in the center of the floor.

Four others without a clan slept on the benches lining the circular walls. Manaha carefully surrounded the flame with some kindling. It was summer, but she felt chilled.

Most of her life she had dreamed of a brown bear chasing her. Sometimes she ran fast. Other times she could hardly move. Even so, the bear had never caught her—until tonight.

As the first morning light slid through the only door, Manaha stood, crossed her arms, bad over good, and crept out. She hurried around the plaza, following a wide, dusty path along the steep bank of the creek to the far side of the growing fields.

Over the short stalks of corn, whiffs of smoke from the nine lodges of her small village rose to the brightening sky. She tested her arm again. Nothing. *What will happen when they find out about my arm?* No matter how the others would react, she knew she had to tell the tribe about her dream.

That evening, she gathered with the others around the square-ground west of the plaza. In the warm months, the sunken clay-packed clearing, enclosed by four open-front sheds, served as the village council site. It once was a place of stories and words of wisdom. The sacred fire still burned in the center, but no one told stories anymore.

Now they gathered with a common face of despair to watch the flames consume wood like so many flickering memories. Her own memories, stirred by last night's dream, forced her to look upon her people differently.

Manaha gathered her courage and stepped from under the thick thatched roof of the Blue Lodge. She pulled the woven scarf she always wore even tighter and marched to the center of the grounds with her arms hanging as if both were the same.

Stepping inside the fire-circle, she turned toward the White Lodge. "I wish to speak to the village." She did not wait for a reply. "I must tell a dream that came to me last night."

Voices of protest from the Red Lodge clamored above the murmurs of general disapproval. Ta-kawa of the Cougar clan, the best hunter of the village, shouted the loudest. "Go back to your place, woman! You have no right to speak before the village fire."

"I must tell my dream," she said.

"No. You cannot speak here." Ta-kawa stood tall and proud of every war scar. "Tell your dream to an elder if you must."

"Hold your tongue, warrior!" Hazaar commanded. The honored elder slowly rose from his position at the center of the White Lodge. Sad eyes, set deep in his taut, weathered face, drifted from lodge to lodge.

"She will tell her dream," he said. "If it has meaning, it will be for each listener to regard or cast away, on their own."

After both men sat down, Manaha breathed deeply and spoke out in a strong voice. She told of a great peaceful valley, where she found death, annihilation, and a brown bear. She stammered as she relived the pain of losing her arm. And she repeated what the Great Brown Bear told her: *"Become the storyteller your people need, and you shall have your arm back."*

~~~

Manaha bowed her head. She could feel every eye staring at the arm hanging at her side. Murmurs swelled all about.

"There are no more brown bears," Ta-kawa shouted above all the others. "Your dream means nothing here." Manaha closed her eyes to her surroundings. After a moment, she bent over, cupped her hand, and extended her good arm to Mother Earth. Raising it to her face, she blew into her palm. Then in a sweeping circle, she cast the power of the dream to those gathered about. A second sweep circled slower, and the third silenced the last voice.

She spoke. "Grandfather told me long ago, 'a man without a story is one without a past, and a man without a past is one without wisdom.' If we do not teach the children as our elders taught us, all that has gone before will be lost."

"Teach the past?" Ta-kawa shouted. "The past should be forgotten and with it any talk of the *strangers*. The deaths and the defeat of the ancestors have no honor here."

"Listen, Ta-kawa. Listen all of you," Hazaar said. "I believe the dream is a warning."

They all turned to look at Hazaar. The elder held out his arms and opened both hands. "This was a family in Nine-Rivers Valley." Wiggling his fingers, he said, "Brothers, mothers, sisters, children—this is a family before the *strangers*."

Hazaar sadly studied each of his flexing fingers then slowly closed both fists one finger at a time except for the last one, wrinkled and bent. He held it up and turned it in front of his face. "When they left," he said, "this is all that remained of that family."

He walked the circle, pointing at each of the four sheds. "We are all that remain. Our ancestors were from different nations, but together we are the last people of Nine-Rivers Valley.

We cannot hold the gifts of our ancestors. We have lost them. We cannot visit their graves; there were none. We cannot speak their names because we have forgotten them. Stories are all we have."

~~~

Morning found Manaha gathering wood on an island in Long Creek, downstream of the village. The large raised open plot, ringed in willows, was ignored by most. She felt close to her childhood there, separated from the world by a deep channel of simple creek water.

The council made the decision late in the night that she could tell her stories, but only at a fire outside the village. A high point near the center of the island was her choice. Manaha dropped her small collection of firewood and began digging a fire pit. As she struggled, her determination of last night gave way to apprehension. _Why did I say those things in front of everyone?_

Never had she stood before the tribe, and never had her words been so eloquent. _Could the telling of the dream hold as much power as the dream itself?_

The pit dug, she picked up her axe. She crossed the creek and wandered lost in a flood of doubt. No birds sang away her troubles. No coyote howled a resolution. No eagle flew overhead to show the way.

"What did I expect?" she asked. "Why was I given the dream?"

In the time between one step and the next, her thoughts cleared. A simple realization flowed over her. *The dream came to me. I only have to believe, and like the dream, the words will come.*

Turning back toward the island, she came upon a large red oak that had been struck by lightning. Split by the force, the charred tree lay in pieces all about, but for one large splinter that stood straight and defiant in the center of the once-great tree.

As she gathered a pile of broken branches, she sensed someone watching.

"I know you are there. What do you want?" she called.

Two girls and a boy edged into the opening. They wanted to sit at her story-fire, they said, and offered to carry wood.

"I have chosen a place near the center of the island for my fire," she told them. "You may put the wood next to the pit."

The children filled their arms and hurried away.

The spirits of the past were with her. They surely had led her to this lightning tree with the proud splinter still standing tall at its center. A piece of oak stouter than lightning should offer a bright flame and lend power to the telling of many stories.

She pounded at the splinter with her dull axe. Her useless arm flopped about until she tied it to her side with leather twine from her pouch. She swung the axe until the last standing piece of the great oak fell. It was flat-sided, wide across the bottom and lighter than she had expected. She dragged it in one piece all the way to the island.

In the center of the fire pit, she placed a large slice cut from the bottom of the splinter. Everything had to be proper, just as her grandfather had shown her: each piece selected and carefully stacked. When she finished, she walked down to the creek to wash.

Children soon began to gather quietly around the unlit fire, their probing eyes watching Manaha. She did not see the boy who had helped with the firewood, but the two girls were there, smiling up at her. Manaha exhaled and turned away to Father Sun.

In the warmth of the day's last breath, Manaha caught the scent of her grandfather and knew then where to begin. With her back to the children, she prayed so all could hear:

It is not the death;
it is the sadness that stole my hopes.

It is not the misery;
it is the sadness that stole my tears.

It is not the hunger;
it is the sadness that stole my strength.

Great Spirit, hear this humble prayer;
carry away the never-ending sadness.

Manaha turned to the circle of listeners. "Some of you may have heard an elder recite that prayer to the setting sun. It speaks of a time long ago and to the loss of our ancestors."

She slowly circled the pit, lighting the kindling. Soon a fire crackled and popped. Manaha returned to the storyteller's place

as the sky smoldered in a soft purple glow behind her. In front, the fire lit young faces aglow with curiosity.

"Our people have always told stories. Telling is how the Old Ones remember, and listening is how you, the Young Ones, will learn." For a moment, the flames pulled her deep into her own youth. The children began to stir. Her voice returned, strong and determined.

"I, Manaha, shall tell the stories I lived and the ones I learned from my grandfather who witnessed the arrival and journeyed with Hernando de Soto, the one our ancestors called the *Son of the Sun.*"

Chapter 2: Island in the Sky

Manaha's childhood
Forty-nine years after "their" arrival

As a child, I lived alone with Taninto, whom I called Grandfather and who called me Nanza. One morning, late in the season of my twelfth winter, Grandfather woke me early.

"I will be gone all day," he said. "Before sunset, meet me on top of Narras."

Narras was a high, narrow ridge that stood in a crook of the winding Buffalo River on the edge of the valley we both called home.

This was a sacred place to him, but the skeleton of a long-dead mountain to me. Its soil had fallen away, exposing bony rocks to the sun and the wind. Grandfather went there often to lament and to be with the spirits of the past.

He had told me many times, "You are too young to climb the sacred mountain."

Now he had instructed me to meet him there. I knew the importance of this event. My emotions leaped from fear to hope and back again. The day lasted longer than the patience of my youth. I was at the Narras early. I walked around its base to the Buffalo River, keeping an eye on the rim for Grandfather.

From the bend in the river, it is possible to see both the north and south side of Narras. One side followed the old trail that I had just walked, and the other bordered the churning river. At the water's edge, I could see its highest point almost straight above me. More than once, I saw Grandfather standing on that ledge, but not today. I ran all the way back around to where the trail to the top of Narras started.

The beginning is not difficult. When Grandfather left me alone in the valley I had climbed the lower part several times. The roots of an old cedar tree growing into the rocks made the first steps easy and tempting. Above that, layers of rock formed natural steps worn by the wind and Grandfather.

The climb went quickly until the point where I could see no other place to grab. I tried to convince myself that I had always turned back at that point because of guilt rather than fear.

I had no reason to feel guilty now. Fear alone tested my resolve and seized me as tightly as I gripped the rock. My fingers crept across the surface as I searched for a handhold, a crack in the rock. I could not see the handhold, but I could feel its strength as I pulled myself up and found more, but none within an easy grasp. The rock face began to slope inward. Soon, I could crawl. I stood and laughed at myself for having given up in the past.

A grove of trees shared the high ground with me. Short with thick trunks, twisted but strong, they seemed as old as the mountain. Their gnarled branches forced me to stoop as I followed a well-traveled path.

A few steps into the tiny forest, the view opened to clear sky and a straight drop to the river. Wind rushing up from the blue waters below chilled my face and stole my breath. My legs buckled. Never had I witnessed a more powerful sight. I cowered back and hugged the closest tree.

Rooted to its trunk, I took in the beauty of Mother Earth. The Buffalo River snaked around hills and valleys until it stretched out of eyesight and beyond my knowledge. Off to my right, Taninto's valley, the world I did know, lay peacefully in the crease of two great mountains. The boundary between the worlds, known and unknown, was a ledge no wider than a single stride.

Across that narrow rim and up another steep climb loomed the top of Narras, Grandfather's sacred place. The path twisted and turned before me. Patches of grass grew between the rocks, but either side fell away to jagged cliffs.

A crow's caws drew my attention.

"*Haw . . . haw . . . haw,*" I called back, thrilled to be looking down on his flight as he soared over the river and disappeared into a darkening forest.

"I cannot be afraid," I said and straightened up. I let go of the last branch and focused on my next steps. Few had been taken when I heard the crow again, returning to taunt me.

Circling overhead, he called out, "*Caw, caw,* who is proud, now? Who is brave, little girl? *Caw, caw, caw.*"

I tried not to listen as he flew closer. "You are in the world of the Winged Ones now. Look up to me, the Mighty Crow. *Caw.*"

I held my arms out like a soaring bird but looked only at the path. Before I reached the other side, I stopped and gazed out over the river into the unknown from the world of the Winged Ones. It was a grand view, but brief. I lunged forward and grabbed the rock wall. I might have shown courage to the crow,

but I had proven little to myself.

My legs shook, but I could not turn back. I forced myself to reach up. Like a snail, I clung with my whole body. The crow gave one last *caw* and flew off downriver.

I pushed up and up, determined to reach the sacred grounds. At the top, I peered over. An island of rock in a lake of sky lay before me. Grandfather stood at the other end, his back to me, arms lifted. Faint sunlight glowed over everything in both worlds, and Grandfather seemed to float between the two.

Without a thought for myself, I climbed on top and walked toward him. He lowered his arms. The vision of his power faded. Fear drained the strength from my body.

The land under me was so scant that I could see death on either side. I fell to my knees and reached for all the earth I could grab.

"Nanza, look into my eyes," Grandfather said.

His voice gave me balance.

"Do not look away." He picked me up and carried me on his back down the rock wall and across the rim. He sat me down at the edge of the stunted forest, facing west. In the last light of the day, he began to sing.

I had never heard him sing before, nor had I heard the language he used. He sang to Father Sun while the yellow disk slid toward the distant mountains. Wisps of clouds drifted in the golden light like giant flames from a world on fire. I remember well what he said when he finished his song.

"My child, whom I rescued, raised, and will always cherish, you have shown great courage and strength in climbing to the top of Narras. Use that power well—hear and remember every word."

Turning from me, he said, "Time has come for the story I kept far too long."

After a painful pause, he raised his arms and said, "Let the trees and the ancient mountains be the circle of listeners and the Great Father Sun be our story-fire. May the spirits of all the wise and honorable men who sat at the fires of my youth hear these words as truth."

Chapter 3: One Slash
Grandfather's story
Forty years after "their" arrival

I, Taninto, lonely wanderer for thirty-eight winters, traveled for seven days from my valley along with my dog, provisions, and an offering. The pilgrimage took me up the White River to the Blue Spring on the edge of the Healing Mountains. Mother Earth gives forth pure water from springs all over Nine-Rivers Valley, but from these mountains flow many healing springs, each with different powers.

Blue Spring is the greatest of these. Its water flows never-ending down into the White River and on to mingle with all the rivers and streams that bless our land. The closer I came to the spring, the harder the current pushed against the canoe. The quiet comfort of tree-lined banks faded, and the sight of an open field broke the rhythm of my paddle.

Always quick to take advantage, the river forced me to the shore. Several turtles slid into the water as I pulled my canoe next to a fallen cottonwood. Though on its side, the tree still grew strong and mighty.

My dog, Chachiz, climbed onto the tree and scampered up the roots that clung to the steep riverbank. He scouted the area while I tied the canoe under a spread of limbs. I unloaded my offering and the supplies we would need for the climb over the mountain and down to the spring.

Chachiz waited at the top of the bank, ready. That was all I needed to know. I had lived alone since my seventeenth winter. Those are sad words for an old man to boast about his life. My home in a valley so far from any villages, made it easy to avoid people. Sometimes the hunger to travel—to wander over the next ridge—challenged my isolation.

Chachiz walked in front, smelling and listening with every step. My hearing was almost as sharp as his. Sharper that day were the memories of my distant childhood.

I last traveled through this land in my youth with my uncle Tecco, a Tassetti or Wise-One from the temple town of Casqui on the banks of the Little Muddy River. He brought me on his second pilgrimage to Blue Spring. I recalled those happy times with my uncle, but I could never let my thoughts turn back to Casqui. There, memories lurked, ready to snatch my spirit.

Chachiz and I traveled most of the day without seeing anything more than a few squirrels. When we came upon a path, I could hear my uncle say, "The only safe path is your own." Thorny briars scratched at both of us as we followed the overgrown path in the quiet before sunset.

The path led to a larger trail on the edge of open land. I knelt at Chachiz's side and whispered, "My friend, this must be the road to Blue Spring. Come, we will find a place where we can wait for the night." We crossed the road and climbed up through the undergrowth to a spot where I could see the road. Chachiz and I settled into the growing shadows.

As the last rays of sun lit the road, I saw a small group—two

men, three women, and two children. Judging by their brightly colored garments, they were from the Nation of Palisema, known for its dyed skins. They hurried away from the river. I soon understood their haste. Warriors painted and armed for war followed close behind.

"War is forbidden here!" I wanted to shout. All nations considered this as sacred land. Who would violate the code? The world slipped into darkness. My thoughts ran on, but I remained rooted in my own terror.

"*Ahaya . . . Ya, ya, ya, yaaaa.*" The cry hushed the night's creatures and doused my hopes.

Chachiz lunged to his feet. I grabbed him. The new songs of the evening were yelps and war cries.

Every sound of the massacre reached into our hiding place and ripped at my soul. I could do nothing. There was no way to turn that I did not hear the attack.

Then silence spread over the forest. Every creature stood still, straining to hear the next sound. Screams. It came as screams. Torture of the survivors began. I thanked the shadows that I could not see what I was forced to hear.

What could I do? I had to leave. I had no weapons. I was an old man with no strength or will for fighting. If I stayed, if I listened, those old memories would find me again and overrun my soul.

"I must go," I whispered. Pain cracked my stiff legs as I stood. "Chachiz, we must go."

I hurried through the night forest, rambling. "I must go. I must go." Louder than their screams, I said, "Chachiz, we must go!"

He did not lead, but stayed by my side. I stumbled often, cutting and bruising my arms and legs, but I could not stop. "Hurry, Chachiz. I must go."

So it went until blind haste brought us back to the trail, the most dangerous path, but the fastest way back to the canoe. I stepped onto the road and turned toward the river. Chachiz circled me and dashed out front, grinning at the sight of an old man running. My chant became our pace. "I-must-go, I-must-go, I-must-go."

We ran until the road curved out of sight around a steep hillside. Uncertain what might be around the bend, Chachiz turned toward the hill and the cover of trees. I had had enough of running through the forest and started for the open field to the left.

Chachiz hesitated a moment, then raced ahead to scout the field and disappeared among the tall weeds and morning fog. I saw him again at a distance, standing above the meadow grasses waiting for me. I crouched and crept toward him. He stood on a pile of freshly dug earth.

"Ch . . . a . . . ch . . . iz . . .," I whispered more like a sound than a name. He remained still and resolute.

"Chachiz," I said. He sat down on his back legs. I stood and walked away. He did not move. "Chachiz, we must go."

I stomped my foot. "Come, dog, come. I must go."

He lay down. Again, I edged toward the small mound, close enough this time to peer over.

A glimpse, a forgotten sense of hope to one who had seen so much tragedy, was a great surprise. Hope did not spring from the sign of life, those whiffs of breath meeting the cool morning

air. Nor had hope returned at the thought of having someone to fill my empty life.

Hope came from a smile—a child's smile. A child ill with Black Sleep, smallpox! I knew the signs well: the painful, oozing boils, the fever and confusion. The child, a girl properly wrapped in a cougar skin, lay in an open grave. She wore a copper and crystal necklace. A red-striped water bottle rested above her left shoulder, with a basket of cornmeal above her right. A child's toy bird fashioned from clay and painted blue perched above her head.

Her family must have brought her to the healing springs after she grew sick. When she did not improve, they prepared a burial site. Fear of the disease was so great that many parents refused to touch a child who died of the sickness. Her family could do nothing but place the small child in the grave and wait for her death.

An even greater fear of men had caused the loving family to abandon her. Unable to wait for her passing and unwilling to do death's deed, they left their hopes in a bundle for me to find. I did not fear her sickness. It could do me no harm, for the disease is *my* curse.

Waging a battle in my thoughts were things I must not remember, must not see, must not do—and one sick child. As I paced, she followed with tiny eyes struggling to stay open. Then I heard her voice, weak and frail, but crashing like thunder.

Terrible, choking memories bubbled up from deep inside. I fought for breath.

A small voice repeated the question. "What is your name?"

How long has it been since another person spoke to me?

"Ta . . . nin . . . to," I stuttered.

"Ta . . . nin . . . to," she repeated.

It sounded good to hear my name.

"Taninto, the Wanderer," I said.

She echoed back with even more confidence. "Taninto, the Wanderer!"

I knew then, I could not leave this child. I tried to speak, but the words lodged in my throat. I climbed over the piled earth, scooped the child from her grave, and held her close to my heart. She nuzzled her face into the hollow of my shoulder, looked up, and smiled. I had lived those miserable, lonely forty-two winters if for nothing else than this child.

"Come, Chachiz," I said as I wrapped the child in my old deerskin. "We must get her into the forest."

Before I took a step, Chachiz growled. I knew the sign and fell to my knees in the center of the grave, carrying the child gently to the earth.

I pulled Chachiz in with us then peered over the top. Through the tall grasses, I saw three warriors trotting east on the trail. Blinded by the morning sun, they might pass us by. I crouched down and listened. They ran as one, but I heard each set of feet.

When they rounded the bend, I could hear only two. Had one of the warriors stopped? Did I hear true? *There must be three*, I told myself. Chachiz told me differently. One of the warriors headed in our direction. He would find us soon.

An old man of frail spirit, my torment would be short, but Chachiz's death would be slow. I could not let that happen. Because of me, they would torture him.

What of the child? If they saw the signs of Black Sleep, they would not touch her.

I pulled my old companion close and buried my face in his fur. He sat on his back legs and licked my chin. I pointed his head to the sky.

"Spirit of my good friend, be free of this wretched world. Soar to the clouds. Lead my way as you have always done." I reached for my knife. I had no choice. Once started, I could not hesitate.

One slash. One quick slash.

Chachiz rolled his head. His eyes fixed on mine. That brief gaze has lingered for a lifetime. He fell into my arms. I fell apart, crumbling into the bottom of the grave. His blood ran down over my body as I pulled the deerskin and the child over my face. The warrior would be upon us any time.

I untied the child's cloak and slipped out her small arms. For her to live, the warrior must see her sores. I took a deep breath and whispered, "Be still, small one."

I waited . . . and hoped. I could see nothing. My nose filled with the smell of blood. How long could I endure?

The morning songbirds were interrupted by the sound of a blue jay. Even with my ears covered, I knew it was not a bird. The warrior had alerted the others to the grave. Soon I heard voices.

One yelled, "The intruders from Palisema have honored us with a sacrifice and gifts. This is truly our land."

"Aquan, do not take anything," a more powerful voice shouted.

The first warrior spoke again. "Who are you to tell me what

I can do? I helped kill the intruders from Palisema, and these skins belong to me."

"The grave is cursed. The child has the sickness. We should leave this place," the other said.

I heard movement, but I could not tell how many were leaving. My body begged for relief.

"*Ahaya . . . yaaaa.*"

"Aquan, come back," someone yelled.

He did not heed, but ran to the edge of the grave and shouted of his bravery in a flurry of war cries and boasts. "I, Aquan, great warrior of Pa-caha, fear no man. I fear no curse—"

~~~

"*Stop!*"

Chapter 4
Manaha's Journey
Ninety-four years after "their" arrival

The magical web the story and the fire had woven around the children vanished with a sudden roar.

"Stop!" Ta-kawa roared again and threw water onto the fire. It slapped the flames; in the hiss and mist, the children disappeared into the shadows.

Manaha snatched up the remains of the splinter she had cut from the lightning tree. Holding it like a staff between her and Ta-kawa, she spoke so all those in hiding could hear. "I have the right, and the guidance to tell this story and many more."

"Woman, I say you have no right to speak of the old nations. And never again say Pa-caha, never—"

Manaha cut him off. "I will hear no more." She sat down, and closed her eyes.

"The Council will deal with you." Ta-kawa shouted, disappearing as quickly as he had come.

After a time, Manaha rose. She walked to the village without ever looking back at the smoldering fire, took her bedding from the village-lodge, and returned to the island.

The story-fire flared up around its wet edges as Manaha spread out her bedding. She thought about her day. She stood on her own. Her fire had burned bright, and her words had been true. She thought of the children and their faces, and she thought of her grandfather.

Somehow, she did not feel her age or her troubles. Her prayers were short but thankful. A blanket spread on the ground was not as comfortable as her bench in the village-lodge, but she took little notice.

Manaha overslept. She sat up quickly but slowly got to her feet. Mother Earth had been hard on her. "I did not have the sounds of others to wake me." She excused herself.

A group of young children stopped their play as she approached the village. Each one stood silent, staring at her and an older boy who stood apart from the group. Manaha felt certain he had been one of her listeners. She studied his face, but he remained mute, never looking up.

A smaller boy tugged at his folded arms, pulling them apart long enough for her to see a punishment scratch. The shallow scratch hurts only a short while. Real pain came when others began to tease. The boy stood for a moment, surrounded by ridicule, before bolting.

What had he done to deserve a punishment scratch? Manaha wondered, as she left the children and walked into the village. There were no smiles from the women around the plaza—not one greeting.

She saw another child from last night. The girl clung to her mother, Asnewn, a good friend of Manaha's. Asnewn continued her work without looking up. As the girl squirmed, Manaha caught a glimpse of a scratch down her arm.

She glanced from face to face around the village plaza. Every

eye turned away. The children were punished because of her. Manaha felt the sting of her own punishment scratch, not on her arm, but across her heart.

Ta-kawa must be responsible. She marched up to his sister. "Where is he?"

"He is with the men on the square-ground planning for an early hunt."

Manaha turned to leave.

"Ta-kawa knows," his sister taunted.

Manaha spun around. "He knows what?"

"Your stories will only bring the sickness again."

"Stories are for healing and learning." Manaha moved around to the sister's down-turned face. "You know that."

She avoided Manaha's glare. "When Ta-kawa returns from this hunt, his voice will lead our village."

Manaha walked away from the troubling boast then turned toward the square-ground. *Ta-kawa's charge should not be taken lightly.* She paused near the Blue Lodge long enough to hear that Ta-kawa and most of the men of the village would be leaving soon.

After collecting the remainder of her belongings, Manaha walked proudly through the center of the plaza and back to the island. The smell of wet, charred wood welcomed her return. She sat where she had the night before and let her bundles fall. Her arms hung limp as if both were now dead.

How can I ever regain the life in my cursed arm if I cannot tell stories?

The wind, the sky, and the world of Mother Earth moved around her, but Manaha sat in opposition. After long, empty moments, her thoughts traveled back to the days spent with her grandfather. His spirit influenced every step of her life's path, good and bad. Just telling one of his stories filled her with a pride she had never known.

Manaha did not know if anyone would sit in her circle of listeners tonight, but she determined to carry on. The remains of last night's fire had to be removed before building a new one. As she pitched the wet wood to the side, something caught her eye. A speck gleamed in the blackened dirt. She rubbed the soot and dirt off the small stone to reveal a tiny arrowhead, the finest she had ever seen, crafted from pure white flint.

She rolled the sharp edges over and over in her fingers, before putting it deep into her pouch. From the same secret depth, she pulled the quartz crystal she had carried for many seasons. Holding it up, Manaha turned it in the light until its reflection twinkled. She placed it where she had found the arrowhead and filled in the pit.

The glow of Father Sun's departure surrounded Manaha as she admired her day's work: a new pit dug and a larger story-fire built. She waited, ready to light the kindling. Slowly, night settled over her, stealing her sight and hopes.

Then behind her, with a crunch of leaves, a twig snapped. She looked around the darkness but saw no one. More sounds came from all sides. Whoever they might be, they were unwilling to be seen by her or by Ta-kawa should he appear. She hurried to remove most of the bigger logs, and soon tended a smaller fire to draw her listeners in closer.

With a short prayer, she dropped three shavings from the lightning tree onto the flames. She took her place in the empty

circle and spoke out in a loud voice.

"Manaha, the rejected will finish the first story and many to come."

Chapter 5: Nanza, My Child

Grandfather's Story
Forty years after "their" arrival

Killer of friends and a friend of enemies, I cowered underneath a deerskin in a pit of death as a warrior danced around the grave. Aquan shouted and sang of his bravery. He proclaimed his part in the torture and killing of the child's family. The girl did not stir throughout his rant, but my resolve swayed as I listened.

I killed Chachiz to save a dying child and myself. I squirmed in his blood, searching for the courage to face the punishment I deserved. My hand brushed his side. I stroked his thick coat. Even in death, Chachiz gave me calm.

A different warrior yelled, "That will be an arrow you cannot retrieve."

I heard the arrow leave Aquan's bow. I heard nothing more until the crack. Pain cut through me. Chomping down on the deerskin, I fought to keep my eyes open. I prayed, *Oh, Great Spirit, guide these souls as we cross into the next world. Return peace and prosperity to all who remain upon this land.* Then I slipped into the darkness.

When my eyes opened again, I saw nothing. I felt nothing but burning guilt. Rolling my eyes in every direction, I feared that my spirit had been carried to a place of never-ending

suffering. Above and behind, a golden light rimmed an edge to the blackness. I reached for it. My arm would not move. It was numb, but I could feel a pain stabbing at my side, a dying child pressing on my chest, and a dead friend tearing at my heart.

The child moved as I pushed my hand toward the pain. I touched the sticky shaft of Aquan's arrow and flinched. My own breath cut through me like a knife. I exhaled slowly, and slid my fingers down the shaft to the arrowhead. It had not gone into my chest, but had cut a gash down my side and cracked a rib.

I eased the deerskin off my face. The late-day sun slammed my eyes shut. A blink at a time, I glimpsed the tops of the trees then the edge of the dirt piled around. I pulled myself into the light from the bottom of the grave.

Eyes forced wide, I still could not see the child, the grave, or the world that surrounded it. I saw only Chachiz and the blood-red arrow in his side. It had pierced his stomach before it had reached me. I had killed my only friend who in death saved my life.

"What have I done?" I cried. All my life, I had run from the deaths that I caused. What could I ever do that would not be stained by this deed? My movements were slow and my thoughts cloudy. I took the sleeping child and her toy bird from the grave. Before anything else, I had to honor and provide for the departed spirit of Chachiz.

I broke the arrow above his chest and pulled the shaft through the other side. I hurled both pieces toward the east, the land of the Pa-caha. Around Chachiz's body, I arranged the red-striped water bottle and three strips of deer jerky from my pouch. I laid a blanket of cut grasses over my friend then shoved in the surrounding dirt. My side stung and my heart ached with each push. I was responsible and would always be responsible for what had happened.

I stood to sing the mourners' song but stammered to silence. The words—I forgot the words. It had been so long since I had heard them, longer still since I wanted to. I could not remember. Who will teach me?

"Spirits of my people, send the sacred words. Sing the mourners' song in the rustle of the wind." The words did not come. I fell to my knees in the fresh earth and spoke to Chachiz's spirit in my own song of mourning. Those words I hold close, never to be spoken again.

I picked up the child and held her out over the grave, waiting for the wind to settle. I wanted my words not to scatter but to fall where I stood.

"Spirits of my ancestors, hear this. Chachiz's last breath gave life—my life and the life of this child. I promise to respect and protect that gift to save this child from Pa-caha warriors and the Black Sleep. By my word, it will be so."

My pains were many of the body and of the soul, but my choices were few. I strapped the child onto my back with my bundles and limped toward the road. The ache in my side eased, or I was growing accustomed to it, but I could not escape the emptiness in my heart.

Who will sing the mourners' song for me? I wondered as we crossed the field. Not a sign of anyone on the road. I glanced back a last time. No one there either. I trotted across

the road and up the hillside into a forest filled with the natural sounds of the night.

Chachiz always warned me of any danger. I had not only lost a friend; I lost a large part of my courage. Without Chachiz, I became a frightened old man. Loneliness had been a reality most of my life, but I never felt it heavier than that night.

The task of walking and running in the dark filled my head. The shadowy moon, which I kept to the right, offered little light. I rested many times that night empty in heart and mind. However the child would not let me forget her. If I stayed too long, she would begin to squirm and remind me of what I had done. She fell back to sleep as soon as I started walking. *Would that my troubles were as easily put to rest.*

As the faint glow of morning spread across the sky, the child began to twist and turn, even when we were moving. Her fitfulness grew to a moan. I knelt down and slipped the child off my back. I held her, still bundled, in my lap. Her eyes were closed and her cheeks hot to the touch. She gasped for every breath.

I untied her burial cloak. Once released, she kicked and fought. Her eyes opened wide in a frozen gaze that looked but did not see. She screamed. I tried to cover her mouth, but she twisted out of my grip and screamed louder. Her legs raced and her arms thrashed the air.

"Go away, go away!" she yelled.

I could see that she fought something unseen—not me. She scratched at my face as I pulled her in close. I forced her head to my chest to muffle the screams and spoke for the first time since leaving the grave.

"Child, you are safe. I am your friend, but your enemies are listening. You must be quiet." I repeated, "You are safe . . . you are safe," until she stopped crying.

I eased my hold on her. "Do not be afraid."

She looked up and studied my face.

"I am Taninto. Do you remember? I am your friend . . . I will protect you." I hoped she could not hear the doubt in my voice.

Doubt or not, the words seemed to comfort her. After a moment, she fell limp against my chest, sleeping as only a child can without worry.

Every nearby warrior would have heard the child's screams. I grabbed the burial cloak and slipped on my back-bundle while I glanced around for what I might be leaving behind. My head slumped over the child. "If only you were here, Chachiz, old friend."

I ran until I could no longer hold her. I laid her on the grassy bank of the stream we had just crossed and drank my fill of the sweet water. Scooping another handful, I returned to the child, who was lying on the ground, unbundled. I truly saw her for the first time. A large sore covered her left cheek. Smaller ones dotted her chest, legs, and arms. She looked so fragile.

"My child . . . that is what you are now . . . my child. I will call you Nanza."

I wiped drops of cool water across her lips. Her eyes opened. She saw me and not a vision. Still, fear crept across her face. I reached out, but she did not resist.

"Do not cry," I said. "I will take care of you, my brave child, my Nanza."

"I am afraid," she said.

"Nanza, a fever-dream frightened you, nothing more."

Her eyes fluttered.

"Now, sleep, my child," I whispered as I lashed up her burial cloak. With her on my back once again, I waded into the stream. It would take us to the river, and if I were careful, it would hide our trail. I stumbled over the rocky bottom too many times for Nanza to sleep soundly. She began to ask questions. Questions, I did not want to face. Answers, she did not need to hear.

"Hush!" I snapped.

She whimpered, "Mother . . . Mother . . . I want my mother."

I hoisted my burden, child and all higher on my back, so that her head rested on my shoulder. I looked around at the small face struggling to see mine. "Nanza, your mother and father love you very much. That, above all, you must never forget. You are ill, and it is their wish that I cure you. Now, you must do as I say. Be quiet and rest."

Her eyes closed. I continued down the stream until I noticed a rock sticking above the water with two dark spots across the top. I studied the banks on both sides while I drank from the stream. The last drops I let fall onto the rock.

Something or someone had crossed the stream. It was not an animal, no tracks on either side. A man, I was certain. More than one, I could not be sure, but only one had been clumsy enough to leave a sign of his passing.

I continued down the stream, hoping to see the river around the next turn. My side ached and my legs were tired, but I pushed on through the water, stumbling along until I finally fell. The deepening stream broke the fall. After the second time, it seemed easier to stay down. Crawling and paddling, we moved with the current. The stream grew wider and cooler. I knew the river must be close.

Nanza yelled, "Looo—," but stopped. She twisted around to me and whispered, "I saw someone."

I stood and began running.

"*Ahaya . . . yaaaa.*"

The lone war cry overtook us. Without slowing or turning around, I pulled the back-bundles and Nanza over my head. To lighten my burden, I pitched the bundles to the bank, unwrapped the child, and dropped her wet burial cloak. She held onto me as tightly as I did her.

Around the next bend, I saw the White River. Racing across the shallows, I plunged in. We were one-person, swimming with two heads above the water, looking in every direction. The mouth of the stream disappeared without a sign of any warriors. Could it be the child had seen another vision, and I had heard only the scream of an eagle?

The river widened. The cold current raced. I waded into the shallows. Nanza shook all over. I held her in one arm, and she held me with both. The rapids and the round river rocks made running difficult. I did not look up until I heard something in front of me.

A warrior stood defiant at the edge of the river. He must have known the country, left the stream, and traveled

downriver by land. I froze in the middle of a long stride. Nanza, still watching behind, had not seen him. She squirmed as I struggled to stand on the river rocks shifting beneath my feet.

"Old man," the warrior shouted.

Nanza jerked around.

"Old man!" he yelled again.

Nanza screamed and kicked, throwing me off balance.

"Behold a great warrior," he shouted. "What gifts have you brought for me?"

I turned back upriver, trying to keep my footing.

"*Ahaya . . . Ya, ya, ya, yaaaa.*" He ran at us with his war axe raised. His yelps echoed up and down the river until he sounded like a great war party.

No time to plan, no time to pray, I ran back up the rapids with Nanza hanging on. The warrior ran along the edge of the river, over the larger rocks, and through the shallow pools.

I reached deeper water and waded in. The warrior ran faster. I shifted the child to my back and dove into the river. She clutched my neck as I gasped for breath and swam for the far bank.

The war cry wavered and ceased. He had slipped in a moss-covered flood pool, falling with a crack that brought a hush.

I froze chest-deep in the running water. The whole world held its breath. The river spoke first, then the insects and birds began to sing. I turned to see the warrior on his back at the edge of a pool. His war axe lay off to one side and out of his reach.

He did not move as I crept out of the water and around to

where the axe lay. I picked up the poorly crafted weapon. For the second time in my miserable life, I held a tool for killing another man. With the child still on my back, I turned toward the warrior.

A sense of power filled me as I gripped the weapon. With each step, I raised the axe higher. My fear turned to anger, and that anger grew to a consuming rage for the evil that had killed so many of my people.

When I reached him, I no longer stooped but stood tall with both arms raised and the war axe clutched in my only hand. I swung with the strength of a wild beast and the anger from forty-two winters of guilt.

"No. Noooo!" the child screamed.

My sight cleared. I no longer saw the faces of dead and dying friends and family, only the face of a boy. Whether that or Nanza's scream diverted the axe, I do not know. The killing tool died with a shattering sound next to his head.

My whole strength and resolve had been committed to the swing. Unbalanced by the change of heart, I fell on top of the warrior. He did not move as I scrambled to my feet, and stared into the open eyes of my enemy. His young, rounded face had not begun the change to a man's. I knew then I would always remember those unseeing eyes.

A piece of the shattered axe had cut my arm. Blood ran down onto the broken handle that I gripped so tightly; I had to force my hand open to let it drop. The wooden handle floated in our mingling blood, then out into the main current and down the river. I raced against the red flow while Nanza hung on, frightened beyond speech.

The White River deepened once again, and I waded in. Over my shoulder, I could see that the boy warrior remained where he fell. In the cold river, the warmth of Nanza's fevered body felt good as she sat on my shoulders, hugging the top of my head. We swam down the river, watching for other warriors and searching for my canoe.

Fear, anger, and a promise had carried me to this point; now the river chose the path. Its power absorbed the last of my strength as it had the warrior's blood. I could no longer touch the bottom, and the banks were too muddy and steep to climb. My legs refused to move. They hung like weights while I struggled to keep the child above water. Even though I could see the fallen tree where I hid the canoe, I could find no more strength.

Only the river could save the child now. The current moved our bobbing heads toward the cottonwood so fast I feared we might be swept past it. I grabbed a branch. It bent and broke. We hit the tree hard. I pushed the child up onto the trunk.

The river pulled me down. Dragged under the tree, I turned over and around, tangled in a web of its limbs and broken branches. Panic filled me. I fought to free myself, losing all sense of direction. A ball of light rippled behind me. I turned and swam for it.

On the other side of the tree, I came up coughing and calling, "Nanza, Nanza."

Father Sun shone down on her. She was crying but safe.

"My child, crawl to the canoe," I said as soon as I reached her. I drew in a breath, full of pride. For in that moment, youth no longer felt like a memory. I bounded onto the fallen tree. But Chachiz's blanket lying at the front of the canoe reminded me of my weakness. I wrapped Nanza in his blanket. I knew he would not mind.

A younger old-man, I pushed out into the White River and began the long, peaceful journey home to my valley and my purpose.

Chapter 6

Manaha's Journey
Ninety-four years after "their" arrival

The last flames of the story-fire danced among dying embers. Manaha glanced once around the empty circle, then spoke with effort. "The fire is consumed. The story told. Sunset next, there will be another fire and more stories."

She bowed her head and closed her eyes, but strained to hear every sound from the departing listeners. In the slight evening breeze, leaves rustled off to her right. In front and behind, she heard footsteps.

Her face flushed. Her wrinkles smiled. How many there were she did not know, but she did have listeners. The telling ritual gave her peace, and having someone want to listen made it worth all her troubles.

Next morning, she woke before sunrise, determined to resume her duties in the village fields as if nothing had happened. She had a bounce in her step as she returned from her morning bath. Alone with the beginning of a new day, Manaha not only had the time, but the desire to offer a prayer.

"Great Father Sun hear the words of one so worthless. For all that you have given, for all that I have failed to receive, I can but ask for another day to try and follow the good path through the wonders of life you make possible."

It was a morning prayer her grandfather often recited. She hoped he was pleased with her telling of his story.

Manaha arrived in the fields long before the other women. Working with the soil and helping crops grow always comforted and nurtured her. She tried to use her hoe with only one good arm. The flint blade landed where it wished and the dry earth gave little.

She remembered her grandfather using that same blade. He would swing it by grabbing the handle with his good hand and bracing the end under the arm that was missing a hand. She could do the same, and soon learned to strike where she wanted with more force. If she wrapped her bad arm around the handle and held both as she swung, she felt almost whole. Rehearsing the deception, Manaha did not hear Asnewn until she stood in front of her.

"Greetings, my friend," Manaha said with a smile.

Asnewn stared at her awkward hold on the hoe. As Manaha waited for a reply, she raised the hoe higher and higher. The two locked eyes but exchanged no words.

A swift breeze followed the heavy blade as it slammed to the ground in front of Asnewn. She jumped back but said nothing. Manaha never looked up, then or ever again, at her old friend.

Her next greetings were returned with more silent rejection. She lost her desire to speak to any of them. She dropped the hoe and her effort to use it, knelt, and began scratching at the earth with a digging stick. None of the others worked close, and no one spoke to her.

Toiling in the heat and the silence, she grew only more determined. She had learned the strength of persistence from her grandfather. They were not going to chase her away. Manaha straightened her back and glared once around the field. No one returned the look.

Still, she moved as though she had an audience and, with great dignity, tied the dangling arm against her waist. Her banishment could be overcome, with hard work if necessary, but the stories could not stop. She wedged the hoe handle under her bad arm and swung her grandfather's flint blade as he had done.

"A good worker is always needed," she said loudly enough for all to hear, and swung again.

Murmurs grew from the far edges of the field and spread to those working closest to her. Soon they were talking around her as though she were a bothersome old stump that stood between them and their morning chat. Much of the discussion swirled around the wedding ceremony to take place once the hunting party returned.

The younger women giggled as they talked about the upcoming marriage of two couples. Most saw the ceremony as the long-awaited sign of growth and new birth. There had not been much to celebrate for many seasons.

Manaha paid little attention as she tried to imagine what a wedding ceremony must have been like back in her homeland of Palisema in Nine-Rivers Valley. The others talked with hope for the coming feast, and she thought of a time when the land offered abundant feasts every day.

In a fleeting moment, more a sweet sensation than a memory, she tasted *piarchi*. Her grandfather had made it on special occasions. Once her favorite food, she had not thought of it in many summers. Could she be the only one who could remember that wonderful taste?

The day's fieldwork done, the women turned to the festival preparations. Manaha had had enough of their chatter. She had her own ritual to tend. Her treatment in the field gave little hope for any new shadow listeners, but it had further sharpened her determination. She spent most of the afternoon gathering wood but used only a portion to build her third and smallest story-fire.

The day ended with a glorious sunset. Father Sun warmed her with his colors and lifted her spirit with his greatness. She thought it sad that she had watched so few sunsets. It happened every evening whether she cared to look up or not.

"The Sun, the Moon, and the Stars are the constants around which all other things change," her grandfather would say.

She had seen many changes. Even the ceremonies were different now. Rituals had been lost or hidden away in the hearts of the Old Ones. Manaha realized then that she had hidden more than most. What her grandfather had taught her must not be forgotten.

The crack of a misplaced step broke into her thoughts. She turned from the darkening skies to the fire pit. Winds stirred. The flame she put to the kindling flickered.

Once the fire took hold, Manaha dropped in a shaving from the lightning-tree, chanting, "I hear listeners round about."

Forest shadows rustled here and then there. She dropped in a second piece. "I hear listeners round about."

Whether it was the fire or a presence nearby—a warmth spread over Manaha as she dropped in the third piece. "I feel listeners round about," she softly chanted.

She turned from the fire to visitors unseen. "It is good to have listeners," she said. "But my heart is saddened to see that you must hide. I know that we all hide something, each one for a different reason."

She untied the scarf she always wore as she spoke to the shadows. "I have always hidden my face for fear of rejection, yet I am rejected."

She stepped fully into the light of the fire. "I can never ask another to come out of hiding if I remain there."

With a tilt of the head, she snatched off the scarf. The night breeze cooled her bare cheeks. All survivors of the Black Sleep sickness had scars. Some carried them without thought, but Manaha had always concealed hers.

She raised the scarf over her head and flung it down. The fire gasped as the tattered cloth settled over it. Her useless arm jerked as if reaching to save an old friend. Flames shot out from under the edges.

Manaha looked away to the stars. She watched them grow in number as she slowly traced and retraced the circular scar on her left cheek. When she looked down, the scarf had fallen to ashes. Not one listener had come forward.

She shouted at the night, "All in the shadows and beyond, listen to the last child of Palisema. I will hide no more! I will tell the stories of all that I know."

Chapter 7: The Hiding Cave

Nanza's Journey
Forty-nine years after "their" arrival

I, Nanza, a child who does not know her own real name or the names of her mother or father, had lived in Taninto's isolated valley for all of my remembered life. If what Grandfather said on Narras Mountain last night was true, what I had always believed about my parents was a lie. He destroyed all my dreams of a family with one story.

New found emotions boiled over in flashes. I began to hate my lonely life and his empty valley. I hated the warriors who had killed my family.

Last night he had said, "I will guide you to Palisema, the land of your people."

How could I ever again believe anything he promised? Once I loved the grandfather he pretended to be, the one who cared for me when I was sick. Now I longed for my mother's people. I needed to walk upon the land of my ancestors.

"I will be down at the creek, preparing the canoe," he had said when he left early. "We will leave in a day or two as soon as we are ready."

Grandfather had given me several tasks to complete before we left. The most important for me was making and packing my own travel-bundle. For as long as I could remember, he had kept a travel-bundle at the foot of his bed.

Sometimes, I would wake to find his walking stick and bundle missing. He always returned by dark from his *wanders* as he called them. Always, except once, when he woke me and said he would not be back for several days. I pleaded, but he would not let me go with him.

Since that day, I feared that I would never get the chance to leave. Now the time had come for my first journey out of Taninto's valley. Grandfather said he would never return. That was his choice. I placed no boundary around my hopes.

I knew that to reach those hopes, I must look forward. I must forget the story, forget what happened to my family, and busy my mind with thoughts of never-before imagined possibilities. I had to control my emotions, but my anger toward Grandfather came without warning. Each time, it left a taste more bitter than before.

I gazed around the only home I had ever known. There had been so many mysterious objects about me as I grew up, most had not sparked a moment of wonder until that day. I studied the collection with new curiosity. Feathers in many colors hung about the lodge. Rocks and crystals of all sizes lay among the shells, berries, nests, and Grandfather's clay figures. The most intriguing sat on the shelf above Grandfather's bed.

"Nanza, you are not to touch anything on my shelf," he reminded me often.

The one object I had stared at and wondered about occupied a special place in the center of his shelf. It was a pot, the size and shape of a head, fashioned in the likeness of a young woman. She had a beautiful face with eyes wide, but full of fear. A large hand covered her mouth and part of her nose, with long thin fingers pressing into her cheeks.

I realized then it was not a likeness of someone older, as I had always assumed, but it was a girl now my own age. I had often compared my reflection to the memory of that face. It looked smooth. My face had pits and scars. I did not understand until that very moment the unspoken words behind the story of my family and my sickness.

Black Sleep had left its mark on me. Ugliness was my shame. Dark emotions rushed through me. *What else is he keeping from me?*

Suddenly, he was at the door. "Nanza," he called.

"What else have you not told me?" I wanted to know.

"Gather up your bundle," he said as if he had not heard me.

He began snatching objects from around the lodge and piling them on his bed-skin. "Gather your things. Hurry!"

Bewildered, I sat down with my travel-bundle half filled.

"Get up, child!" he yelled. I had never heard fear in his voice until that moment. He pushed me and my bundle out of the lodge.

With my shawl, his cloak, and our bundles on his back, he wrapped the stuffed bed-skin around his bad hand and carried his walking stick in the other. We crossed the edge of the cornfield heading toward the east mountain. He did not run, but I had to just to keep up.

Once in the woods, Grandfather stopped. "I saw a hunting party coming from the north," he said as he rearranged the bundles. "Should they cross the river, they will find our lodge."

His words had no meaning. I watched him tie the walking stick to his left hand. Then I understood.

"They have come for *me*!" I shouted.

"Quiet, child." He threw the shawl in my face.

I screamed.

"Nanza," he whispered, "be quiet." He grabbed my arm, but fear had the stronger hold.

"They have come to torture and kill me," I said.

"Listen to me, Nanza. No harm will come to you."

"The warriors who killed my family have come for me."

"No. No! That was a long time ago. These men are Nadakos—hunters, not warriors."

He waited for his words to reason with my panic then turned toward the mountain. "Now pick up your shawl and follow my path." He looked back over his shoulder and smiled. "I will take you to a place where we can watch without being seen."

We crossed the valley creek and started up the mountain. Grandfather climbed the steep slope quickly in spite of the load he carried. I never thought of him as having only one hand, except when he used his walking stick. The short stick had a jar-like opening carved into the top which was lined with rabbit fur. He placed the hand without fingers or a thumb into the opening and strapped it tight. On a mountainside with his walking stick, he had the advantage over others with only two hands.

Whenever I asked about his missing hand, he acted as

though he had not heard my words—as he was still doing.

"Grandfather walk slower, please . . . wait. Wait for me."

He did not wait or slow his pace until almost out of sight. He turned around to survey the valley. I stopped to catch a breath and have my own look.

"Hurry, Nanza. There is no time for you to be lazy."

Before I turned back to the mountain, I caught a glimpse of distant figures on the river trail. Grandfather began climbing, and I followed with new commitment. Almost out of sight, he stopped again. This time, I did not slow until I reached his side.

"We can see the valley from this ledge," he said as I came up.

I sat close to him. We watched together. Small figures appeared and disappeared between the branches and the few remaining leaves that shielded us from their view. Eventually, they reached our home.

I was seeing other people for the first time in memory. I had always imagined that it would be a joyous event, not frightening. It made me angry to think of someone in our lodge, touching our belongings. I hoped they would leave soon.

Two hunters ran up the valley while two others started across the cornfield.

When Grandfather saw them heading in our direction, he said, "We must go. I know a place to hide."

"But . . ." I stammered.

"Do not speak." He scowled. "I know a place to hide. Now, be silent with every step."

Inside I shouted, but I followed without a word. His path headed to the south and always up. He stepped from rock to rock to fallen trees whenever he could. We never stopped or looked back, although I wanted to. The light faded as we came to a bluff overlooking a small ravine. He climbed down one side and unloaded his bundles at the bottom.

"This is no place to hide," I mumbled.

He began clearing away the dead branches that lay at the base of the cliff.

"Grandfather, what are you doing?" Confusion twisted inside me as I looked down on him. "You expect us to hide in the brushes, old man?" I asked.

He ignored my disrespect and said with no emotion, "I will go in first. You follow." Pushing all the bundles in front of him, he crawled into a crack in the earth.

Left behind with no time for doubt, I followed. The small opening forced me to crawl on my belly. An earthy smell filled the blackness in front of me. I tried to turn around, but it was too tight.

"Do not be afraid, Nanza."

I could almost reach his heels, but his voice seemed far away.

"This is the entrance to a great cave that reaches into the heart of the mountain. Nothing ever found me when I hid here."

His words gave me a vague sense of direction, but little assurance.

"Not much further and you will be able to stand."

The tunnel shrank as the darkness closed in on me.

"Will there be light?" I wanted to know before I crawled any deeper.

"In time, your eyes will adapt," he said and scrambled out of my reach.

I stopped. In front and to either side, I could see nothing but black. Behind me, the opening glowed in soft sunlight. I had started backing toward it when something grabbed my arm. Dragged from the light and stood upright in complete blackness, I could see no more with my eyes open than I could with them closed.

Darkness spoke without form or substance in a hushed voice. "Do not be afraid."

Once I was certain the voice belonged to Grandfather, I reached until I grabbed him.

"Nanza stay here. Do not move until I get a fire started." He pulled free of my grasp. "You will feel better once we have some light."

At that moment, I wanted more than a fire. I needed something familiar to hold.

"Stay where you are." The words came from everywhere and nowhere.

I squatted down until I found the crack through which I had been pulled. The light at the other end had turned orange. The outside would soon grow dark, but it would be nowhere close to the dark nothingness of the underworld. From the thick dust around me, I picked up a small rock and rolled it in my fingers, hoping for something familiar. I dropped it when a crash of tumbling boulders echoed from across the unknown.

"Grandfath . . ." I started to yell but stopped myself. My own voice sounded strange in this world. I called out again but in a whisper, "Grandfather, are you hurt? Where are you?"

"Nanza, speak softly in the underworld," he said in a low, stern voice. "I am close. We will have a fire soon."

Leaning and straining, I began to see the outline of his movements. I was hopeful that my vision was returning but frightened by what I witnessed. Unnatural shapes and forms loomed all around. Some seemed to float and glow.

"I have found my torch. It will not be long now," Grandfather whispered.

I hated the cave. At that moment, had the burden of destiny been within my power, I would have preferred to be captured or even killed by the intruders rather than be left alone in that darkness.

Somewhere across the unnatural night, water trickled. Grandfather's constant fumbling spoiled its comforting rhythm. Sparks of a fear I had never known lit up my mind. *Why has he brought me into this horrible place?*

A loud crack shattered my thoughts. A flash of light froze an image of him hunched over his flint and a pile of kindling on the floor of a vast room.

A second flash and then another, like a lightning storm on a dark night, the world appeared and disappeared. However, what appeared looked nothing like the world I knew. Burned into my memory are those flashes of the underworld. Moments before, I had struggled to see anything; now, I saw more than I ever wanted to. I closed my eyes and jerked with each new crack of the flint.

When the last echo faded, darkness returned, except for the faint glow that Grandfather held in his hand. The small ball lit up his wrinkled face as he gently blew into it. He laid the burning kindling onto a bundle of pitch-soaked cane, then raised the torch high. Its light pulled me in and warmed my spirit.

Dancing above Grandfather's head, the flames chased darkness into hiding at the far edges of its reach. In the torchlight, what I had imagined as floating demons became glistening rocks, like giant icicles hanging from the ceiling and growing from the floor. Behind each one, the darkness peeked out at each flickering chance. I pressed close to Grandfather, and he put his arm around me, something he had not done for a long time. I felt content but not secure.

"When can we leave this place?" I asked.

"Not until the hunting party has gone. Come, I will take you to my secret cavern where we will be safe."

I stayed close to the light and Grandfather as he led me through the underworld. He picked his way with experience.

"I will return later and get the rest of our belongings," he reassured me.

Losing our bundles did not worry me. I feared the darkness that could forever conceal the way back. It held a power so great in this cave so large that the torchlight could not reach any walls. The size of the cave could be judged only by the distance we walked.

When the ceiling sloped down to a wall, I felt some sense of relief. It was not the endless dark world I had imagined.

Grandfather climbed over a boulder and slid down its dusty slope. The dancing torchlight exposed a narrow opening between the boulder and the wall.

"Come, Nanza. We are almost there."

I hoped to see sunlight, but beyond the short crawl, it opened to another dark cavern. On the other side, he stood proud, holding his torch high. The light reached every part of this cavern.

"This is my hiding place," Grandfather announced.

I studied the cavern as he tried to reassure me.

"You will be safe here. Only I know of this place."

He could see that I questioned his boast and led me to a huge, flat boulder lying in the center of the room. On top, an old buffalo hide lay draped over a pile of wood next to the burnt remains of previous fires. He had been there, many times.

Grandfather handed me the torch while he cleared the pit. I could not resist the chance to chase dark demons from the cracks and crevices with the power of torchlight.

"Nanza," he grumbled, "hold the light over here."

I clenched my teeth and squeezed the torch, but I held it steady. He arranged the kindling and four logs, took the torch from me, and lit the pile. Flames shot up from the dry wood, crackling, then echoing back from every side. Only the bravest of the dark demons danced at the edge of its light.

"Watch the fire while I go back to get our bundles and cover the opening to the cave." He gave me a piece of jerky and walked away before pride would let me disagree. "I will return soon."

He left me alone with nothing but a fire. It warmed my exhausted body as I fought the urge to sleep in the strange place. That struggle and the task of tending the fire occupied me until he returned.

"You need to rest. I will watch the fire," he said as he handed me my blanket.

I wrapped it around me, longing for the escape of simple sleep. My mind stirred with questions. "Do you come here often?" I asked.

"No, I have not been here . . . in a long time."

"Why did you come here at all?"

"The spirits of the forest showed me this cave when I needed a place to hide. This is the Hiding Cave."

I sat up. "Hiding from what?"

"My child, I know you have many questions, and in the past, I have always avoided them. Things have changed now, and so must it be with your questions. But be warned that answers found in the past are often filled with sorrow."

He paused, and together we watched the flames prance their ancient dance.

"Nanza, I tried to give you a good childhood," he said, "but I raised you without stories. Now, I see it differently. I have come to understand that stories must be passed down or those who follow will lose their place in the world and the guidance of knowledge gathered through many lifetimes."

He stood and spread his arms wide. "The mountains above and around us are ancient and weathered. Their valleys are but deep wrinkles. Their once lofty peaks are worn down like stooped old men to rounded hills and mountaintop meadows. But these mountains possess ancient wisdom. They offer tranquility and healing, a gentle peace that slips away so slowly when you leave, you will not know that it is gone until you return."

He looked up as if he could see the sky, pointed and said, "Several days to the east across the Mountains of the Ozarks, the Little Red River flows out of its foothills onto the fertile land of Nine-Rivers Valley. Along its banks, just above where it joins with the White River, your people, the people of Palisema, built their villages. They are a peaceful nation, generous with their abundance. Known as great hunters, they cover the floors of their homes and adorn their bodies with many colored skins."

His next words came slowly as if each one hurt. "I first traveled to Palisema as a young man—the willing servant of a band of *strangers* from Spain, a land beyond the great waters. Their warriors called themselves *conquistadors*. Many stories could be told about those evil times. I know the truth of but one, my story. I pledge to tell all, but from the beginning, for that is what I know."

Grandfather circled the fire three times, chanting in a low, sad moan. He stopped across from me and spoke out as if youth had returned to him.

"I shall tell my story from the time of prophecy and triumphs, a time before the Great Dying."

Chapter 8: The Son of the Sun

Taninto's Journey
Two days before "their" arrival - June 20, 1541

On the third day of my fifteenth summer, I started down the twisted path that ended in the dark depths of this Hiding Cave. That day, as with most, my friends and I roamed the river's edge, swimming and hunting. Then we heard, "Taninto, Taninto!"

Two younger boys ran from the village, calling my name. A messenger was close behind them. The boys reached me at the same time, each talking louder than the other. My friends gathered around. Curiosity and confusion swelled until the messenger spoke.

"Taninto of Togo." His words rang out over all others.

Two of my friends laughed, but quickly fell silent.

"Heed these words. Tecco Tassetti, Wise-One of the High Council, charged this humble servant with the duty of escorting you back to the main town of Casqui."

Throughout the nation of Casqui, people respected and recognized Uncle Tecco as a man of honor.

"Why has he sent for me?" It was his responsibility as my mother's oldest brother to guide me to the path of manhood, but he had never sent a messenger before. And it had been only

three days since I stood with him on the Temple Mound for the Raising of the First Summer Sun.

"Is he ill?" I asked.

"He gave me orders, not answers," the messenger said. "Come."

"Are we leaving now?" I asked as I ran after him. "Can I tell my family where I am going?"

True to his word, he said nothing. I could only assume the worst about my uncle.

"Tell my father where I have gone," I shouted over my shoulder to the friends and the boyhood I was leaving behind.

It is less than a half day's run from Togo to Casqui. On the road, we met people who seemed to be fleeing, struggling with their belongings. We ran past other travelers loaded with baskets of gifts as if on their way to Casqui for a festival.

"What are the baskets for?" I asked one group as we ran by.

They gave no more answers than my escort.

The days of Green Corn had passed. Tribute from that early harvest already filled the storehouses of Casqui. Who were these tributes for? My uncle? If so, he was dead. Why were some people fleeing? My questions only grew in number as we approached the south gate.

Baskets of beans, bread, corn, and skins dotted the strip of land between the canal and the walls of Casqui.

"This is all for someone of great importance . . . outside of Casqui," I muttered to myself.

"Boy, what have you to say?" shouted one of the two warriors guarding the entrance. War axe at the ready, he waited for an answer.

"Just a . . . a thought," I stammered.

The messenger stepped between us. "I am Watubi, noble messenger returning as charged by Tecco Tassetti, to bring this boy before his uncle." He stood as proud as the two warriors in their ceremonial headdresses—a brimless cap of bear hide with the fur pulled up to a point and tied with a knot.

All three remained rigid in a test of will. Finally, the warrior who had questioned me waved us through without a word of explanation. I stepped into the gate first. Watubi followed. The mud plaster walls around Casqui overlapped to form a gate in the north and south sides. Guarded at both ends, the long narrow passages were only wide enough for a single man to walk through.

I had never before seen a guard dressed for ceremony but painted red for war. Of all the nations in Nine-Rivers Valley, only the Pa-caha would wage war against our most sacred site. For generations, their war parties had crossed the Chewauhla Swamp to raid our small villages and carry away people and crops. The Pa-caha might well attack, but no Casquis would ever offer them a gift.

Even before I reached the end of the gateway, I could hear the excitement inside. The town hummed with anticipation and uncertainty. The center plaza, where I had seen so many games played, swarmed with warriors from up and down the Little Muddy River. Some wore ceremonial dress, others war-paint. Most seemed as uncertain about their summons as I felt about mine. I slowed to watch the dance of confusion.

"Come on, nosy one." The messenger jerked at my arm. "I have a duty to complete."

"I know the way to the lodge of Tecco," I said.

He released my arm but continued to lead me around the plaza to the north side.

"Watubi," I said, hoping he might answer if I used his name, "why are so many people in Casqui?"

No answer; we ran on in silence past lodges all built alike, square with steep thatched roofs and plastered walls of upright posts, mud, and grass.

"Uncle Tecco," I called out before Watubi had a chance.

"Taninto, we are out here," Aunt Miluka said from the summer patio. I knew that "we" meant her and her friend for many seasons.

"Where is Uncle Tecco? Why did he send for me?" My aunt looked up, but before she could answer those questions, I asked more. "Why are warriors gathering on the plaza? And why are gifts being brought to Casqui?"

She hesitated, then turned to the messenger and said, "You may go."

I nodded to Watubi as he backed out of the patio.

"I am happy to see you, Taninto," she said once he had left. "As for your uncle, he is well. He climbed the temple steps late yesterday and has not returned."

My aunt's visitor could not wait a moment longer to repeat what she always said to me. "I believe you have grown since I saw you last."

I looked down at my feet. What could I say?

"I know nothing about your summons," my aunt said, "or a reason for the gathering of warriors, but I am glad that you are here." She paused and asked, "How is your family?"

I knew she would say nothing more about the strange events unfolding around us. I wanted to run back to the plaza. Instead, I passed the time with the two women and waited for my uncle. I had little news to share, but my aunt's stories about her two daughters, both older than I, had no end.

Against the sounds of the plaza, the often-repeated stories faded to a drone. From my place on the summer patio, I could see the top of the Temple Mound steps and the warriors that hurried up and down them.

The sun set without the return of my uncle. The daughters prepared an evening meal, which I ate more quickly than I should have. I paced about until my aunt said, "Taninto, maybe you should go down to the plaza."

I started off before she had finished speaking.

"Hurry back if you hear that the High Council has broken the circle," she called after me.

Outside, I breathed in the night air and ran to the plaza. Once there I walked around the edge, watching and absorbing all the grandeur of the mighty warriors of Casqui. For each of the six traditional weapons, a band of warriors shared not only the skill and training in that weapon but a code and a color. Six colors circling six fires surrounded one great fire. Pride swelled my chest.

In the midst of all who had gathered, I saw Saswanna. She and I had become friends during the first summer I visited my uncle. Since that summer, Saswanna and I were often together on days of celebration.

She put her arms around me. We embraced.

I felt awkward and uncomfortable. I felt wonderful.

She pulled away but held onto my hand. "Taninto, have you heard?" Her voice sang with excitement, and her smile shone like a new sun.

I shook my head.

"He is coming from the East, from across the Great Waters as the legends said. The healer, the unconquered warrior of our grandfathers' stories, is coming."

I had never noticed her smile. I had not noticed how perfect her hand felt in mine.

She squeezed it hard. "Have you heard anything?"

I studied—admired—her face.

"They say that he is the Son of the Sun," she said.

"Saswanna," someone behind me shouted.

She dropped my hand but not her smile. The youngest of Saswanna's two older brothers and three of his friends surrounded me. The bad feeling between her clan and my family was most evident in Saswanna's brothers. Their presence accomplished its intent. I turned to leave.

"My . . . my aunt, I . . . promised to . . . I must go before my uncle returns before I can." My words twisted on themselves, making a fool of me.

The older boys laughed, and Saswanna's beautiful smile slipped away.

Drumming drew their attention from me to the plaza. The boys rushed toward the sound, Saswanna with them. I stood like a rock in a stream of people flowing by. When all had passed, I took my first step slowly, the second running. I thought of nothing but the embrace and its mystery.

I ran hard, passing my uncle's lodge onto the palisade and

around. Between the wall and garden plots, I scrambled, dodging winter lodges and corn cribs. Passing the guards at the south gate, I followed the wall to the old wart tree, north of the Temple Mound. That is what Saswanna called it because of the knotty bulges on its trunk. We used to sneak out of Casqui at night by climbing up its warts to a huge branch that stretched out over the wall. I stopped underneath, caught my breath, and trotted back toward the lodge.

My aunt stepped out. "Your uncle returned while you were gone." Her head tilted one way and her smile the other. "He will talk to you in the morning."

I nodded, and she disappeared back into the lodge.

It was too hot for me to sleep inside. I laid down on a bench on the summer patio. Stars sparkled in spaces between the saplings laid across its roof. Longing and confusion smothered me like a heavy blanket. I tossed between the sounds of the plaza and images of Saswanna, unable to sleep. Reliving the embrace, I imagined clever words I could have said, hating all over again what I had said.

I would feel different with Saswanna from that point on. And I sensed that, with what I had seen and heard that day, all of Casqui would soon be different.

Chapter 9

Manaha's Journey
Ninety-four years after "their" arrival

Manaha stretched her back as she stood. The storyteller needed nothing, but the old woman needed to walk. She circled the story-fire, rallying the flames with her lightning stick. Her stirring and the fire's crackling did not mask the sounds of retreating footsteps. *I still have listeners.* Sleep came easily after a story well told.

The next day began bright and warm. For the first time, Manaha slept as well on the ground as she had on her bench in the lodge. On her morning walk, she met several women also on their way to bathe. Their conversations ended in a common gasp—few had ever seen Manaha without her scarf. She did not slow but walked among them. When they reached the creek, she continued downstream and bathed alone.

Only five women worked in the fields that day. The others either wanted to avoid Manaha or had given up on the summer crop. Almost everyone had turned their thoughts and efforts toward the joining ceremony and the abundance of meat and skins the hunting party would surely bring back.

The harvest of green corn had its traditional ritual but only a halfhearted celebration. The smallest harvest that anyone could remember offered no reason for joy. Prayers for the summer crop had accomplished little. It was already the month of the Sun, and the cornstalks, which should have been taller than Manaha, stood no higher than her shoulder. Almost no rain had fallen, and the men who should have been carrying water to the fields left with the hunting party.

"Sad for so much hope to be placed on a hunt before the harvest," Manaha said quietly as she tilled around another stalk, seemingly unaffected by the burning heat and the still, heavy air.

Even if the corn withered, the stalks had to remain stout enough to hold up the twisting vines of the beans and the squash until they ripened. The dirt she piled onto the shallow roots gave the stalk extra support against the thunder-winds that came when the nights were hot and dry. She packed down the center of the hill of dirt, creating a bowl shape around the stalk to hold the little rain that might fall or a splash of water that one of the boys might carry from the creek.

"This land is old and tired," Manaha grumbled. All around, the signs spoke of unknown people who had abandoned this place long before her tribe arrived. The island where she had her story-fire was their island. Manaha knew that, but no one else cared.

Who were they? Where had they gone? Had they left their home because this land would no longer grow corn and beans? Had they been chased away by enemies or the sickness?

Even the oldest of the children around Manaha's first story-fire had little memory of their villages before this one. They could not understand the grief of people forced to leave their homes. More than possessions were lost with each move. Yet, in this land, Manaha found something of great value—her true

path.

Over the next three days, she worked in the fields with fewer and fewer women. Each night grew warmer than the one before, her story-fire smaller, and the listeners in the shadows quieter. She retold the ancient legends as she heard them from her grandfather in the dark depths of the Hiding Cave.

On the third evening, she sat at her place west of the fire pit, carving thin strips from her staff of lightning wood. She took the cuttings from around her feet and placed them in a basket. The last three she held up to the sun as it sank behind a wall of threatening clouds.

"Oh, Father Sun, symbol of all that is great and wise, bless this fire and the words spoken around it that they may be pure and true."

Lightning flashed off to the south as Manaha waited for her listeners. When she heard the first footstep, she put a flame to the pile of sticks and small logs. In a ritual becoming more natural and complete, Manaha placed her three offerings on the story-fire, chanting each time, "I hear listeners round about."

Chapter 10: Looking Down on the Sun

Nanza's Journey
Forty-nine years after "their" arrival

As a young girl, I hid from a party of Nadako hunters in a cave with my grandfather. I slept most of the time, but when I could not, Grandfather's stories kept my thoughts off the darkness. He had never told stories before that night on Narras Mountain. Now ancient legends flowed out with hardly a breath between the last and the next.

He spoke with such conviction, I believed him when he said he could feel Father Sun even underground and knew the time of his coming and going. Before each new foreseen sunrise, Grandfather would say, "I need to gather more wood if you want to keep a fire burning."

I followed as he climbed out of his secret cavern and crossed the rocky, uneven cave floor, hoping that I would not have to come back. He walked straight to the cave opening every time, but I never saw its warm glow until we were upon it.

I would rush toward it, but Grandfather would force his way past me, blocking out the light. "Nanza, stay here," he said like he had each day before. When the light returned, I knew he had reached the outside.

"Do not come out unless I call for you," his distant voice commanded. "I will be back soon."

It mattered little when he would return, only that he had left me alone, once again. I marked the passing of the morning by the light's slow march across the rocks at the other end of the opening. When the light vanished, time stopped. I held my breath and waited. Grandfather should have called out "Nanza" as he had done each day before, but the shadow remained, silent.

"Nanza, you can come out," a voice roared through the opening.

I jumped into the tight passage, fearing nothing on the outside as much as I feared the dark demons behind me. Grandfather reached in. I dodged his grip and clawed my way up his arm and out.

My eyes would not stay open, but my legs were running before I could stand. I knocked him aside, stumbled over a small tree, and fell. Instead of pain, I felt alive, my senses overwhelmed by a bright world filled with sweet sounds and wonderful smells. I strained to keep my eyes open as I scrambled to the top of the cliff above the mouth of the cave.

He watched my flight, his arms still bent at his side in a broken embrace. I shouted down at him, "I will never go back inside that or any other cave."

He pulled a blackened chunk of flint from his pouch and bounced it in his hand as he looked up. "I am going back in for our bundles and supplies." Sadness filled his eyes. He started to say something, but turned and slipped into the cave, leaving the black stone behind.

It seemed longer than three days since I had crawled into that cave. The ground felt soft and moist. Rain had fallen on the mountainside. Tender green leaves glistened as their curled brown ancestors rustled in a warm breeze, smelling of spring. A sky of pure blue was marred only by a thin wisp of smoke rising from Taninto's valley.

I watched the smoke for a moment before I realized. "Grandfather is wrong. The hunting party is still there." I backed up the mountain, trying to find an opening in the branches. Side to side, up and down, I moved until I spotted a patch of black.

Is that the cornfield? I wondered as I eased to the right. I gazed at the knoll I knew so well. "They burned our lodge!" I screamed. "They burned it!" All that remained, the faint trails of smoke, would soon be lost in the blue sky.

"Grandfather!" I shouted as he crawled out of the cave. I pointed to the valley and the smoke.

"I know." His face showed more torment than surprise.

Pain stabbed my heart. "Our lodge?" I asked.

He again said, "I know."

Did he understand what I asked? Sliding most of the way, I ran down to where he stood. He reached out to me. I resisted for a moment. Then without a word, we held each other and wept the same tears.

"Child, we are safe," Grandfather said, "but our home and our fields are gone."

I pulled away.

"The hunting party has taken all that they found of value and burned the rest."

I turned and started down the mountainside.

"No, you will find nothing there but bad memories. I know of what I speak."

"But why . . . why did they burn our home?"

"Nanza, my child—"

"I am not your child!" I stiffened and demanded, "Why did they burn my home? You said you would answer all my questions."

"I cannot answer that which I do not know." He knelt with his back to me and spread out the bed-skin, so hastily packed three days ago.

The head-pot of the young woman rolled to the center. He gently stroked her face and said, "Lay to one side the things that we will need for the journey."

I did nothing.

"I will get the rest of our supplies," he said and took the head-pot with him into the cave.

I sat, staring at the wisps of smoke rising from my past life and the odd collection in front of me. I could not find order for one thing over another. Each piece now held a special place. I handled every treasure with honor as the last tokens from Grandfather's life of wandering and my childhood of wondering.

I retrieved the stone Grandfather left near the opening, the flint blade he used on his hoe. The handle and the binding had been burned away, and the alabaster flint blackened. I added the blade to the collection as Grandfather pulled himself out of the cave.

In anger I had called him an old man. My words of rage had become words of truth. He said nothing as he laid down my back-bundle and shawl, the buffalo cloak, and the other provisions from the cave.

He loaded the back-bundles with all they would hold: rope, twine, leather, tool pouch, axe, blackened hoe blade, and all the jerky and hard-bread we had. There was little room left for his treasures. He selected a few pieces and placed the rest just inside the cave, then covered its opening with branches.

He handed the shawl to me and put on the buffalo cloak. "Turn your face and thoughts toward Palisema," he said. "Remember our home and valley as it was."

We started up the mountain in a wide zigzagging path. Grandfather climbed slower than he had three days before. I had no trouble keeping up with him, and we rested at his bidding.

Near the end of the day, high bluffs spread across our path. The tops the bluff boulders were smooth and flat, like giant river rocks. From there, I could see over the trees that had stood tall and proud at the bottom of the ledge. Beyond lay more trees than one could imagine: a tangled web of bare limbs covering the mountains in an endless gray haze without any fields or lodges in sight.

"Where is our valley?" I asked.

Grandfather walked to the edge and pointed off to his left. "See that glistening, there, through the trees? That is the little creek that flows through our valley."

Following a line in the trees with his hand, he said, "It flows around this mountain, past our fields, and into the Buffalo River." His last words were lost in winds gusting up from the valley. He sat down on the boulder, faced the setting sun, and took on a quiet reverence.

For as long as I could remember, I had lived in the valley and always had to raise my eyes to look at the sun. Now I saw something I never expected. I looked down on Father Sun. I could not help but feel pride in my lofty position.

I tried to grasp all that surrounded me. I saw further than I could ever imagine, mountains beyond mountains beyond mountains. Those to my right still glowed red with the setting sun. Behind me, night settled over rolling black peaks and, to the south, more mountain tops created a thin purple line. I had never seen so much or so far in my life.

"How will we ever find our way across these mountains?" I asked.

Grandfather sat unmoving.

Throughout my whole life, I had been able to see the boundaries of my world. Now before me spread a world with no limits. Every direction seemed hopeless. In all that vastness, the world of my youth was lost.

"The moon will give us little light," Grandfather said without notice for my despair. "We need to find a place to camp."

"You never answer my questions." I raised both hands and tried to push it all away: him, the mountains, his stories, my family, all of it.

"Why is everything so different?" I wanted to know.

"Change is upon both of us," he said. "I walk in my last season." His face softened, and his eyes turned down. "You are young and beginning a wondrous time when you need to be among the women of your people."

"But how will we find my people?"

"I can find Palisema. Of that, there is no doubt," he said and walked over the ridge down to a large pine tree.

I was not satisfied. I had my doubts, but I was glad to be out of the wind, and started gathering firewood. When I dropped the wood near the pit he was clearing, he looked up. "Bring me several of those pine cones for kindling."

Soon he had a bright fire burning. Grandfather placed his hand on my shoulder. "Tonight, Nanza, you will tell the story."

I pulled away.

"Listeners can never truly understand the power of telling a story until they become the teller," he said.

I wanted to ask questions, not tell a story. I wanted to know more about my people, and how we would find them.

Grandfather gripped my arm and urged me to stand. "Nanza, amuse us with a grand tale."

I resisted his push for a moment, but I did as he said. I stood and told one of the stories I had heard in the Hiding Cave, "The Great Turtle and the White Bird." Grandfather listened closely, encouraging and helping me when I lost my way. When I finished the story, I was smiling.

"Good, good."

His praise turned my smile to a giggle. I forgot all about my anger and doubts.

"Very good," he sounded as proud as I felt. "Now," he said, "I shall tell the legend 'Cula and Mother Wolf.'"

"No!" I yelled, surprising both of us.

"You promised to tell me the truth, not another legend. Tell me about the land of my people. Tell me about Nine-Rivers Valley," I demanded.

He stared long into the fire. I begin to wonder. *Did he really know anything about my ancestors or Palisema—if such a place ever existed?*

"Nanza, you are right." He stood and circled the flames. "I am an old man as you said and weary of the long struggle to forget."

He stretched his arms wide, looked to the sky and said, "As promised I shall tell my story of Nine-Rivers Valley."

Chapter 11: Uncle's Hat

Taninto's Journey
One day before "their" arrival - June 21, 1541

I awoke my first day after Saswanna's embrace to the thundering voice of my uncle, "Taninto, lazy boy . . . get up."

"I am here," I said as I struggled to stand.

He grabbed me, a hand on each shoulder. "A large band of strange warriors has crossed into Nine-Rivers Valley," he said, "and they march toward Casqui."

"What are we going to do?"

"When change comes, the wise are prepared," he said.

"Who . . ."

"Listen, Taninto. Pass this day as you will, but at sunset, be in front of my lodge." He pushed down on my shoulders.

"Uncle Tecco, your command is my will," I said.

He released me and marched off toward the Temple Mound. The demand and his manner only added to my puzzlement as I ran toward the plaza. It did not take long to find Saswanna.

"A son . . . of . . . the . . . sun," she shouted. "Taninto, he is coming." Waving her long arms, she jumped up and down. "Taninto, can you believe that he is coming to Casqui?"

I smiled.

She continued without an answer. "They do not look like

us."

"What do you mean?" I asked. "What do they look like?"

"I do not know, but that is what I have heard." She must have seen the doubt on my face, but did not hesitate. "They have traveled from nation to nation conquering all who met them with war."

Several of the king's servants trotted by carrying two litters of gifts: one of fine shawls, the other of tanned, dressed skins.

"The king is sending a party to greet the Son of the Sun and present gifts on behalf of all the people of Casqui," Saswanna announced and turned to follow the gift bearers.

They continued through the south gate and placed their gifts with all those sent from the different villages of the Casqui Nation. We joined the growing number of people mingling among and examining the variety and craftsmanship of the offerings. A hush spread over the crowd when Akahahi passed through the gate.

"He is the best speaker in all of Casqui," Saswanna said.

She talked as if I knew nothing. I knew Akahahi. I had heard him many times. He would speak for the people of Casqui with dignity and truth no matter who stood before him.

While the bearers gathered up all of the displayed offerings, Akahahi assembled his party in proper rank and position. He led with three nobles trailing off each side like a flight of geese. One warrior ran ahead. Three marched on each side of the bearers and their burdens of gifts. The last two warriors guarded the rear.

Women in the crowd began to sing the song of "Good Journey." Saswanna joined in. I turned away, uncertain about what I had seen or what I felt.

"A smaller party of gift-bearers left two days ago," she said over the singing. "But none have returned."

Did she know everything?

"Traders from the east say that the *strangers* command savage dogs and other great beasts on which men of metal ride faster than a frightened doe."

I shook my head.

"And my brother told me that when the *strangers* reached the Mizzissibizzibbippi River, the king of Pa-caha sent two hundred longboats to prevent their crossing."

"Saswanna," I interrupted, "do you know how many men that would be with twenty paddlers and twenty warriors in each of those boats?"

"Yes." She stomped her foot.

I watched the dust puff up around her ankle.

"The Pa-cahas," she resumed undaunted, "descended the river every day for seven days hurling arrows and curses at the *strangers*, but they never stopped building their barges. The *strangers*, their beasts, and the slaves from many conquered nations crossed the mighty river in one morning. All the boats and warriors of Pa-caha could not stop them."

"I do not think—"

Saswanna threw her hand up in my face.

"And my brother said that if a Pa-caha boat drifted too close, the *strangers* could kill with a weapon that smoked like burning leaves and roared like thunder."

"A son of the sun and men from beyond the great waters that can kill with thunder?" I laughed out loud.

"You are just a boy from down the Little Muddy. What do you know?" she shouted, spun around, and stomped away.

"Saswanna, I did not mean to make you angry," I called after her. "I . . . I believe you."

She stopped.

I measured my words. "I believe you, Saswanna. I know a band of strangers approaches our land, and they must be powerful to have crossed the Mizzissibizzibbippi River against the will of the Pa-cahas, but I just cannot believe that their leader is the Son of the Sun."

I hoped for a smile, but her lips tightened as she pushed past me. I followed her around the canal, past the north gate, and toward the Little Muddy. My heart and mind wrestled in a search for the right words.

"Tell me how you would explain what you have seen today?" she asked when we reached the riverbank.

I shrugged my shoulders while screaming inside, *Say something. Say something!*

Saswanna glared at me, waiting for an answer. I looked away, up to the huge birch tree stretching out over the river. *I had always been able to talk to her,* I thought as I pulled down a dead branch.

I broke off the end and threw it over the dried shoreline into the river. She turned and watched it float away. I broke and threw in another piece. The silence deepened with each new crack of the dried wood.

Saswanna snapped, "Stop that."

I flung the branch into the river. The muddy waters carried it silently out of sight. "Let me tell you what my uncle did this morning." I had to say something, but the moment I did, I wished I had not.

Saswanna shook her finger at me. "If you cannot believe what I say, then I know I do not want to hear what your uncle said." She walked away.

I did not follow.

"Someday, I will be a man of respect, and my words will be sought out," I said, but not loud enough for her to hear. I spun around and shouted at the river, "Someday. You will see."

I crossed the dried riverbed to the water's edge. I had never seen it so low. Baked by the summer sun, the barren strip of sand and clay curled up and cracked like so many broken pots. I walked upriver, crunching the dried clay with my feet. It stung with a pain I could understand—somehow that felt good.

"Saswanna . . . Saswanna." I wanted to see her. I wanted to apologize, to take back everything I had said. I wanted to hear her sweet voice. I could do none of those things. It was time to be at my uncle's lodge.

Aunt Miluka waited in the front of the lodge. "Stay here until called," she said, and went inside.

I began to pace, wondering what my uncle would say. Finally, I slumped down next to the entrance and thought just of Saswanna.

"Taninto," my uncle called.

I stepped into his lodge.

"Son of my only sister, come." He motioned for me to sit at the fire. Two woven mats lay on either side. A buffalo robe covered the mat north of the fire. A smooth, well-tanned beaver skin stretched across the other. I sat on the south side, hoping

I had not failed in my choice.

Uncle Tecco sat on the buffalo robe. "Taninto, enjoy my gifts," he said and, motioned for the feasting bowls to be brought out. The two daughters and my aunt placed all four bowls in front of me and left the lodge.

I ate in silence while my uncle filled his pipe. When I had eaten all that he wished, he waved his hand and stood. I set the bowls aside. Still without a word, he lit his pipe. With his first draw, he blew smoke up to the sky and down to Grandmother Earth. Another long draw and he blew smoke in each of the four sacred directions.

He turned back to the fire and began to chant, "Sacred smoke, purify this lodge. Sacred smoke, purify this circle. Sacred smoke, purify this man."

Uncle Tecco loomed over me. The eagle tattooed across his left eye from chin to his topknot seemed ready to swoop. He offered the pipe—a sight of wonderment that I had only seen once before. I felt its power the moment it touched my hand. I did not want to choke and only pretended to take a deep draw.

"Listen well," he said.

I slowly exhaled into the fire.

"As a young man, I had a vision in which I saw a great change coming to the people of Casqui—war growing from peace and sickness flowing from reverence. I feel that time is close at hand."

He took the pipe from me and sat. "Close also is the change within you, the time when you will become a man. That path cannot be complete without training and proper ritual. Even so, I fear if you do not walk as a man soon, your time may never come."

I did not understand what he meant, but I nodded.

"You are a boy of great stamina with regard for all things." His silver ear spools sparkled in the firelight as he spoke. "I know you will toil and question until you understand all that is needed to become a man."

"Taninto, you partook of my food as a boy." He waved his arms. "Rise now, a man, and receive my blessings. Look behind you, beneath the skin. It is a feza, the hat of manhood for our clan. You did not kill the bear from which it was made as is our way, but I know you will meet that challenge in time."

I had seen my uncle wear it on many occasions. I felt different as soon as I put it on. My whole body stretched to fit: my shoulders wider, my heart beat stronger and my head swelled.

"Tecco, honored brother of my mother, I am indebted by your gift and your trust." My words felt hopelessly inadequate. It seemed as though in two days I had lost my ability to speak. I backed toward the doorway, hoping to escape any more ceremony. I wanted to find Saswanna. She would respect me now. Everyone would. She would have to forgive me for not believing.

"Taninto, you have not yet earned the honor needed to wear that hat," he proclaimed. "Tomorrow, and only tomorrow, you are given permission to wear it in tribute. You will walk beside me dressed in your hat of manhood when our people welcome the one some are calling the Son of the Sun."

The Son of the Sun! Could Saswanna be right?

"Take it off for now," he said.

I removed the hat, but I still had to get out of the lodge. I

needed to jump, run and yell. I had to see Saswanna. The fire roared above the silence. I did not know what to say or how to leave.

Finally, my uncle said, "You may go."

Outside, the endless night sky seemed full of possibilities. I ran in leaps toward Saswanna's lodge, but shortened my steps as I came closer, then passed it by. What would I say? *Saswanna, I have a feza, but I cannot wear it.*

I wandered back to the river where we last spoke. The warm water swirled around my legs as I waded in. I buried myself in the river and let the current carry me past the west wall. From down in the river, the Temple Mound loomed high above like a mountain. From that place of power, a blazing fire could be seen by the villages up and down the river and off to the east.

The ancestors had built up the land on which Casqui sat to protect it from the spring floods. They dug a canal around it to feed and water the people. They built walls on all sides to defend against attacks. *How could a wandering band of strangers be more powerful than this place?*

Could I be wrong? Could Saswanna be right? Either way, I knew tomorrow our world would change.

Chapter 12

Manaha's Journey
Ninety-four years after "their" arrival

Manaha finished her story with a sigh. The small fire hissed back. She made no effort to save it. *Nine-Rivers Valley must have been wonderful*, she thought. All of her images of that land and time came from her grandfather's stories. Only now did she realize how important they were to her and the tribe.

"I wish I could have seen it as it was," she mumbled while her shadow listeners slipped away. She did not always hear the listener who hid behind her, but she had felt him since that first night.

The storyteller studied the long splinter that she had taken from the center of the lightning-struck oak tree. An offering of three shavings from that special wood became an important part of her ritual. She had carved away ever-smaller pieces, giving little thought to the form revealing itself—a light, stout walking stick. Leaning on it, she stood and turned toward the creek in search of a breeze.

She followed a path cut through the steep bank that surrounded the island down to the water's edge. Here, the creek spread wide and shallow. She hung her shawl over her walking

stick and propped it against a young sapling. For a moment, she thought about bringing the stick with her into the creek.

The water seemed warmer than the day before. She waded upstream toward the village. Clear sky surrounded a moon—bright, but not yet full. The threatening clouds from earlier in the day had vanished. A breath of wind brushed past her, carrying the soft murmur of young lovers. Smiling at their joy, she sank into the dark, gentle current.

Manaha rose early the next day so she could be in the fields well before the heat. No one else came to tend the crops, but she did not mind working alone. Twice she glimpsed a group of boys watching her from a distance. One of those could be her faithful listener.

"What am I thinking?" she asked. "I believe he is a boy. How can I know that?" *I do not know that there are any listeners at all*, she thought, but refused to say it out loud.

She worked until she had added to and packed down a bowl shape into the top of the hill around the base of each cornstalk. This late in the season, it should have been their third hilling. Father Sun had not reached the top of his climb, but it already felt too hot to be in the open. Manaha retreated to the shade and spent the afternoon chasing away crows—usually the task of young boys, now just another neglected duty.

Late in the day, Manaha heard shouting and yelps coming from the village. When she reached the plaza, a crowd had already gathered. A swarm of boys shouldered Gasapa, the oldest of them and the youngest boy to have gone with the hunting party. They carried him around the plaza like a hero.

He raised his arms. The boys struggled as Gasapa

straightened his back.

"Listen all," he shouted, "I bring the words of Hazaar." He paused and then said, "The hunting grounds are empty."

Everyone gasped, some for breath, others for the hope of better words.

Gasapa continued, "Hazaar says, 'As chosen leader bearing the trust of many and the counsel of Ta-kawa, I have turned the party toward the Akamsa River. Our scouts have spotted herds of elk and buffalo on the far side. Rejoice, people of Hachie. You will soon have meat to fill your bellies and skins to cover your bodies.'"

The boys lowered Gasapa to the ground. The message offered hope to some and uncertainty to others. Tulla, a nation of mystery, lay somewhere on the other side of the river. Their people spoke an unknown language. They did not plant or trade and were known to be vicious in war. Never had they crossed north of the river, and until now, no one from Hachia had ventured into their land.

In a few days, the people would be either celebrating or grieving. Anxiety could be seen in every unguarded eye. Someone shouted, "Gasapa, tell us. What did Ta-kawa say?"

"Ta-kawa?" Manaha questioned a little too loud.

Everyone heard her and looked away. She wished someone would turn on her. She could fight that, but they just stepped aside as she marched through the crowd.

"Do you think Ta-kawa's words matter over that of Hazaar, Elder of the White Lodge?"

Two from the crowd shouted, "Gasapa, tell us what Ta-kawa said."

Gasapa stretched as tall as he could. "As a trusted messenger, I can give you no more than my charge."

He repeated the message again and then again, for any who would ask. Manaha could learn nothing more, but she stayed with the crowd. They would have to push her out if they wanted her to leave. Not a true relation to the tribe, she had been captured during a raid many winters ago. Only hard work, devotion to the clan of her dead husband, and her age had given her any standing.

More than an outsider, Manaha had become a ghost: one who worked and moved among the women and old men of her tribe, but seen only by the children. As such, she saw a larger world than most, hidden from view by their daily struggle. Farming and hunting were necessary and important, but without a connection to the past, their efforts would always be incomplete.

Manaha left the village in her own time, but hurried back to the island. More than fulfillment or joy, she had come to need her storytelling. Once darkness and the last unseen listeners had settled in around her, she began her ritual, chanting and circling the flames three times. As she dropped in the third offering of lightning wood, she caught a glimmer of firelight twinkling in a pair of wide eyes back deep in the shadows. She turned to them and boasted, "I, Manaha, will tell all the stories that I know."

Chapter 13: Grandfather's Last Day

Nanza's Journey
Forty-nine years after "their" arrival

A girl of just twelve winters, I woke from my first night in the forest to a rush of emotions and meaningless chanting. "Stop that!" I said.

Grandfather chanted louder.

I rolled over, my back to him. Taninto's valley was home as far as my memory reached. I missed the roar of the Buffalo River and the wide, open meadows. Father Sun smiled on every rock. In the dense mountain forest, huge trees with thick branches, even without leaves, blocked most of the sunlight.

I had my fill of change. I did not want to feel different. I wanted the same. My heart ached for our lodge and the valley. I longed for the child I was.

I flung off my bedding, put on my moccasins, and jumped to my feet. Taninto was still chanting.

I turned in circles, kicked my bedding, kicked until dirt flew into the fire. He stopped.

I grabbed up my bedding and bundle. "I am going back," I said over my shoulder and set out, without plan or means. My determination was blind and my march short.

Yanked from my stride, I fell backward onto the ground.

Grandfather glared down at me. His fist clenched in a knot of my hair, his face full of anger.

I screamed and pulled at his only hand with both of mine. He jerked me to my feet. We stumbled and fought all the way back to the campsite. He shoved me to the ground.

"You are not going back." His face hardened.

I struggled to stand. "All this time, you let me believe you were my grandfather. You are not my family." Fighting the tears, I shouted, "You are not my grandfather."

A hush fell over the morning songs. Finally, he said, "Your words are sharp. Their cut is deeper than you will ever know." One shoulder dropped. "I did deceive you about your family. I lied to protect you."

I turned away. I did not want him to see me cry.

"Now listen, Nanza look at me," he said. "The truth is you are deep in the mountains and I am your only guide. It is also true that I am not your grandfather . . . nor can I ever be."

Those words changed the man before me. He stood newly unburdened and determined. "I am Taninto, the Wanderer," he said.

After a time, he spoke in the calm, reassuring voice I knew so well. "I will take you to Palisema, but you must do as I say."

Grandfather, Taninto the Wanderer, or my guide—I did not care what name he wanted. I was not going to speak to him again.

He handed me a strip of smoked fish. "Roll up your bedding, proper. We have a long day ahead."

I did believe he could lead us out of the mountains. Beyond that, I had lost faith in the things he said. I followed in his path, but never looked up at him. Head bent, I stumbled over rocky slopes through the bushes, briars, and the maze of countless trees.

When he stopped and whispered, "Nanza, look." I refused.

"Nanza, a white squirrel." Still whispering, he showed his amazement. "A white squirrel."

Curiosity overpowered my mood. I looked in the direction that he pointed. On a limb high up in a black walnut tree, a white tail fluttered in the sunlight as if to say, *Here I am, the grand White Squirrel.* White as a cloud, except for a thin gray streak that ran up his back to the noble head he held high as he surveyed his domain.

"A white squirrel is a rare creature, which I have never seen." He tried to catch my smile. "This is a good sign for our journey."

The white squirrel stood so regal, high above my world. Could he see where the mountains stop from his perch? As graceful as an eagle, he soared to the branch of another tree. A wave of his tail and he vanished around the trunk—another flash of white before he faded into the gray tangle of bare limbs and the reddish brown of new buds.

"This is a good sign," my guide said again and stepped off in the direction of the white squirrel.

Squirrel or not, I still had nothing to say, but I found that I could no longer keep my head down. I searched the forest for the white squirrel. I studied the trees, and they opened their branches to me. For the first time, I began to appreciate their beauty, to admire their strength and generosity. If as he often said, "All things listen; all things speak," then trees must have a

great lot to say, were one only patient enough.

The forest thinned to a small meadow with a stream, little more than a stride across.

"This is good water. You must be thirsty," my guide said.

He stooped beside the stream. "It is cool and sweet. Drink some."

I waited until he had his fill, jumped the stream, and marched off. I made myself heard without having spoken a word.

At my side in a few steps, he led the way by the time we entered the forest again. I had to follow him. I could never find my way alone, not to the land of my ancestors, or even back to the valley of my youth.

We traveled from mountaintop to mountaintop, staying just below the ridge line. He watched the horizon constantly for campfire smoke and avoided valleys when he could.

"I have a guide who is afraid of the whole world," I mumbled behind his back.

We came to another stream.

"You need to drink."

I walked on.

"Look, Nanza, the first flowers of spring," he said as we approached a third stream.

I stepped over the purple clumps growing in the rocky channel, knelt at the stream and drank slow and long.

With daylight nearly gone, we climbed to the upper side of a small clearing. He stopped and untied his walking stick. Mountain ridges stretched to the eastern horizon in ever fading shades of blue. I found little hope in the sight.

He set up camp without a word or a command. Finally, he had nothing to say. He had given up trying to talk to me.

The empty victory did not last.

As soon as a fire burned brightly, he turned to me, "I will tell a story as I have every night since we left our valley if you will but ask."

My determination would not be broken for want of a story. I lay down with my back to him and the fire. No matter how many times he asked, I was not going to speak.

The next day began without words from either of us. His first steps turned down the mountainside, but the pace soon slowed. The closer we came to the valley floor, the more often my guide stopped to listen. At the bottom, he crouched and studied the empty flat land in front of us, certainly not a grand valley with nine rivers.

Without warning, he grabbed my arm and pulled me across the meadow. In the distance, water churned like the Buffalo River. We hurried toward the sound, but it was not a river, only a flooded stream tumbling down slabs of black rock into a swollen pool.

"Bear Creek," he said, wading slowly across just above the waterfall. I took off my moccasins and stomped in. Two steps onto the smooth rock bottom and I slipped, falling half onto the bank and the other in the creek.

He turned and, without any expression, offered help. The outstretched hand only angered me. I pushed myself up and rinsed off my hands. Head high and my skirt wet, I scooted to the other side.

He kept the creek to our right as we hurried across the

valley. A smaller stream joined our race. At a sharp bend in the creek, we came upon a standing stone. My guide walked straight to it. I followed him around it once. Three-sided, its sharp edges came to a point high above my reach.

He walked around a second time, as I searched for a way out of Bear Creek Valley. Quietly chanting, my guide danced another circle about the stone.

In every direction, a cliff or steep mountainsides loomed.

How will we get out of here? I asked myself.

He centered his back on the edge, which had once been painted red. "Our path is there," he pointed straight in front of him, "to Little Red Creek."

After a long, steady climb up out of the valley, we reached a wide plateau. On every side, mountains shouldered dark clouds. We stood at the highest point around. Over the distance, only three ridges stood as tall, and I still could not see an end to the mountains.

The wind turned cold as we started down the other side into an open forest with little underbrush. He kept a quick pace. The wind steadily blew harder.

Night approached when he pointed and said, "Little Red Creek."

I shrugged my shoulders. *Not red, but it is little*, I thought.

"The water running here," he said, "will twist, turn and swell until it becomes a river that will flow down into Nine-Rivers Valley and past the villages of your people."

I wanted to ask how many days that would take.

He waited. I did not ask. He walked away. "We will camp there below the bluff," he said over his shoulder.

It felt good to be sheltered from the wind and warmed by a fire.

As with the night before, he said, "I will tell a story if you will but ask."

It had not been an easy day to remain silent. My resolve had waned at times, and youthful curiosity almost tricked me more than once. I had not faltered. I felt that was the only thing I had control of.

The next morning, we broke camp in our new routine of silence. We left Little Red Creek behind, climbing most of the morning. The steep hike wound about chunks of rock that lay strewn on top of the earth as if thrown there by giant hands. Few trees grew on the slope and even fewer on the mountaintop, which opened onto wide grassy fields.

I saw the old path before my guide said anything.

"Once many traveled this trail, but even I have not passed this way for many seasons." He marched off.

As I studied the eastern horizon in front of us, I wondered. *Are there really towns beyond the mountains as marvelous as he describes?*

We turned downhill, and the mountaintops disappeared. The last light of a cloudy day faded. Soon, the trail slipped away, lost among moss-covered boulders.

He stumbled across a stream and topped a small mound on the other side. "We will camp here," he said.

"Nanza clear a circle. I will gather some wood." He walked down the other side, muttering to himself.

I hurried to clear a pit near the center of the mound. It felt colder than the night before, and we had no shelter to break the wind. I surrounded the pit with rocks that I carried up from the stream. When he still had not returned, I gathered some wood on my own.

He came back with only a few limbs under his arm. I started to ask why, but stopped. With the wood I had gathered and his skill, we soon had a fire. The flames warmed my feet and burned away the last of my commitment. We stared hard at each other across the flames, a determined old man and a stubborn young girl.

I wanted to learn about people and about my homeland. He lowered his eyes and leaned forward. Before he had the chance to ask his nightly question, I stood and looked up into the darkness between the stars. He waited. I was still angry, but I chose to speak for my reasons.

"Taninto, the Wanderer, tell me a story."

He waited for me to sit then nodded slightly.

Chapter 14: Men of Metal

Taninto's Journey
Their arrival - June 22, 1541

As a boy-just-turned-man, I could not wait for my first day to wear Uncle Tecco's *feza*. In the light haze between dark and dawn, I bathed with thoughts of strutting about the plaza in my hat of manhood, for everyone to see, most of all Saswanna.

I raced back to my uncle's lodge, but he had already left. The *feza* could not be worn without his permission. The town bustled with people in their finest cloaks and headdresses, and I had nothing on my head.

My uncle was not on the crowded streets or the plaza. He had already climbed the Mound and disappeared into the Lodge of the High Council. The guards at the top of the stairs indicated as much, but without Uncle Tecco at my side, they would not allow me up the steps.

A confusion of voices churned the air. Drums rumbled on all sides as I ran back to my uncle's lodge. Aunt Miluka and the two daughters were resting in the summer patio as if nothing were happening. Neither daughter looked up from their hair braiding. It was their place to wait, but I could not. I quickly stepped inside the empty lodge.

"Did you talk to your uncle?" Aunt Miluka asked from

outside the door.

"No," I answered.

She bent slightly and looked in. "He is on the Temple Mound," I added.

Her shadow remained in the door while I took down a jar of bear grease and rubbed the oil over my chest and arms. I slipped on my deerskin shirt. She grumbled when I picked up the *feza*. I put it on and pulled it down in the back, snug like every other young warrior wore his.

The daughters giggled as I stepped out of the lodge. I spread my arms wide and spun around. They giggled louder. Before my aunt could speak, I let go with my best war cry.

Two steps toward finding Saswanna, Aunt Miluka called out, "Your uncle will not be pleased to find you gone."

I stopped and mumbled, "I will wait for him in the lodge."

I sat where I had the night before. What meager skill I had in patience, I learned from my father. A quiet man of intricate moves each action considered and precise. In the two days since my uncle had summoned me to Casqui, I had little time for thoughts about my family or friends.

"Taninto," my uncle called from outside.

"I am here, Uncle Tecco," I said as I stepped out.

He wore the ceremonial mantle of a *Tassitti*, a wise-one. The cloak of white bird feathers reached from his knees to his neck, leaving only his head and left arm exposed. I stretched tall and looked him in the eyes. The white feathers in his topknot fluttered in the breeze as he studied me. I noticed he had replaced both of his silver ear-spools with wooden plugs.

"Son of my first sister," he said, "today, you shine. I am

proud of you, Taninto." He put his hand on my shoulder. "Never let that light fade. Walk with pride, but always step with respect."

As he spoke, the daughters came from the patio. Both wore flowing blue cloaks hung over the right shoulder and a single braid over the left with a blue feather tied at the end.

Uncle Tecco shook my attention away from the daughters. "Listen, Taninto," he said. "Keep what you have learned up to this day above all that you will see in the days that follow."

I nodded.

"It is time," he said.

As he must, Tecco Tassitti led the way. I followed two paces back with Aunt Miluka and her daughters close behind. All along our path, people stepped aside in honor of a wise-one. Pride gleamed in every face. Uncle Tecco seemed proud of me, my aunt of her daughters the people of their nation and me of my new status.

The crowd around the south gate parted as Uncle Tecco approached. He led us through the gate without hesitation. As soon as the daughters stepped from the other side, the opening filled back in.

Many things had happened in the days since I had returned to Casqui, but nothing compared to the sights around me. More people than I could see gathered outside the walls on both sides of the canal. A formation of warriors and elders from every village of the Casqui Nation stood before me. Together, they completed four squares, each one inside another.

Twenty stout warriors with one captain formed each wall of the outside square. All faced away from the center square, each one gripping a long-handled war club in one hand, and a buffalo hide shield in the other. Behind every warrior with a war club stood a man pointing an antler-tipped lance to the sky. Bowmen completed the third square, with every bow taut. The most feared warriors, skilled in the use of the war axe and the long blade, protected the open square inside all the others. Scattered about the inner square, village elders and the other wise-ones waited.

Three warrior chiefs stood in front of the formation. To the left, the Warrior Chief of Upper Towns wore a breastplate of woven buffalo hide and a headdress of hawk feathers. He held a war club of white flint, rubbed to a high shine. Like the other warrior chiefs, his weapon was for ceremony, not fighting.

In the center, the Warrior Chief of Casqui carried a white bow. Thirteen red feathers circled the rim of his hat. Two large copper discs hung around his neck, polished but pitted with the marks of many battles. A quill bag with one red arrow hung at his left side.

To his right the Warrior Chief of Lower Towns held a white lance, tipped with the horn of an elk. A round breastplate of copper protected his heart. He wore the orange-brown skin of a mountain lion over his head and down his back. Spread around the formation of warriors and elders, eight scouts carrying copper-tipped spears waited, ready to race out in every direction.

Uncle Tecco walked toward the wall of warriors. I hesitated. He said, "Remember, step with respect."

He marched through the layers to the inner square where three other Tassettis, all wearing white, greeted Uncle Tecco.

They looked past me as I followed my uncle to his position on the south side. A circle outlined on the ground in purple paint and covered in skins lay at the center of all those squares.

I hoped Saswanna could see me inside with my *feza*. I searched the crowd for her face. My heart jumped. Saswanna was there. She looked up. Through and above it all, our eyes met. I smiled, but felt uneasy. I lowered my head and looked away.

"Uncle Tecco, what does it mean to see a face and grow weak?"

"This is not the time for such questions," he said without regard for my pain.

A rhythm of deep drones began to grow. The crowd grew silent. The ranks on the north end opened. Wise-ones, elders, warriors and all who had gathered bowed their heads and eyes, except for one.

Uncle Tecco pushed my head down but not before my vision filled with all the honor and wealth surrounding the eighteenth mico, King of all Upper and Lower Towns of the Casqui Nation. I had admired and watched him speak from the summit of the Temple Mound during many ceremonies, but I had never been in the close presences of King Issqui.

On four strong shoulders, King Issqui floated above the mass of bent heads. He sat perched on a carved throne under a canopy of fine woven red cloth floating in the breeze of two large fans of white birch bark. The deep, rich tones from a pearl-wrapped cypress flute led the royal procession. Three warriors painted white and clutching shiny copper-tipped lances marched on each side of the throne. At the center of the assembled circle the flute playing stopped. The royal bearers steadied the throne on stout poles forked at the top.

King Issqui stood and spoke. "Hear me, the honorable, the wise and the brave joined here as one. I come to walk with you as just another man following the same path of duty. Together, let us meet the Strangers."

The bearers lowered the throne. King Issqui stepped to the ground as Uncle Tecco spun me around. Everyone turned toward the east. Out front, the three commanders called the formation of warriors and peacemakers forward. And so began the grand procession of the Casqui Nation to meet the one Saswanna called the "Son of the Sun."

The scouts ran to the front as the bearers struggled at the rear with baskets and litters overflowing with gifts. The march moved slowly. Many feet pounded the dry earth to a choking dust. In the hot months, I normally wore very little. The hat and shirt I had put on earlier with great pride had become an irritation that I wished I could remove.

We passed the edge of Casqui territory where it dropped off into the swamplands, further than I had ever gone. Trees with trunks thicker than the reach of six men blocked most of the sunlight, except where it shimmered off the dark swamp waters in the distance. The lowlands and its swamps were a natural defense that separated Casqui from its neighbors and enemies.

Two scouts ran in from the southeast. The warrior chiefs signaled and the grand march stopped. A bellowing cloud of dust raced toward us.

"Men of Casqui," King Issqui shouted from the center of the formation, "do not betray your people. Stand proud, stand strong, but stand in peace."

The formation opened to allow King Issqui through the ranks. He walked past the three warrior chiefs with the four wise-ones following. I stayed close to Tecco Tassetti. On orders, bearers hurried to the front and began laying out the many fine gifts on either side of the king.

Odd shapes led the rolling dust. Thirty or forty of these figures galloped toward us like a stampede of buffalo, but not buffalo or any known animal. Each moved with such grace and certainty that from afar it appeared as one creature.

At a point where no arrows could reach, they stopped. When the dust settled, I could make out men—strange men—sitting atop beasts the size of a bull elk, but with a long neck and a noble head without horns. Each man and beast sparkled as their shiny cloaks rippled.

One of the beasts reared and danced on two legs. Its rider shouted commands, and two raced back to where they had come from. Those that remained fell into a single line across the road. Each one pulled a gleaming sword of silver from a sheath at his side and held it across his chest as they marched forward.

King Issqui turned and shouted, "Men of Casqui, regard the unknown, but do not fear it."

I straightened my back and squared my shoulders like those around me. The strangers halted. Stance to stance, men of different worlds waited with hardly a movement as an odd sound of rumbling, pounding, screeching, and clanging grew ever louder.

Where the road enters the forest, four flags of three colors, black, white and blue, appeared against the trees. More men of metal carried the flags, followed by another hundred beast-riders, and two hundred or more men on foot carrying weapons known and weapons never seen before. Three or four hundred gaunt and bound slaves trudged at the rear. Out front, three giant fierce dogs circled a great prancing black beast carrying the greatest of all the riders.

The King of Casqui called for his throne. He mounted it as the strangers moved closer. The one on the black beast waved his hand, and the advance stopped. Their dust washed over Issqui.

The strangers had thick beards, wore hats of metal, and too many garments for the heat. But the beasts on which some rode held my greatest wonder. Beautiful and frightening, yet they carried their master where and whenever commanded.

King Issqui ordered his throne bearers forward. Between the line of beast-riders and the Casqui procession, he dismounted alone. The king of all Casqui faced the direction of the rising sun and made a long, slow bow, kneeling in silent prayer. When he stood, he turned in the direction of the setting sun and made another long bow, but remained humbled on the ground only a short time. Turning to the strangers, he made a sweeping bow, but bent only his back, not his knees.

He returned to his throne. His bearers raised him above all others, even the strangers on their great beasts. From behind the front ranks of the pale strangers, three red men stepped out. All three bowed to our king. One announced that they were interpreters in the service of their great lord, Hernando de Soto.

Issqui studied the interpreters, then looked up at the strangers and shouted loud enough for all to hear, "Very high, powerful, and renowned Master, I greet your coming. Soon as I had notice of you, your power, and your perfection, I determined to conform my wishes to your command."

One of the interpreters ran back to the strangers. Issqui waited while his greeting was translated to an insignificant man on a smaller brown beast.

"Is that their leader?" someone behind me asked.

The man rose up, turned to the strangers, and shouted in a language like nothing ever heard by my people. When the translator returned, the king continued his speech.

"Although you entered my land, capturing and killing the people who dwell upon it, who are my brothers, I will hold as right all that you might do, believing that it should be so and for a good reason that to you is perceivable, but from me is concealed. Since it is known that an evil may well be permitted to avoid a greater evil, I trust that this will be so. For from so excellent a prince, no bad motive is to be suspected."

King Issqui paused and glanced back at his people. He motioned to the gifts of skins and foods arranged on either side.

"My ability to serve is small, according to your great merit. And though you should consider even my most abundant will and humility in providing you all manner of services, I must still deserve little in your sight. If my ability to serve you can, with reason, be valued, I pray you receive it, and with it, my country and my people. For though you were the lord of the earth, with no more goodwill would you be received, served, and obeyed."

King Issqui put his hand to his mouth and bowed his head. My chest swelled to hear such an elegant speech given on behalf of the Casqui people. Surely, the words of their leader would be as grand.

The black beast strutted forward. His master rose-up spread his arms wide, hands open and empty. Then he spoke through the interpreter.

"I, Hernando de Soto, as governor of all these lands by the grace of the one true God, and on behalf of the Emperor and King of all Spain in the year of Our Lord 1541, accept your kind words and many gifts, but most of all your offer of peace and servitude. In return, I shall release all of your vassals whom my conquistadors have captured."

The interpreter paused. No one moved. Like me, they waited, expecting more.

"Now, may we go in peace to a place where I might find rest for my army?" The interpreter bowed his head.

"He offers no gifts?" someone behind me mumbled.

"No words of respect for the Great King of Casqui?" another asked.

"We have offended the Son of the Sun," some said.

"No," others shouted, "he has offended us."

King Issqui turned around. The grumbling stopped. He turned back to the translators.

"Very powerful Master, all that I have said and that which I have given is small and unworthy in your sight. However, it is my sincerest desire not to offend, so I offer that which has been my home and the home of my ancestors for many generations. You may rest in comfort surrounded by all that is the best of Casqui."

The translator quickly returned with Lord de Soto's reply.

"Though I am governor of this land, I wish to cause no

inconvenience. I desire to camp close to your town, but outside its walls, for I need an agreeable spot to accommodate all my men and horses."

"Horses," I repeated to myself. "This is what the strangers called their magnificent beasts. *Horses.*"

Issqui, the King of all Upper and Lower Towns, had given many fine gifts, offered his servitude and the ancestral lodge atop the sacred Mound of Casqui. He received little in return, but the right to lead the grandest procession ever to enter Nine-Rivers Valley.

Chapter 15

Manaha's Journey
Ninety-four years after "their" arrival

Story finished, the fire faded. Manaha's listeners slipped away, leaving an old woman without comfort or companion. The stillness around her invited little notice, but a flicker from above caught her attention. Did she blink or did the sky?

There was no moon and the only stars she could see were off to the west. Another blink. She heard no thunder. Not the slightest breeze stirred, but the air tingled.

In the village, they would be watching the same sky with concerns for their crops that needed rain, but not too much. Tension lay as thick as the dry heat. Young and old worried about the empty hunting grounds and the men crossing the river.

Light flashed across the dark sky. Manaha recalled the Hiding Cave, and the strange sights captured in the spark of Grandfather's flint. She promised herself once more. *I will never again go into that cave or any other.* The next flash brought the first lightning bolt. Manaha remembered an old song children would chant to tell if a storm was getting closer.

"When Brothers Thunder and Lightning race, know rain is near. When Brothers Thunder and Lightning race, know a storm is close. When Brothers Thunder and Lightning race, know it is best if Thunder is last."

Brother Thunder rolled across the island, down the creek, and back. *A storm from the northeast is rare,* she thought. "Maybe I should sleep in the village-lodge." Lightning answered with a strike from cloud to cloud.

"When Brothers Thunder and Lightning race, know rain is near. When Brothers Thunder and Lightning race, know a storm is close. When Brothers—"

Thunder grumbled. Manaha shook her head. Only her stubbornness would keep her out of anyone's lodge on a stormy night. Lightning filled the sky, spreading out in branches too quickly to count.

"When Brothers Thunder and Lightning race, know rain is near. When Brothers Thunder and Lightning race, know a—"

Brother Thunder rumbled around and around. Manaha began stacking up her firewood in a square around her basket of cuttings from the lightning wood, the pot of *sofkee*, a bag of hominy meal, and her pouch. Another flash lit up the island.

"When Brothers Thunder and Lightning race, know rain is near. When Brothers Thunder and Lightning—"

Wind came with the Brothers, tugging at the buckskin she had pulled over the pile of belongings. *Not much to cover up,* Manaha thought as she fought to weigh down the buckskin with rocks. Lightning ripped across the black sky.

"When Brothers Thunder and Lightning race—"

Thunder shook. Manaha wedged two pieces of firewood under her bad arm, took up her walking stick, and started for the village. "No reason to suffer," she told herself.

Lightning.

"When Bro—"

Thunder.

The wind began to howl, the trees to sway. She crossed the creek. Lightning . . . thunder, she could see the village. Then it was gone.

Lightning! Thunder!

The Brothers ran side by side. Manaha lost her race. The storm was on the village and there was no shelter nearby to keep her dry. She dropped her two pieces of firewood, untied her deerskin skirt and wrapped it tightly around the wood.

A large drop of cold rain smacked her shoulder as she turned toward the creek where an old willow tree hung over its bank. With her back against its trunk and the storm, she placed her walking stick across her lap and bent over her bundled firewood. Like so many strands of hair, the willow tree flowed with the wind. Other trees around her moaned, wishing they could bend like the willows. Branches snapped and blew across the creek where the great oaks danced with the thunderbolts.

The rain washed over her like a waterfall, like the healing waterfall her grandfather had taken her to long ago. She could see it all, even now, the clear pool, the giant boulders. She could hear the roar of the falls and most of all, feel the peace.

How long it rained, she could not know. In her mind, she was swimming beneath the waterfall. Manaha pushed up from the mud and memories with her walking stick. She put the firewood still wrapped in her skirt under her good arm, and started for the village.

The two women huddled around the small fire in the center

of the village-lodge did not look up when Manaha entered. No one objected as she walked to her old bench. It was empty and had not been used. She lay down without looking for approval. None was given.

She had no blanket, but she was not on the wet ground and there was fire close by. She fell into an uneasy sleep and woke to a ruckus of voices.

"The corn is gone!"

"Thunder-winds knocked it down," someone else shouted.

"It is all gone."

Everyone rushed out. Manaha followed after she had gathered her dry firewood. People came out of every lodge and ran to the fields.

Broken by the wind and pounded by the rain, almost all of the cornstalks lay on the ground, pointing like morning shadows to the west. Blackbirds had already discovered the tragedy. No one even tried to chase them away.

"We cannot let birds take our food," Manaha said.

No one wanted to hear her.

"Listen," she called out, "it was not a good crop, and it is not yet ready for harvest. But what is standing will grow, and many of the green ears on the ground can be saved."

No one responded. One by one, they turned away, leaving Manaha alone with the blackbirds and crows gathering in the surrounding trees.

"*Ah yie, ah yie, ah yie!*" Manaha yelled at the birds.

She turned and shouted at the village, "When the snow is deep, you will want for a cob of green corn."

She tore an ear from a crumpled stalk. The green shuck,

with dry patches of brown, opened easily. Rubbing her hand over the few kernels, she mumbled, "It will take a lot of ears to make a meal." Still, she could not let her work go for nothing.

Pulling up one stalk at a time from the mud, she picked off every ear no matter how small. With her bad hand tucked in her skirt, she cradled as many ears as she could hold and carried them to the edge of the field. After her second trip, crows swarmed the pile as though it had been gathered for them. Manaha chased them off, but they returned before she could get back in the field. She sat down next to the pile and stared across the field. How could this happen? Did her stories bring the thunder-winds?

"I cannot let them think that," she said as she watched a young boy run toward her. It was the shy boy who had carried wood for her first story-fire.

"I can help gather the corn . . . if you like," he said.

"You have helped me before, but this time, you must give me your name."

"Ic . . . hisi . . . Ichisi," he stammered.

"Ichisi, I should know that," Manaha said. "But as a woman grows older and slower, youth becomes more an object of disdain than interest."

"I can help," he repeated.

"Are you the youngest of Ta-kawa's sons?"

He looked down and nodded. Any boy with three older brothers had to be either a fighter or a loner. Small for his age, he did not look like a fighter.

"Yes, Ichisi, I believe you can help," Manaha said, "but I do not want to cause you any trouble with your father."

He stood for a moment before bending down and pulling an ear off one of the broken stalks. Manaha smiled when he laid his ear of corn on the pile she had started.

"Gather what you can around here," Manaha turned and walked back into the field, "but stay close enough to keep the birds away."

She carefully stepped over the bean pods and gourd vines. With the blessing of Father Sun, they would continue to grow. Harvesting was slow, hot, and messy and, in the end, disappointing. Manaha eased down next to their meager heap of corn.

"Ichisi, could you bring us water and something to eat?"

He returned with a gourd of water, hickory bread, and a bearskin to cover the pile and keep the birds out. After they had eaten, they gathered the few remaining good ears. Then Manaha and the boy marched off toward the village with as much green corn as they could carry.

Several boys ran out as they approached. A few tried to help Ichisi carry his load, but he held on tightly. Manaha marched across the plaza to the raised mud hut where green corn was stored. She placed her gift near its entrance. Ichisi added his load and ran back for the rest, leading a pack of boys.

Someone yelled, "Get Casinca to open the door."

Manaha began shucking the corn in the shade under the storehouse, between the four tall greased poles that held it up and kept the mice out. Others joined in, creating a stack of ears, a pile of shucks, and a basket of corn silk.

When he arrived, Casinca climbed a short ladder and yanked open the sealed door. Manaha had earned the right to

place the ears inside. She stood them on end, starting a new row along the back, behind the layer of shucks covering the very last of the winter corn. The door was resealed with a mixture of straw and mud.

Manaha had proven her worth and her loyalty to the village, but still no one spoke to her. She walked back to the island, alone, telling herself she did not need to hear their thanks. She had her listeners, but soon she began to doubt them. As darkness crept over the island, a half-moon cast a dim light across her empty fire-circle.

Is no one coming? She wondered.

The answer came in a rustle of footsteps off to the left, then behind her. When they settled, she circled the fire. Dropping in her offering of lightning wood, she chanted three times, "I hear listeners about."

Face to the fire, she spoke out in a loud voice. "Manaha, gatherer of corn, child of Palisema will tell you a story."

Chapter 16: Cayas Trace

Nanza's Journey
Forty-nine years after "their" arrival

My first thought, *Do not talk!*

"Nanza, get up," he yelled again. We were five days across the mountain forest from my burned home on the Buffalo River. I had not talked to Taninto in three days and last night only to ask for a story.

"Get up," he said and shook me.

I pressed my lips tightly.

He shook harder. "Did you hear me?"

"Today, we will cross Cayas Trace." He glared until I nodded. "We have to be cautious. There might be others about."

What did he know? I thought. Last night, staring into the fire, surrounded by darkness, I fell into his story. I walked through the crowded streets of Casqui, followed a grand procession of hundreds of warriors, and witnessed strange men on stranger beasts. With the light of morning, I saw only one old man surrounded by the damp, overgrown mound he had chosen for a campsite.

"Time to go," he insisted.

I stooped to drink from the stream.

"Wait," he said, "there is better water close by."

I took a drink anyway. He started across the field to a massive red oak growing at the edge of the steep hillside.

"Oak Springs," he announced when I walked up.

The spring flowed around and through boulders and a tangle of exposed roots, trickling down into a pool formed from smooth flat river rocks. I took a drink and a second while Taninto filled the water-skins.

We walked through the morning without another word. Glimpses of a valley appeared and disappeared off to the left.

"Valley of White Oaks," he said as we approached the rim.

Larger than Taninto's valley, but this was not a great valley of nine rivers. Distant ridges rose up as high on the other side.

He pointed down. "Can you see the creek?"

I stepped forward.

He jerked me back. "Not too far, someone might see you."

I pulled away.

"You can see from here, if you just look." He waited. "Can you see it?"

I shook my head.

"Cayas Trace runs this side of the creek and follows it until it flows into the Little Red River. The trail turns south, down to the land of the Cayas people and the Akamsa River."

Through the bare tops of countless white oaks, I could see flashes of sunlight reflecting off the water. I saw nothing of a trace.

"It is a path traveled by beast and man since ancient times," he said. "We must cross the trace, the creek," he pointed across the valley, "and climb that mountain without stopping."

I shrugged my shoulders.

"Stay here until I find a way down." He walked off to the north, still talking. "Eat some jerky and be ready to climb."

I nodded and watched him leave before venturing further out on the black slate covering the ledge. I could see the mountain curved off to the right and back in a face of sheer rock. A chunk of slate snapped under my feet, pieces slid over the edge and tumbled down into the forest.

I glanced around, hoping he had not heard. Looking out over the valley reminded me of standing on the edge of Narras Mountain. *Will I ever feel at home again?*

Thump, thump, thump. Taninto stood behind me, pounding the slate with his walking stick. "Come away from there," he demanded.

He led me to a dry wash that ran between two bluffs. We zigzagged from one side to the other down the steep gully. The further we went, the lower Taninto crouched. When we reached the bottom, the old man was hunched and skittish.

The trace lay only a few steps away. Beyond that, I could see the far bank of the creek. He threw his arm in front of me. I waited as he crept out into the opening. He motioned me forward.

"Follow me," he whispered, then bolted across the trace and kept running.

I strolled onto the old trail. It was like a shallow streambed that had never seen water. Wide enough for ten men to walk abreast, it was not dug or cut, but pounded into the earth. Nothing grew there, but it vibrated with the spirits of all who had passed. By the time I started up the other side, his panic had taken hold of me.

I ran for the creek and started down at the first place I came to. Taninto stepped from behind a thicket, grabbed my arm, and turned me upstream.

"The bank is too steep and muddy there," he mumbled.

At the bottom, we took off our moccasins and waded in. The knee-deep water ran strong and cold over solid bedrock. Across first, I easily climbed the other side, and waited at the top with a smirk.

He said nothing, put on his moccasins, and started running again. Almost no brush grew under the spread of the white oaks that filled the valley floor. His pace slowed as the land sloped up toward the far hilltops. I stopped to look back over the valley.

He rapped his stick against the ground and waved his arm.

"What are you afraid of?" I blurted out.

He ran back to me. I ran at him.

"Is this the place where my family was murdered?"

"Not here. This is not the place for talk," he growled through clenched teeth.

I did not care. I had broken my commitment. I had spoken, and now I wanted an answer. "Is that why you are so frightened? Did they torture my mother and my father here?"

"No!" He took a deep breath and whispered, "You are just a child, Nanza. You know nothing, nothing of this world."

"I am not a child. I am a woman, a woman returning to my people," I boasted in full voice.

"If you are so, be a woman of good sense. Speak in a whisper."

I wanted to yell as loud as I could, but I stomped my feet instead.

"This is not Blue Spring or close to it," he said.

I shook and snorted at him.

"It did not happen here."

"How can I believe you?"

"Not now," he said and trotted away.

I knew he would not stop or say anything more. I followed as he climbed the ever-steepening slope to a plateau of brown switch-grass rustling in the warm breeze. Long blue ridges stretched in every direction, layering one mountain beyond another. Across the endless forest, scattered blossoms of red and pure white brightened my spirit. Patches of faint green and dark yellow marked a new beginning.

We traveled east. The land became more uneven, broken up by jagged stones and boulders. Taninto led us down to a small creek. The water sparkled and raced past as we slowly made our way along the bank. High bluffs of knotty boulders closed in on both sides.

Long ago, one of the boulders had tumbled from its lofty perch down into the creek. Behind it, the water spread wide. In the shallows, he crossed to the other side and climbed up to an overhanging ledge. "We will camp under here," he said and did not speak again until we had set up camp and started a fire.

"Nanza." He gently laid his hand on my arm. "I know you are angry at me, but I have told you all that I know about your family."

Instead of pulling away, I stared down at his hand, tracing the deep wrinkle to nowhere.

"I kept all stories from you—at first because you were too young, then because I wanted to protect you in my valley. Now, to be safe, you need to know all that I know." He waited for me to look up.

"Nanza, listen and always remember."

Chapter 17: Shadow-Wind

Taninto's Journey
The day after - June 23, 1541

Like all of my people, I was humbled by the conquistadors and eager to pay homage to their leader Hernando de Soto, the Son of the Sun. Issqui, the Great King of Casqui, had stood before him and spoken elegant words of honor, service, and peace. He presented many fine gifts and offered the comfort of his own lodge.

Lord de Soto gave in return no gifts, few words, and a rejection of the finest lodge in all of Casqui. At his wish, the Spanish camped outside the walls, east of the north gate, among the town grove. Orders were given for poles, branches, and twine to build shelters and for firewood.

After I put away my shirt and feza, my uncle sent me to help where I could. I knew the groves of Casqui well. I had spent many summer days eating early-ripes from the mulberry and pear trees, climbing to the top of the tallest pecan tree, or wandering among the walnuts and persimmons. Keepers of the grove burned off the brush and the undergrowth each spring, making newly fallen limbs easy to find.

Before I could gather an armload, the Spanish had posted guards around most of the grove. One of them, with his sword

drawn, stepped across my path. I raised my collection of firewood. He motioned me around to the west past two other guards.

Although the Spanish language sounded like no other and their weapons seemed magical, their manner was not so different from ours. Their unusual appearance owed much to their clothes, armor and hats of metal. Yet for all the power and uniqueness of these strange men, their beasts intrigued me the most. I felt drawn to them. I could not keep my eyes off the proud animal they called "horse."

Young servants who all appeared to come from different nations tended to each horse as if it were an honored elder. With my second armload of wood, I risked a closer look at three of the animals tied to a rope stretched between two pecan trees. A horse tender worked to undress one of the horses. He swayed under the weight of the shiny cloak pulled from the animal's back. It was a cloak woven of metal like many of the conquistadors wore.

The true measure of these beasts lay bare; every part of their body rippled with power. Their eyes were deep, black, and full of understanding. Grace could be seen in their slightest movement. When they held their head high, there was no manner of man that stood prouder. Their skin glistened, each one a different color. Two were brown, one lighter than the other, and the largest and proudest, a dark gray.

A boy, not much older than I, wearing nothing but the bruises and scars from a long journey, stroked and brushed the gray horse. He worked his way around to the other side, and I crept in closer.

The gray broke his stance. His ears flicked in my direction. The fine black hair atop his head ruffled as he turned his long, graceful neck. He cast his eyes on me. I looked into the blackness and wanted no more at that moment than just to touch the great beast. When the horse snorted, the servant looked around. He grabbed the leather strap around its head, but did not say anything. I smiled. He smiled. I took another step forward.

With a sound like none I had ever heard, the gray jerked his head up, throwing the servant off to the side. Growing ever larger, the beast rose, standing upright on hind legs. Lips curled. Teeth flashed. And heavy hooves kicked about my head.

I turned to run, stumbled, and crawled away, trying to get back on my feet when a Spaniard grabbed me. He held me by the arms and yelled at the servant. I could not understand the words, but I understood the threat. I wiggled one arm free. He gripped the other harder and reached for his sword.

"Señor, Señor de Guzman," the horse servant called out. The Spaniard drew the weapon. With a blade raised above both our heads, the servant knelt beside me, bowed, and humbled himself in the language of the strangers. He pointed at me and the horses as he spoke. The Spaniard slowly eased his hold.

I took my first breath of the foul air that surrounded my captor. The strangers bathed little for many had a great fear of water. Among the Spaniards, he was a large man, taller and thicker than most. Without his headdress of metal, I could see his small eyes set in a round face with a great wooly beard. Altogether he was more a point of regard than fear.

The horse tender shouted, "*El desea servir al español,*" twice.

"*¿El desea servir al español?*" the conquistador asked.

"*Sí*," the servant answered.

The servant turned to me and said, "The man who holds you is Master Diego de Guzman, and I am his servant." He spoke to me in a language I had learned from travelers and traders. "Those are his horses," he said as two other servants tried to calm all three animals.

"I told my master a snake had frightened the horse and you intended no harm."

I started to explain. He held up his hand. "Before you speak, know that I also told him you wish to serve the Spanish masters." He repeated the words in Spanish, "*El desea servir al español.*"

"Tell your master," I stammered, "for his mercy, I offer my humble service for as long as he remains in the lands of Casqui."

As the servant repeated my words in the strange language of the Spanish, I could hear flutes playing in the distance. The Spaniard seemed pleased with my pledge and released his hold. I nodded to the servant and bowed deeply to my new master, Diego de Guzman.

Three men of different lands reached an understanding then with a common curiosity, all turned in the direction of the music. Women's voices mingled with the sound of flutes. Led by the singers, King Issqui and a party of headmen, tassettis, and old warriors advanced on Hernando de Soto's camp.

Diego ran toward the party as fast as a man of his size could. The horse servant returned to his duty, and I followed my new master. The conquistadors quickly formed a line in front of Lord de Soto's tent. They stood feet spread, fists clenched, but their swords sheathed.

I moved in behind Master Diego. The man to whom I had just pledged my loyalty pushed me out front. I stood between the line of conquistadors and the approaching leaders of Casqui. Of all those gathered, I was the least worthy. I knelt, and tried to make myself appear as small as I felt.

The music stopped when Lord de Soto stepped out of his tent with guards at either side, their swords drawn. Every Casqui knelt. King Issqui rose first. As the singers scampered to the back, he walked past the flute players, unchallenged by the guards.

"Hernando de Soto, my Lord," he said and bowed from the waist.

De Soto nodded and sat down on a throne that had been carried from his tent by two guards.

Issqui straightened and said, "Receive these gifts and the headmen, who brought them."

One by one, the leaders from each village came forward, bowed, and presented their gifts of fine cloaks, baskets, and pottery.

When all had passed, King Issqui said in a loud voice. "My Lord, I stand before you the worthiest among all these noble men to speak in your presence. I know, and have been counseled by many, that you are a man with great power. Some say a son of the sun."

As he spoke two men were led from the back.

"Though I am the leader for all the people of the Casqui Nation, I regard each one as if they were my own children." He motioned for the men. "The two sons before you are blind."

The men knelt where they were left.

"My Lord," Issqui called out, "I beg you to give sight to these empty eyes."

The blind men waved their arms and shouted, "Oh, Son of the Sun have mercy. Have mercy."

Lord de Soto raised his hand. Everyone fell silent. He turned to his interpreter and spoke without looking at the blind men or Issqui.

"There is one and only one," the translator began, "who reigns from the heavens above and has the power to make these men whole. That one is the Lord Jesus Christ to whom my army and I bow and from whom all blessings come. For He alone can grant your request."

Every Casqui head, bowed or not, sank a little lower. The translator paused and looked back at Lord de Soto. He motioned for him to continue.

"As governor of all these lands, I will pray to my Heavenly Father on behalf of your sons."

The two men were led away still blind, but hopeful. Issqui took another step forward.

"My Lord, for one to hear your words is to know that you are a man from the sky." King Issqui raised his voice and declared. "The Son of the Sun!"

The people cheered, and Issqui continued. "As such, it is necessary, I know, for you to go away. Our crops have long needed rain, and so it is, our people suffer. I beseech you, leave a sign which we may honor and pray to in times of need."

De Soto stood. "My Lord is Lord of all Lords. He suffered and died for the sins of all men on the earth. So that you may know Him, and your faith continue once I have gone, I will place within your town a blessed sign of Our Lord."

Issqui, King of all Casqui, fell upon his knees at these words, as did all those in his party. De Soto turned and walked away, giving several orders before entering his tent. The line of conquistadors remained in formation as the king and his party retreated.

I ran back to where Master Diego's horses were tied. The servant who had spoken on my behalf stood between the two brown horses.

From a safe distance, I called out, "I have returned to fulfill my promise to your master."

He looked me over while shaking his head. "For too long, these confused Spaniards wandered about the swamps in your land," he said. "The horses are in need of fresh, flowing water."

"I would be hon—"

"Show me," he demanded, "a cool creek where we can bathe the horses."

"The River of Casqui," I boasted, "is not far. Its waters are cool, but muddy. Some call it the *Little Muddy*."

He stared at me and said nothing.

"I can take you to a place upstream where the water is clearer."

He turned and called to the other horse tenders.

"If you will, but answer my questions," I added.

"And you talk of honoring a promise." He scowled.

My head dropped.

"As to answers," he said, "I abide few questions. Choose your words and time well."

I said nothing else while I led him, the great gray horse, the two browns and their tenders out of the grove. When we approached the north gate, my chest swelled with pride. People gathered on either side of our passing, some followed along. I strutted out front, nodded to anyone I recognized, and some I did not.

The horses cautiously crossed the dried riverbed to the water's edge. Their tenders waded in without hesitation and played like children as the horses drank. I watched in amazement as they took each horse out into the river and bathed it.

"He is called *Sombra Viento*," the tender said as he led the big gray horse out of the river. "It means 'shadow wind'."

"Shadow Wind," I whispered. I started to ask about the other horses, but stopped myself.

He said nothing more. The other two chattered all the way back to the Spanish camp. I listened closely, but understood very little.

Saswanna stood among the crowd who watched our return. I straightened my shoulders, swelled my chest, and acted as though I had not seen her.

Close to the grove, I let the other servants take the lead. I fell back alongside Shadow Wind and the servant.

"I am called Taninto by my friends," I said. The young horse tender stopped and turned to me. "And I, Taninto, ask of you only one question."

Shadow Wind tugged on the rope. The horse tender motioned the others to walk on.

He looked me in the eyes until I flinched, then he nodded.

"By what name would a friend call you?" I asked.

Slowly, a smile turned over his sneer. "I am Cooquyi of Ocute on the Ocmulgee River," he said with pride. His gaze slowly drifted down. "The land of my ancestors is many days far to the east."

I took a step back.

He looked up and chuckled. "Taninto, you have chosen your question well."

We both laughed. A question, an answer and we parted friends.

Chapter 18

Manaha's Journey
Ninety-four years after "their" arrival

Manaha watched the clouds rolling up from the southwest drift past the half-moon while her shadow listeners slipped silently away. She placed a night log on her campfire and fell asleep with little effort.

The next morning, with no need to go into the fields, she ventured down the island channel and around to where a tree lay across the creek. Blown over in the storm, water had built up behind the tangle of its roots and other limbs. Manaha enjoyed a tranquil morning bath in her own pool.

She decided to spend the day away from the clamor of the village and explore her island. *Could I become a hermit like my grandfather?* She wondered for a moment.

"A . . . ya . . . ya . . . ya . . . ya."

The single warbling yelp came from across the creek to the south.

"The hunting party is back." She waited for the flurry of yelps that should be coming from the rest of the party. When they did not come, she mumbled, "Only one returning?"

She hurried back to her campsite, stirred the cook fire, and added a log. Another messenger, she hoped, this time with good words. Those not already in the plaza scurried in with Manaha.

"Ta-kawa has returned," she heard as she wandered in between people and bits of conversations.

"No others?"

"Where are the others?"

"Only Ta-kawa and two outsiders."

"Two outsiders with a slave?"

"One old, one young."

"They wore war paint."

"The young one and Ta-kawa."

"Ta-kawa painted for war?"

"He said nothing."

"The outsiders are in the village-lodge."

"And Ta-kawa."

"He would say nothing?"

"Nothing of the others?"

"Only to the Council of Elders."

Suddenly, the crowd parted. Casinca and Koyota, the only elders remaining in the village, walked through the plaza, each carrying a gift of but a single skin: one a fox, the other a beaver. The elders passed in silence and disappeared into the village-lodge. No one had a guess as to what it all meant or knew what to do.

Through the eyes of an outcast Manaha watched trouble settle over her people. She could be silent no longer.

"We must treat our visitors well," she said, "if we are to hope for good in return." Whether it was the power in her voice strong from nights of storytelling or the truth in her words, she drew their attention.

"Why should we do your bidding, old woman?" someone shouted back.

"Generosity toward a guest is our custom, not the bidding of an old woman," Manaha said.

No one could argue against that.

"Wives, who fear for your husbands," Manaha called, "bring out your best foods. Brothers and sons, offer your best tobacco."

Still, no one moved.

"Hurry!" Manaha shouted. "Do not let our guests go unattended and think ill of our people."

Some turned to what they knew was their duty, but others remained in the plaza to ask the same questions and find no new answers. The wife of Ta-kawa returned first with his council robe and a loaf of acorn hard bread. The village had little to spare. One by one, worried wives and mothers humbly entered the council lodge with their gifts of berries, pears, nuts, dried fish, and some meat.

Manaha had no food to offer, but she could gather wood. A council fire must burn bright for the elders to find the best path. Near the door of the village-lodge, she placed her gift of firewood and added three shavings from her lightning-staff. She could do nothing more in the village, but she could prepare for her next story.

Darkness settled in, well before her story-fire flickered. The moon and stars hid from her and the Hachia people. A large fire burned in the plaza. Manaha could see its light dancing in the treetops. Most everyone would be there, waiting through the night.

For a moment, she imagined herself before such a fire

surrounded by listeners, telling her stories. She shook herself. Nothing surrounded her, but an empty circle.

She stood, faced the darkness, and chanted, "Listeners come round. Come round, come round. Listeners come round."

To the right, a shadow listener stepped close, maybe another one, then the faithful listener settled in behind her. She let the three cuttings clutched in her hand fall into the flames.

"I will tell a story."

Chapter 19: Meadow Creek

Nanza's Journey
Forty-nine years after "their" arrival

The seventh morning of my journey to Nine-Rivers Valley, I woke well before sunrise. He poked at the dying fire. A few embers flashed to a flame, lighting up the rocks all around and above me. I sat up, ready to jump to my feet before I saw the night sky beyond the edge of the overhang.

"This is not a cave," I reassured myself and turned my back to sleep.

It was still cold, but it was light when I woke the second time.

"Nanza." He shook me. "A late-winter wind blows from the northeast; we must cross Meadow Creek before the storm catches us."

I rolled over and took some jerky from my back-bundle.

The results of heavy morning dew dripped from the ledge and floated in the air with the musky dark odor. He kicked dirt over the fire while I tried to eat then he yanked the bundles onto his back and started off. Even with his walking stick, he slid twice on the way down the bluff.

"Nanza," he called from the stream at the bottom.

I tied on my bedroll and stomped after him. When I reached

the bottom, he had already crossed further up the stream. It split into two fast-moving branches around a bed of rocks and pools of stagnant water. I jumped the first channel and danced across the rocks. A thin layer of ice rimmed the puddles. The other channel spread wider than the first, but if he had jumped, so could I.

The shelter bluffs on either side vanished into forest-covered hills as I ran to catch my guide. The valley between was flat and open with few trees or briars. Pale shades of orange, red, and yellow mingled with new green in the distant gray forest. A cool wind twirled the brown waist-high stalks of purple-top as wisps of clouds raced across a dark blue sky.

My guide followed a slight depression meandering across the field as Father Sun topped the tree line. "In the shelter of that hillside," he said and pointed, "where the stream we just crossed joins Tick Creek, there was a village full of people, but that was a lifetime ago."

"What happened?" I asked before I thought.

"Sickness," he said as I stepped to his side. For a moment, his eyes turned on mine. I wanted to ask more, but the pain in his expression stopped me. He walked away. I followed with the word "sickness" still resounding in my thoughts.

Before high sun, we reached Tick Creek. The swollen stream would have been difficult to cross if not for a spot where logs were jammed one against the other. On the far side, the forest closed in and started downhill. Everywhere lay green-gray, moss-covered rocks, large and small, but not on the trail that he followed. Nothing but an occasional tree grew from the leaf-covered depression, attesting to its great age and lack of use in

recent times. Rocks pushed to the downhill edge lined the trail as it began to zigzag against the steepening slope. Each time we cut back to the right, the sound of crashing waters rushed up.

"Meadow Creek," he said.

A few paces off the trail, the mountainside dropped almost straight down to a boulder-filled ravine, too deep and narrow to see the bottom.

"It is there." He had learned to read doubt in my face.

I could hear it, but I wanted to see. With a good hold on a young oak, I leaned out. The churning creek roared and twinkled in between the tumble of boulders.

"You will see it again," he said and continued down the trail.

The descent was long and slow, but not difficult. Even so, Taninto, the great wanderer, fell once. He pulled himself up before I could reach him. I did not notice his limp until we were on the valley floor. The path that brought us down the mountainside disappeared among river-worn rocks and patches of brown grass. He stopped to listen then trotted across the open field. I followed, stomping on the small hole his walking stick left in the sandy soil.

We quickly waded through a wide but shallow stream. On the other side, the trees stood tall and spread themselves into a dark roof over thick patches of lifeless vines, waiting in the moist soil for a warmer day. A hint of green sprouted from large-leafed plants, no more than a hand high. Pools of sunlight warmed the cool north wind.

We crossed two more streams and another field. Water was all around, even under my feet. I could feel its power surging. I could hear it roar. It was more than just a meadow creek. It was rain-swollen and raging.

"It is higher than I expected," he said. "Still, we must cross it before the storm reaches us." I shook my head even as he continued. "I will carry everything over then come back for you."

He took off his moccasins, pouch, breechcloth, and rolled them in his cloak. Leaving his walking stick behind, he picked up his bundles and wobbled barefoot across the rocky shore.

"We can have a big fire on the other side," he said as he waded in. The further he went, the deeper he sank. Soon, only his head and bundles bobbed above the racing water. He struggled to get up the muddy bank on the far side, dropped the bundles, and returned to the creek without ever looking up at me.

A gust of wind chilled my bare skin as I watched him carry away my clothes and back-bundle wrapped in the buffalo hide. It took longer for him to cross the second time and even longer to return.

He staggered out of the creek and grabbed up his walking stick. Spasms shook his body as his pale lips quivered. His voice wavered, but his steady eyes fixed on mine. "Come," was all he needed to say.

I followed him to the water's edge. He held his walking stick by the bottom and waved the end that should have been bound to his bad hand at me.

"I will pull you across," he said and dragged me in, deeper and deeper into the swift current. Cold spread up through my legs. They moved ever slower. He pulled on the walking stick and it slipped out of my hand.

"Hold on, my child," he said.

"I am not a child!" I shouted back. The frigid water had numbed my body, but inside I burned. I snatched up the stick.

"Use both hands," he said. "Hold on."

He tugged on it. I pushed back. We fought each other and the current on into the channel. Water reached his chest and skimmed over the stick between us. I stopped fighting.

Taninto tugged me across the main channel, his head bobbing in and out of the waves. Water slapped my face, splashed over my head. Against it all, I felt his steady pull.

And I felt him slip. He disappeared. The current grabbed me and pulled. The walking stick yanked back. Taninto regained his footing. He tugged again. My hand slipped. I clutched the bindings. They broke.

"Grab it!" he shouted and shoved the stick toward me.

"Grandfather," I screamed, stretching, reaching for the stick, a low-hanging branch, the bottom—anything. I was separate and apart, moving with the spring flood.

Taninto plunged into the channel and swam toward me. His walking stick floated past as he reached for my arm. The creek had carried us far from the crossing. It was too swift and deep to reach the far side. Against the current, he pulled us back to the shallows. I crawled onto the rocky shore and curled into a quivering ball.

"Get up," he said.

I could twitch. I could shake. But I could go no further.

He yelled, "Get up. We must cross the creek."

"I am too cold."

"Our provisions—our clothes—are on the other side. Get up. Now!"

Large raindrops began to pound the earth around us.

"I cannot do it," I said. A drop hit me on the head. "I need your help." Another stung my back. It felt as if each one bored a hole into my skin.

He jerked me to my feet and marched back up the creek. My body shivered. I could hardly walk. But I followed. Sleet began to mix with the rain.

Taninto waded out until the water reached his chest. The creek felt warm against the wind. He stopped and waited for me. Bits of sleet floated by, as I reached out to him. He picked me up and raised my head above his.

His arms shook. He was unsteady and stumbled, but fought to keep my head above the water. Cold mud squished through my toes when he put me down on the other side. I climbed onto the shore and started for my shawl.

"Brush the water off first," he said as he dragged himself out of the creek.

All around, large drops of ice snapped against dead leaves and the bare branches. I shook and wiped off what I could. He handed me his buffalo cloak. "This will be warmer."

My teeth chattered; I swayed, unsure of my legs. I wanted to lie down.

He pitched my moccasins in front of me. "Put them on," he said, gathering up our clothes and back-bundles. Draping my shawl over his head, he started running, still naked.

"Hurry, Nanza," he called as he climbed toward an outcropping of square-shaped boulders. One large slab leaned against another with its corner buried into the hillside. In the shelter of the two, he knelt down and opened his back-bundle.

He took out his flint and a wad of shredded cedar bark. I stood over him, numb. Sleet and rain fell. His shaky hand could not coax a spark from the flint.

He glared up at me. "Do something," he said. "Get some kindling, some twigs. Hurry."

I picked up the small branches around me and snapped them into kindling. Before I had a handful, a glow flickered in his cedar shavings. He set it against the standing slab and added a few dried leaves and some of my twigs. The slant of the boulder shielded the flame from the wind and rain.

"Bring more kindling before it all gets wet," he said.

I brought what I could carry in one hand with the other holding the cloak tightly. Once he had a good fire burning, he stopped to dress. He warmed himself at the fire for a moment. Then he was gone. I dressed.

"Give me the buffalo cloak," he said when he returned with his load of firewood.

I scowled as he handed me my shawl.

"Keep the fire burning. I will build a lean-to."

He tied one end of the buffalo hide to a tree and the other to a broken limb that he wedged between the two slabs. He staked the bottom out to the west. Before he could weight down the edges with rocks, I had crawled under the lean-to.

"Get out. Firewood goes in first."

We stacked what we had in the back. He went in search of anything else dry enough to burn while I tended the fire. The rain and sleet slowed then stopped after dark.

I heard its soft patter before I saw the first flake of snow. Side by side, we sat and watched snow swirl about the firelight.

The buffalo hide pitched and rustled, but I felt warm inside and out, sheltered.

The fire dried my lips. I licked them and worked my jaw side to side. Slowly, I exhaled in a long sigh—one word followed, "Grandfather."

His eyes flashed from the fire to mine. He dropped one corner of his mouth and tilted his head the same direction, but the rest of him smiled. He put his hand on my back. I stammered, "Thank you."

Grandfather squeezed my shoulder and said, "I shall tell a story."

Chapter 20: Tallest Cypress

Taninto's Journey
Two days after "their" arrival - June 24, 1541

I had worn a hat of manhood for just two days, and had already pledged my service to a Spaniard while they remained in the land of Casqui. My master, Diego de Guzman, a conquistador of good fortune, had three horses where many Spaniards had none. Without question, a warrior of great courage, but he was just one of many in the army of the Son of the Sun.

I spent the night inside the walls of Casqui and, like most of my people, I slept little. Saswanna and Shadow Wind, the best of Master Diego's horses, filled my thoughts whether waking or sleeping. When I could no longer lie in my uncle's summer patio, I got up and wandered about the streets to the plaza.

Word had spread of Lord de Soto's response to the blind men. Most found hope in the promise that the Son of the Sun would pray for their sight. But some distrusted him and doubted his power.

I left the plaza and the arguments, drifting toward the Spanish camp as the rising sun cast an orange glow across the tops of the pecan grove. Light streaked down through the branches in long, smoky fingers across many fires.

Spanish guards stood at the edge of the camp ready to turn back anyone who attempted to enter. Two horsemen and their grand beasts strutted among them. Their presence provoked fear in most Casquis and surely filled the guards with confidence. The horse made its rider more than a man. I admired that power.

I wanted to see Shadow Wind again and talk to my new friend Cooquyi, but I had neither the nobility nor the courage to try the Spanish guards. Instead, I climbed a large mulberry tree where I could see most of the camp. Straddling a thick limb, my back against the trunk, I watched and ate mulberries.

Through the morning haze, I could see the silhouette of horses tied where Master Diego's had been the day before. The largest held his head high. I knew that was Shadow Wind. The men of Spain ambled about, showing little concern for what I could see around the grove.

People gathered and filled the roads. Whole families carried the best of their spring crops. Young warriors in bright feathers ran in groups. Village headmen escorted gifts, and old warriors traveled alone.

Of all the festivals throughout the year, none matched the excitement of this gathering to see the Son of the Sun. I searched the crowd for my family. I had little reason for doing so. If all but one man from all the villages of Casqui did not come, that man would be my father.

My father was a pottery-maker, who cared nothing for ritual or tradition. His water vessels and head-pots were known throughout Casqui, but he thought of little else.

A procession began to take shape outside the north gate.

Like the day before, singers and a flute player led King Issqui toward the Spanish camp. But today, Uncle Tecco walked among the party with two other wise-ones.

I climbed down and joined a group of other onlookers cautiously following the party into the Spanish camp. We huddled together, trying to hide behind the last warriors as a shy child would with its mother. The flute fell silent. I pushed to the edge of the crowd.

Hernando de Soto stood flanked by his royal guard. Issqui approached alone as he had done the day before. He made a great bow to Father Sun in the east then bowed to Lord de Soto.

With his head still bent, he said, "As your humble vassal, I ask first that you forgive this intrusion on your day."

De Soto nodded slightly when the interpreter finished.

Issqui straightened and continued, "I speak for the people of my nation. And I say that all are waiting for the time to serve you and your god. A god so great as to be served by a Lord as powerful and wise as you must indeed be a god greater than all the gods of Casqui."

Two Spanish holy men stepped closer as Issqui's words were translated. Lord de Soto showed little interest.

Bending a knee, then his back, King Issqui cried out, "Son of the Sun, I beseech you." His voice wavered. "Do not leave your humble servants without the promised sign, without a hope of knowing your god."

Some of the conquistadors stirred, ambushed by Issqui's passion. The power of his plea brought tears to the eyes of the Spanish holy men.

Lord de Soto motioned for Issqui to stand. "Do not be

troubled," he said. "I could not depart from a nation of people so in need of our Heavenly Father without leaving behind a manifestation of His true love."

"Return tomorrow," Lord de Soto said as he stood. "I will give your people that which you seek, that which all men should seek."

I could feel joy spreading around and through me as I listened to the translation. Some bowed their heads, some mumbled, and some ran back shouting Lord de Soto's promise to anyone who would listen, but all felt the power. Word of the gift that tomorrow and the Spanish would bring reached into the town of Casqui, out its gates, and up and down its rivers.

Everyone began his or her own preparation for the coming of the greatest of all days. I quietly slipped away to the mulberry tree before Uncle Tecco spotted me.

I could see signs of activity on the far side of the Spanish camp. Two lines of slaves staggered from the back toward the camp guards. Bound together with the Spanish ropes of metal, they wore nothing but a metal collar.

Freedom taken, their spirit had fallen long ago. Every eye downcast, their backs bent under the burdens they carried. *Those wretched beings surely were once men of little courage or evil intent toward Lord de Soto to be so broken*, I thought.

Spanish foot soldiers flanked by horse warriors surrounded the slaves. A tender ran at the side of each horse. I thought that I recognized one as the tender to Master Diego's dark-brown horse. I felt certain that to toil in the service of a Spanish master must be an adventure every day.

The Spaniards and their slaves marched out of sight on the road to the Tyronza River. Soon after, I spotted Cooquyi walking

with Shadow Wind, the other brown horse, and its tender, Wasse. I climbed down to meet them at the edge of the camp. Cooquyi nodded as he approached. Shadow Wind seemed even larger than I remembered.

"Your friend, Taninto, is here," I said if he had forgotten my name. "I come to serve your master, the master of these great beasts, and the one to whom I am indebted, Master Diego de Guzman," I boasted, more for the Spanish guards than for Cooquyi.

"Yesterday, you served my master well," Cooquyi said. He frowned and said something in Spanish. The guard nodded.

Cooquyi turned back to me. "Master Diego is grateful. Your debt has been paid." His expression hardened. "Now you can go back to your family."

"I pledged my service to your master for more than one day."

"Go back to your people," he insisted.

"But I can guide you and these fine horses to the river."

"In my servitude to the Spanish," Cooquyi said, "I have crossed more rivers than you know of and am certain I can find this one again without your help."

"I do not doubt your ability, my friend, but you may not know how crowded the roads and the banks of the Little Muddy River are with so many coming to see the sign that the Son of the Sun has promised."

"You have served the Spanish. Take that and be proud."

"Then I wish to serve the horses," I said.

Cooquyi started to speak, stopped and just shook his head.

"Casqui is a nation of two rivers," I said. "The other is the Tyronza. From here, it is a longer walk, but it is away from town and the crowds."

Cooquyi called to Wasse. "Come on, my friend says he will take us to a better river."

I looked about for the third horse.

"Master is riding the old brown," Cooquyi said.

So it was Master Diego I had seen that morning. I did not let on and waited for Cooquyi to tell me more.

"Master left with a second party taking supplies and more slaves," he said. "They are commanded to help bring back the largest tree they can find."

"The tallest are the bald cypress in the swamps further up the Tyronza River."

Cooquyi tilted his head and shrugged his shoulder. He did not care. I wondered if he already knew what the promised *sign* would be.

I tried to imagine the tallest cypress and the ability of the Spanish to cut it down and move it to Casqui. What could be created from a cypress that would be a symbol of the Spanish god to which my people could pray for rain in times of drought and for peace in times of war?

"The Tyronza River is not as big as the Little Muddy, but it is clearer," I said as I led them alongside a stream to a sandy beach where it empties into the Tyronza.

The two horses and their tenders quickly waded into the river. I watched from the shore, turning over the problem of which question to ask next.

They called for me to join them, and soon we were splashing and laughing like three friends. The horses took little notice of our boyhood games. Later, I watched Cooquyi wipe-down

Shadow Wind, amazed at the taut strength beneath the smooth gray skin. Wasse and Cooquyi took the horses above the bank and tied them up where they could graze.

I started to join the two tenders deep under the shade of an old elm tree. Cooquyi looked up. I hesitated and straightened my back.

"Cooquyi, traveler of many lands, keeper of Shadow Wind," I said, "I have one question."

Wasse looked away. Cooquyi nodded.

"What will you tell me about the Spaniards?" I asked as I sat.

Wasse stood and walked toward the river.

A smile spread across Cooquyi's face. "You have asked wisely, once again," he said. "I will answer your question."

"I am told that two summers ago the Spaniards came from across the ocean in great boats carrying six hundred conquistadors, twelve holy men, and more than two hundred horses. The one your people call the Son of the Sun is known to his men as g*overnor* because the King of Spain granted him the power to govern all the lands and nations that he could conquer and settle."

Cooquyi paused to glance up and down the river. "They came to your land as they did mine, by the greatness of their god with speeches of friendship and peace." He turned to me. "But deceit is their way."

"What do you mean?" I asked.

"Among the Spanish, rank and order are determined by possessions rather than wisdom or bravery. Conquistadors are trained to kill and do so without hesitation, ceremony, or cause."

Cooquyi pushed the sandy soil around with his feet. "Some, like Master Diego, are men of honor, but many will say or do anything to possess the one thing they truly seek."

"What do they desire—"

He cut me off with a wave of his hand.

"It is not safe to even speak of it." Cooquyi stood. "I will say no more about your Son of the Sun," he said then whispered. "I know the torture of his punishment."

He paced away and back. "Let me tell you instead," he said, his eyes sparkling, "about the first time I saw the Lady of Cofitachequi, Grand Queen of Talomico, on her purple throne."

Cooquyi could have talked the morning away about the people and lands he had seen if not for Shadow Wind. The horse raised his head, pointed his ears toward the road, and snorted. The other horse looked up. Both began to prance.

"Someone is coming." Cooquyi jumped up and grabbed Shadow Wind's harness. He pulled the horse's head down and stroked it as he listened.

"Spanish coming from the east," he said. "Taninto, go up to the road. See if our master is returning. He would be angry to see Shadow Wind and the young brown so far from the camp."

The screeching of metal and the pounding of hooves grew closer.

"The Spanish will think nothing of you being there," he said. "Hurry."

What someone might think was not in my thoughts as I ran to the road. I heard Spanish voices and stepped behind a bush just as the first riders approached. Master Diego rode in front of two other horsemen. I waited until he passed before I stepped to

the edge of the road. The conquistadors who followed gave me little notice.

Behind the horses, soldiers leaned on their lances as they walked. In between them, chained slaves struggled to carry Spanish tools and goods. I turned and ran back toward the river. Cooquyi met me, leading both horses.

"Where is Wasse?" I asked.

"What did you see on the road?"

"Master Diego. He led other Spaniards and a party of slaves toward camp."

"He will report to Governor de Soto first," Cooquyi mumbled.

"Where is Wasse?" I asked again.

"He is still at the river."

"What will happen if he does not go back?"

"They will find him. They always find the ones who run away. Those they do not kill, they feed to the governor's dogs for pleasure."

"I will find him."

Cooquyi studied me. "I have to get the horses back to camp," he said and ran off with a rein in each hand.

I did not have to go far. Wasse lay on his stomach at the edge of a steep bank, surveying the river. I crawled up next to him. Men from Casqui waded in the shallows on either side of the river. They pushed and pulled on the trunk of a large cypress tree. Evenly rounded with all the bark and limbs removed, it stretched more than the reach of six men.

I poked Wasse and motioned him to follow me. He shook his head and pointed back at the bank. A horse and rider trotted up to the spot where we had dried off in the sun. The rider studied the hoof prints in the sandy soil. He turned his horse toward us and followed Shadow Wind's tracks up the shore to the trees.

Two more horsemen came down the river. They yelled at the Casqui workers, then at the rider closing in on our hiding place. He turned and galloped toward them.

Face to face, they argued while workers guided another cypress around the bend. Much larger than the first it moved with the river, fighting the effort of the slaves in the water and the Casquis pulling from the banks. It drifted by for so long, it was impossible to guess how tall it once stood.

When the tallest cypress had passed with all the riders and workers, I poked Wasse again. "I can get you back to camp," I said.

He ran with me as I led him away from the river on a short-cut around the road. We caught up with Cooquyi and the two horses just before he reached the camp.

I strutted past the guards with a horse and tender on each side. I held my head high while Cooquyi and Wasse stared at the ground. Their pace slowed and shoulders slumped. Gone were any sign of the two boys I had played with at the river.

Neither said a word as we walked to their campsite. Wasse rekindled the fire. Cooquyi tied Shadow Wind to one tree and the young brown to the other. I stood between the two, awkward and unnoticed. Later around the fire, they began to tell stories. A few stories made them laugh, but all made me wonder how I knew so little. I spent my first night inside the camp of strangers, but among friends.

Chapter 21

Manaha's Journey
Ninety-four years after "their" arrival

Story ended, the teller faded. The island and the trouble around it became Manaha's world once again. She drew a deep breath and tried to imagine Taninto, the old man she knew, living those adventures, seeing horses and conquistadors. Why had he kept those stories from her for so long? She did not completely understand, but she knew what he meant when he said, "The story you hide can become a weight you will bear every day until it is told."

Behind Manaha, a bush rustled once then again. A departing listener's way of saying, *I was here*. Above her, the reality of the vast night sky spread beyond her ability to see or grasp. *A tiny speck in it all*, Manaha thought, *but important to someone*.

Between the surrounding darkness and the sky, light from the plaza fire danced about the treetops. A slow drumbeat carried the sad chanting of the Hachia people. Even though they had rejected her, she would always be in their circle. Manaha and her people, young Taninto and the lost nations of Nine-Rivers Valley were all part of the same great circle.

Manaha began to talk to her grandfather like she had never

done when he was alive. To someone who did not know, she explained late into the night the suffering of the last Hachia village. From someone who could not be seen, she hoped for but found no answers.

"I must also learn to choose my questions," she said and turned to her bed.

Manaha woke uneasy. Today they would hear the reason for the visit of the two outsiders and learn about the hunting party. She bathed and hurried off to the village without taking time to eat.

The fire in the center of the plaza burned low as three young boys beat the drum without dancers or chants. A few women moved about while children played like any day before. Everything known of the guests had been told and retold. Nothing could be done but wait for word from the village-lodge.

The sun had passed well into the western sky before Casinca appeared in the doorway. The drum fell silent. Whispers spread as he crossed the plaza and onto square-ground where he stopped in the center.

Women rushed in behind, filling the benches. Manaha stood between the Blue and White sheds, neither in the south nor the west. Boys and the few old men remaining in the village came from the lodges and children from their play. When everyone had settled, Casinca spoke.

"The men of the hunting party are safe," he said. "All . . . all but four."

Some gasped, but no one breathed.

"I will not speak of those four until I have visited their lodges."

Casinca turned a complete circle as if looking for direction. He raised his voice. "The hunting party is safe," he said and smiled with effort.

No one moved or smiled back. His words "all but four" still echoed in their thoughts. Would he visit *their* lodge?

Casinca spread his arms, "The rest are unharmed. Our men are unharmed, but . . . they have all been taken prisoners by the Tulla Nation."

Muted cries came from all sides. Manaha steadied herself against a shed post.

"The men are unharmed," he repeated louder.

"All but four," someone shouted.

Casinca turned in their direction. "Listen," he said. "In good faith, Ta-kawa has been returned to us with two honored Tulla warriors."

Cries could no longer be muffled.

Casinca shouted over them, "Ta-kawa reports that the Tulla people have treated our men with great respect."

"All but four," they shouted again.

"What four?" another asked.

"Hear me out," he yelled. "Honorable men of Tulla have brought with them offerings of peace and the talk of barter."

"What barter?" some asked.

"Tomorrow . . . " Casinca raised his arms and waited. "Tomorrow at the midday's sun, the tribe will gather in the village-lodge to hear from the men of Tulla." He turned to his clan under the White shed. "Preparations must be made. Our guests will feast in my lodge tonight."

"Tell us!" the angry shouted. "What barter?"

"Not now," Casinca shouted back. "Now is the time for mourning our dead." He stepped back and turned toward the plaza.

No one moved as he walked away. No one hurried off to begin the preparations. No one knew who or what to mourn.

Casinca disappeared into the village-lodge and reemerged leading the two Tulla guests. The younger strutted as he crossed the plaza, teeth clenched behind black tattooed lips. A single tattooed line swirled around his chest and wrapped down one leg.

The thin older outsider had no tattoos but garnered more regard and amazement, for his head was not round but long. From the brow ridge, his forehead swelled up and back to the size of two heads. Some in the village had heard of a race of long-heads, but no one had ever seen one.

A crowd quickly gathered along the short walk to Casinca's lodge. His wife and daughters scurried in behind the guests and closed the opening. More people gathered, waiting for Casinca to come out with one question on all of their minds. *Whose lodge would he visit?*

Mumbled prayers and grumbled outrage rolled around his lodge like distant thunder. Casinca stepped out. It all stopped. He turned in the silence toward the lodges of the Beaver clan.

"Stay away," one woman pleaded.

"Casinca, wise Casinca visit us another day," cried a second.

He did not falter but went straight to the home of Kiatio. He and two of his sons were with the hunting party. Kiatio's daughter tried to push Casinca from the path and hung on until he stepped through the door. The lodge quickly filled with the

Beaver clan. Outsiders surrounded it. Manaha stood back as they leaned in.

"Kiatio and his oldest son are dead," they began to whisper.

After a time, Casinca stepped out and turned toward the village-lodge. As he walked, he chanted softly.

"Where is he going?" the crowd asked. "Who else?"

When he passed the village-lodge, everyone knew. Only one lodge stood to the east on the bank above the creek—the home of Hazaar, beloved elder of the tribe.

No one followed. They turned around and into each other. Their question and the answer were the same, "Hazaar is dead? Hazaar is dead!"

No longer just sorrow, their grief erupted. Anguish breeds despair and still there was another. From Hazaar's lodge, Casinca pushed through a crowd of unbroken silence. Swaying as he approached the plaza, he stopped. His stature, his strength, fell away in slumps. He turned toward his own home.

"Not my son, it was his first hunting party!" Casinca's wife screamed.

The village splintered. Their bonds unraveled. Families and hopes scattered in all directions.

Manaha drifted back to her island but could not stay. When she returned to the village, there was no one on the plaza or in the square-ground, no one chanting, no one beating the drum.

The purifying smell of sweet grass floated from the door of the village-lodge where she left another gift of lightning wood shavings.

"In times of grief, few gifts or words have merit, but stories told will comfort, even heal," she could hear her grandfather say.

Manaha walked to the center of the plaza and shouted for all to hear, "Tonight, my fire will burn bright and long for all who wish to share the stories of those we have lost."

Hoping for the best, she built a large fire and lit it just before sunset. The day's light slipped away until the fire was all she saw, its crackle all she heard. Manaha bowed her head, closed her eyes, and waited for the one sound she had come to depend on, cautious footsteps behind her.

They came and when they settled, she began to chant. Three times around and she said, "We will share a story."

Chapter 22: First Friend

Nanza's Journey
Forty-nine years after "their" arrival

I found myself alone on a snow-covered spring morning deep in the Ozark Mountains. The campfire had burned out. White, silent hills surrounded the cold lean-to. I pulled my shawl tight and climbed out. Taninto appeared from behind.

"I have some dry grass for your moccasins, " he said with a rare smile.

I shook my head.

"It is a wet snow," he said, still smiling.

I took the grass and sat down on one of the rock slabs. He untied the buffalo hide and shook it without a notice of my glare or the snow landing on me. While I lined my moccasins, he searched through his back-bundle. I tried not to watch as he pulled out a piece of deerskin not much larger than his hand and tied a length of twine to each corner.

He held his work up like a sling and grinned. "Come along, Nanza, I know where we might find a friend."

"A friend?" I could not stop myself. "What friend?"

"Come along." He grabbed the buffalo hide and bounded off like a young boy. I followed like a little sister. He slowed down just below a ridge overlooking the creek. We crept along the hillside above a small ravine. Upwind of a fallen tree, he laid the buffalo hide on the snow. He crouched and pointed at a cluster of three trees on the far side, growing from one trunk.

I watched the hillside as I puzzled over the old man's manner. He grinned and pointed. Something moved, black against snow. In the rocks, just below the three trees, a long snout cautiously sniffed a cool breeze blowing up from the creek.

"A wild dog," Taninto whispered and pulled me down.

Through a space between the snowdrift and the underside of the fallen tree, I could see the dog slink out of its burrow. Starting at the head, it shook its thin body out to the tail. Its coat rippled with a shaggy mix of red, black, and brown. The dog sniffed the air then with a quickness of purpose, ran toward the creek.

When it was out of sight, Taninto stood. "Stay here until I call for you." He slipped twice in the snow and wet leaves as he hurried down the valley and up the other side.

At the burrow, he took a fresh rabbit pelt from his pouch and pushed it into the hole. When he pulled it out, three puppies tugged on the other end. A fourth and a fifth pup stumbled out behind the others. I had already started down the hill when Taninto signaled.

"Move slow," he said as I rushed up. I knelt close to him. All the puppies fought over the pelt that he held over their heads. The old man smiled. "Meet your new friend."

"Friend?" I asked. "One of these puppies?"

"That is for you to decide," he said.

I reached for one of them.

He grabbed my arm. "Touch only the one you choose."

I leaned back and watched them and the old man play. They all looked strong and healthy. I scooted in closer, and they scampered away, all but the smallest. With a coat of brown and patches of black or the other way around, it bounced toward me and fell headfirst at my knees. I did not have to make a decision; it was made for me. I took my first friend, yelping and squirming into my arms.

Two of the puppies disappeared into the den. Taninto herded the last two into the hole with a stick. He reached over and lifted my puppy's tail.

"You carry *her*," he said. "Follow me."

The puppy wiggled, but I held her tightly and tried not to fall as I followed Taninto down the snow-covered ravine. Out of sight of the burrow, Taninto took out the sling he had fashioned.

"Lay the pup in here," he said, "on its belly."

I placed the puppy facing him with legs straddling the small piece of deerskin he held in his hand. He stroked and whispered to the puppy until its head rested on his forearm.

"Hold her, like this," he demanded as I eased my hand under her belly and the sling. He took the twine attached at each corner and tied them together in one knot above the puppy's head. Holding the knot, he lifted the sling and puppy out of my hands.

Her feet dangled, and her head drooped as he raised her up to his face. Eye to eye, they stared until she yelped.

"Take her," he said and handed me the sling.

Holding her up to my face, I said, "Do not worry. I am not going to hurt you."

Taninto jumped as high as he could and grabbed an

overhead branch. He used that to pull down a larger limb.

"Bring the pup," he said as he broke off one of its branches.

He hung the sling on the broken limb and slowly eased it up, carrying the puppy out of my reach. She began to yelp and struggle.

"You are hurting her!" I shouted at him.

"She is not hurting . . . but she might be thirsty," he said and pulled the limb back down.

"Get a bit of snow and let it melt between your palms."

He lowered the puppy to my cupped hands. She licked the melted snow and my wet fingers. I giggled for the first time since I had left Taninto's valley.

He eased the limb back up out of my reach. "Come on, before Mother Dog returns."

"Are you leaving her like this?" I asked.

He motioned me up the hillside. I did not understand, but I followed him back to the buffalo cloak.

"The mother will return soon," he said.

"How do you know?" I snapped.

"I surprised her this morning with a rabbit she had just caught. She dropped it when she ran off. I followed her tracks to the burrow. When I saw that she had pups, I knew she would have to go back for her kill."

My new friend soon tired of her struggle. Her head dropped. She whimpered softly. Then that stopped. Taninto raised his hand before I could stand.

"Do not worry," he whispered. "Young pups can sleep anywhere."

As the sun climbed, snow fell in clumps from trees, and

water trickled down the hillside. The puppy woke.

"She senses something," he whispered.

Mother Dog had returned. The puppy let out a weak howl. The mother looked up for a moment, and vanished into her burrow. The puppy barked and barked until its mother came out followed by two pups. The mother tilted her head, sniffed the air and pushed the two curious young ones back into the burrow. Our smell around the burrow troubled her. She knew to be cautious as she followed our trail down into the ravine.

She found her helpless pup, whimpering and squirming above her. Mother Dog circled the tree with her nose in the air. Suddenly she ran and jumped for her pup. She missed her mark, backed up, and tried again. From the other side, from underneath, from all sides, she jumped and jumped.

Her last jump, she fell to the ground hard and did not get up for a long time. When she did, she began to howl. The young puppy joined in. Together, they sang a song of sorrow. After that, Mother Dog did not look back nor waver. She left the puppy in a run and disappeared into her burrow.

"Now, we may go get your friend," Taninto said, "but be quiet."

She wiggled and licked my face as I lifted her out of the sling. "I will take care of you from now on," I said.

"Let her chew on this," he said, cutting-off a strip of the deer hide and tying it in several knots. The puppy chewed it and licked my fingers all the way back to camp.

"What will you name her?" he asked.

"We could call her 'Chachiz'," I blurted out. "He was your friend."

The old man stopped packing his back-bundle and glanced back over his shoulder. For a long silent moment, he stared, seeing things I could not. A deep breath overtook him and he mumbled, "No."

I studied the puppy in my arms. "I will call you . . . Little Pup, my friend."

"Gather your things," he ordered. "We have a long day ahead."

I had to contend with a squirming puppy in my arms, but the old man, without his walking stick, seemed to have the most trouble climbing out of the valley. He led us east, up through a steep, dark forest as bright sunlight slid down the western mountainside. Its cliff of black rock gleamed against the surrounding snow. Before we could reach the top or greet Father Sun face to face, clouds rolled in between.

"There goes our sunny day," I told Little Pup. "Can you see that eagle, Little Pup?" I asked. "When we are out of the snow, I will let you walk." I said. I talked. I asked. I said more that morning than I had since the journey began. And I did not speak a word of it to Taninto.

When we reached the mountaintop, it seemed as if we stood on the top of the world; the plateau rolled off to blue horizons and snow-covered mountains on every side. Small flakes still fell from time to time. The clouds parted but never long enough for the sun to melt much of the snow.

I put Little Pup down. She could not have been happier. She scampered back and forth between me and our guide, barking if I fell too far behind.

"What are you saying, Little Pup?" I asked. "Oh, do not

worry about me," I said as she jumped around my heels. "Just because I am so far behind," I shouted, "is no reason to slow down."

Taninto stopped at a large flat rock, an island of brown surrounded by white. He took off his back-bundle and sat down, face to the sun. I sat with my back to him.

"Are you hungry, Little Pup?" I asked. "I might have some jerky for you."

Over his shoulder, Taninto said, "Puppies are always hungry. Give her small bites and use each piece to remind her that you are her friend."

Late in the day, we crossed a mountain meadow where the melting snow had left behind rows of furrows like ripples across still water. Instead of forming circles, they twisted side by side down the hillside like so many snakes.

"What do you think those lines in the snow are?" I asked my friend.

She said nothing. Taninto said nothing.

He said nothing until he had a campfire burning on a dry eastern slope. "In honor of our new listener," he said as he watched Little Pup search my lap for a place to settle.

"I shall tell a story."

Chapter 23: A Sign

Taninto's Journey
Three days after "their" arrival - June 25, 1541

On the third day of the Son of the Sun's presence in the land of Casqui, I found myself inside the Spanish camp. This was a world far from what I knew with different smells, unusual sounds. As a boy, I longed to be part of something as great as the stories told about the ancestors. The Spanish mystique held that promise.

I found Cooquyi and Wasse around the fire, dreaming but awake. For a time, we shared nothing but the flames. Cooquyi pulled something from his bedroll. He tore off a piece and handed it to Wasse. He saw me eyeing the strip of pale meat glistening in his hand.

"The Spanish call it *cerdo salado*," he said and broke off a tiny piece.

As I took it, he repeated, "*Cerdo salado* . . . salt pork."

I nibbled the strange, salty meat.

"The Spanish make it from the ugly, fat beast they call *puercos*." Hogs

I had seen them at a distance and heard their squeals. "Hogs?" I asked.

Something behind me caught Cooquyi's attention. The

horse, Old Brown, and its tender approached. The small boy, frailest of Master Diego's three tenders, struggled to tie up the weary and disagreeable beast. Wasse jumped up to help. They hugged and laughed like lost brothers found.

Cooquyi called the boy to the fire and gave him a much larger piece of salt pork. "Tell us, what did you see today?"

Cooquyi and Wasse listened closely while he told his story, but I only understood a few of the words.

"What did he say?" I asked when he finished.

Cooquyi stared into the fire—long enough for me to wonder if he would answer. Finally, he looked up. "He has just come from inside the walls of Casqui, where you should be."

I moved in closer. He waited until I settled.

"He said your people worked through the night alongside the Spanish slaves to move the cypress timbers you saw in the river to the top of the Temple Mound."

"It is the sign," I said and tugged at his arm. "Let us go see."

Cooquyi jerked back. "I am not going in there."

"Why?" I asked. "My people would be honored to have you in the temple town of Casqui."

He looked straight at me for the first time that day and said, "I do not embrace your people or anything about them save our friendship. I honor only the people of Ocute."

I shifted to the side of his glare. He turned back to the fire.

"I still dream of my people, from whom the Spanish took much and, in return, gave only death and sickness. I find no joy watching your people receive the blessing of Governor de Soto and a gift of the sacred sign."

He pushed me away with a wave of his hand. "I must stay here. I am a slave." His words hissed with contempt. I turned slowly, leaving him time to mend them.

I ran, not to Casqui, not to see the great sign. I just ran. I ran until I heard the distant vibrations of the ceremonial flute.

King Issqui, in the cloak of a white buffalo, led the flute player and a large procession. Four and five abreast, the line of chiefs, wise-ones, warriors, and elders wrapped its way back to the canal. All wore something white, and no one carried a weapon.

Lord de Soto stood in front of his tent with five Spanish priests. As Issqui approached, de Soto spoke through his interpreters. "Together, let us walk in humility and prayer to the mound where you and your people will receive the sign of our Heavenly Father's sacrifice and great love."

The priests stepped out in front of the Son of the Sun. Unlike the spiritual men of Casqui, who dressed in bright colors, the Spanish holy men wore tattered brown robes. The two called clerics walked in front, swinging small copper pots. The smoke and fumes of an unfamiliar burning sage filled the path before Lord de Soto. The three other Spanish priests prayed softly as they followed. Prayer and cleansing smoke is our ancient way of purification. The Spanish and Casquis were so different, and yet we shared sacred rituals.

The flute player joined in behind the priest until a horseman galloped up and pushed him to the side. De Soto's guards and their proud horses took his place. Sunlight sparkled off their hats and cloaks of woven metal and gleamed from their long swords drawn but laid across their laps.

The governor's black stallion strutted with the guards, outshining them all. Together the great beast without a rider and the Son of the Sun walking behind cast an image of power and yet trust.

Lord de Soto motioned Issqui to his right side. More guards took their position around them. Conquistadors followed their leader according to rank and distinction. Shadow Wind and Master Diego led the horsemen who flanked the march, keeping the Casquis to the outside.

When all the horses and noble conquistadors had passed, the Casquis were allowed to walk with the common foot soldiers. Without proper order, village elders and warriors hurried to find their places in the swelling procession. Spanish soldiers and important Casquis walked side-by-side and one behind the other. Feather headdresses fluttered between dull and dented helmets. Moccasins embraced Mother Earth as heavy boots and hooves pounded her.

From the front, a single lofty voice rose above the procession. The eldest priest was singing. The words were not Spanish but hauntingly distant and ancient. The sound spread awe through the crowds of onlookers, casting a spell on all who listened.

I ran to Uncle Tecco when I saw him join the march.

"Now, you return to walk with me," he said, pressing down on my shoulder.

As suddenly as he had begun, the high priest stopped chanting. Then in one great deep voice, every Spaniard responded. I slowed as did many. Uncle pushed me on. The Spaniards never faltered.

The high priest sang out again. Up and down the line, on horses and those walking, every Spaniard answered, all chanting the same song. For me, the strange words held no meaning, but I took them in like a deep breath.

Too many faces crammed both sides of the procession to see just one. They spilled over the land, pushing for a better view, and crashing against each other like waves of a spring flood. Above that, more people filled the raised land between the wall and the canal. Higher still, boys scurried up the surrounding trees and perched on their limbs. In all, I saw a common expression of wonder and fear.

The procession continued unbroken from the grove, across the canal and through the north gate under a sky of gray clouds that hid Father Sun. The Spanish priests were already climbing the Temple Mound steps when I came through the gate next to Uncle Tecco.

Lord de Soto led his black horse up the side of the sacred mound. On top he remounted the powerful beast and slowly circled the rim, surveying the masses that filled the town, surrounded it and spread across the river.

The high priest stepped to the edge of the mound above the crowded plaza. He raised his arms and silence followed. He spoke in a solemn, yet powerful voice. The Casqui people could not understand the words, but most knew it was a prayer. We turned our faces up to the sky. The Spanish turned down to the earth.

The prayer ended with one word that every Spaniard repeated, "Amen."

Lord de Soto stood in his saddle and pointed his sword to

the sky. It shone like a staff of light against the clouds. He shouted a similar prayer, which ended with the same word. All the Spanish and some Casquis said, "Amen."

He waved the sword as his interpreter shouted, "Behold, people of Casqui. I, Hernando de Soto, give to you the sacred symbol of our Heavenly Father's love for all mankind."

From the far side of the mound, other Spaniards shouted commands. Above all those on the mound, the great cypress rose, pushed up by many hands and poles until it could be pulled by ropes. The promised sign from the Son of the Sun, the hope of my people, slid to the bottom of a newly dug hole with a thud that stabbed at the center, the very heart of our nation, the Temple Mound of Casqui.

Maestro Francisco, a Spanish boat builder, directed the slaves as they twisted and straightened the cypress. The second smaller log was notched and strapped across it near the top. The slaves turned it until the crossing piece pointed north and south then filled in the hole.

The Spanish had cut down the tallest tree in all Casqui and raised it again on the sacred Temple Mound. A union of the ancient ways and new beliefs joined in that moment. For in a fashion, the sign stood as a cross, known among our people as the symbol of the Four Sacred Directions.

Though unbalanced, the bottom being longer than the other three directions, its unevenness gave the Spanish Cross a sense of balance that seemed right. The height and breadth of this new form of the old symbol commanded a reverence for the power of the Spanish and their god. Up and down the River of Casqui and across its flat lands, no one could look upon the wondrous sight and not be in awe.

The hush following that first sight swelled to a murmur, ever growing, spreading and mingling. An unimagined sound flowing from so many: singing, praying and wailing. The Son of the Sun raised his sword once again to our Father Sun. The clamor faded before his voice. The interpreter proclaimed his words.

"I, Hernando de Soto, governor of these lands as decreed by the Emperor and King of Spain, hereby command the people of the Casqui Nation to honor the Cross of our Savior, Jesus Christ, and in my absence pray before it."

He returned the sword to his side, stepped down from the black horse and knelt next to the high priest. The priest sang out a third prayer. All the Spaniards and all the Casquis said in one great, united voice, "Amen!"

One word roared as never before. It soared with hope and vibrated every heart. One word joined two grand circles with one center—the Cross of Casqui. Silently, the great gathering watched the Spanish clerics purify a path from the east side of the mound to the foot of the Cross.

Alone, the high priest walked the path and knelt at the cross with his back to the plaza. I could see his right arm move up and down and across his shoulders. He placed his palms together, hands in front of his face, and bowed his head. The faint mumbles of a prayer spoken only for the sacred sign floated above the stillness. The high priest leaned forward and kissed the thick cypress trunk.

Next, Lord de Soto walked the path with Issqui at his side. Together, they knelt. Together, they mimicked the priest's

ritual. No one could hear either prayer, but all saw the King of Casqui kiss the Spanish cross. The Spanish captains followed. Two at a time they knelt and prayed.

On the plaza the noblest of Casqui's leaders formed pairs behind the last Spaniards. Thousands of voices rose and fell but never faded throughout the long ceremony. I stayed beside Uncle Tecco until we reached the top of the mound. People covered the far bank, spread up and down the River of Casqui, and out into the growing fields.

Uncle Tecco grabbed my arm and pulled me toward the Cross. Father Sun slipped in and out of the clouds, casting a shadow down the purified path. My uncle did not say anything, but I could feel him watching me. I knelt as he did; as I saw the Spanish do. I repeated their motions. I put my hands together. I bowed my head, but I did not pray.

What could I say? What should a boy just turned a man say before the Cross of Casqui? The high priest had shown the Casqui people what to do, but no one had taught us what to say. I stared up at the great cypress that seemed to reach the racing clouds.

Uncle Tecco leaned forward and kissed the cross. I did the same and jumped to my feet before he had a chance to pull me up. I do not remember crossing the mound or going down the stairs. I found myself wandering about the plaza dizzy and dazed, having seen, felt and heard more than I could grasp.

Lord de Soto, Son of the Sun, stood at the top of the Temple Mound. The edge of the clouds hiding the sun began to glow as the interpreter shouted, "I have been most humbled by the manner in which you have received the Cross of Jesus

Christ. People of Casqui cherish and honor that which I have given you. Worship as you were shown and receive the blessing of the one true Father."

As two slaves led his horse down the side of the mound, Lord de Soto descended the stairs without further regard. The priests walked behind, chanting. The remaining Spaniards followed in no particular order or rank. Soon, only Casquis remained on the plaza.

All eyes turned from the departing Spaniards to King Issqui, the lone figure atop the mound with the cross over his right shoulder and the Temple of Ancients off to his left. Issqui slowly gazed over the people of his nation. They looked back for words of meaning, a speech worthy of such a moment.

The King of Casqui lowered his eyes and simply said, "Amen."

The people responded, "Amen."

He bowed to the cross and walked to his lodge. The emotions of the day were like a fleeting dream that I desperately wanted to hold onto. I had felt a closeness to the Creator and my people that I did not want to lose.

I remained on the plaza with others, clinging to the fading bliss. Wise-ones and elders climbed the mound and disappeared into the Council House. Messengers were called. Runners dispatched while fresh-cut cane was brought to the mound.

On that wondrous day, the sun slipped below the clouds just behind the consecrated sign while a cane-fence was hastily built around it. Too late, for the long shadow created by Father Sun and the Cross of Casqui had escaped. Its spirit had flown down the mound steps, across the plaza, over the walls, and out across the land. Nine-Rivers Valley could never be the same.

Chapter 24

Manaha's Journey
Ninety-four years after "their" arrival

The storyteller was once again alone with the night. Her fire burned low, flickering in and around the images of her small tribe and the throngs of hopeful people gathered around a sacred cross. Her head nodded, sleep rousted burdens for a moment. Clinging to the victory, Manaha rolled onto her bedding and slept.

She woke early, rested and lighthearted. Trouble stirred moments later—their trouble, her trouble, troubles from the past, of the future. She did not feel like eating or bathing. With her lightning-stick for support, Manaha crossed the creek and wandered off to the south.

Land around the village lay mostly flat but here and there, hills rose up steep and round, nothing like the mountains where Manaha grew up. Across the creek from the village, a rocky bluff stretched far above the trees. She had often wanted to climb those bluffs. It seemed a good day to turn her thoughts and steps toward that quest.

Morning mist lay heavy on the thick undergrowth below the bluff. Manaha pushed through, parting spider webs, and knocking off the dew with her walking stick. She did not stop until she reached the first overhang, a shelter that had been used many times before. Not the top of the bluff, but it would do as well, Manaha told herself as she sat down. The height, with its view of mountain peaks to the north, stirred longings for her grandfather and his lost valley.

Manaha slid to the right. She could see most of the village and part of the plaza. It seemed more distant than just across the creek, but she could still hear their cries and feel their despair. Her stories did not bring the sickness Ta-kawa had predicted, but neither had they helped the tribe through these sad days.

Squinting at the morning sun rising toward the treetops, Manaha knew that it would soon be time to enter the village-lodge and hear the words of the Tulla warriors. She started down the hillside at the bottom she turned back to the bluff. "I will climb to the top another day," she said. As she made her way through the brush, she began to wonder, *would they let her inside the lodge? Should I speak?*

A storyteller must speak, she thought.

By the time she reached the plaza, most everyone had already gathered around the village-lodge. Manaha watched the anxious struggle for their proper place. Puffed up with his new respect, Gasapa stood grim-faced at the front, facing the crowd. At midday, he pulled back the elk skin that had covered the opening ever since the outsiders had arrived. He motioned Ta-kawa's clan in first. A rush followed. Who should enter, and when, overwhelmed Gasapa. He soon left his post to the bickering.

Manaha kept her distance until the last person entered. She slipped in and stood next to the opening. It looked nothing like the place where she had spent so many lonely nights. The air smelled of fresh paint, sweet grass—and fear.

She knew everyone, but not the faces they wore. Dread and grief forced the difference. Some, casting respect aside, climbed onto the benches along the walls to see over those who refused to sit. Squeezed side-by-side, old men, women, and the children waited in silence.

On a platform opposite the door where Manaha stood, Casinca sat alone on the council bench of the elders. The Tulla warriors sat either side on newly made benches. The few remaining men of importance in the village stood behind them. Ta-kawa, larger and nobler than all in his long mantle of eagle feathers, stood between Casinca and the young Tulla warrior.

In front of the platform, fire danced about the cypress logs laid out in the four sacred directions. Only a thin haze of smoke swirled up toward the hole in the center of the thatched dome roof.

"It is a bad sign," Manaha mumbled, remembering the lazy wisp rise from her burnt home in Taninto's valley. She started to leave.

"Proud people of Hachia," Casinca called out as he stood. Manaha turned back.

"I am here because I am too old to hunt," Casinca said. "I'm an elder by misfortune with few other merits, but that I have always accepted my duty."

He stepped to the side. "The council bench is empty. I stand alone with the charge of speaking to you and for you." He

glanced around the lodge. "The spirits have not been good to our village. Our children are few, the growing fields have withered. The hunting grounds are empty and our men taken hostage."

Casinca turned to the older Tulla. "As a tribe, we came to this place," he spread his arms, palms down, "to find peace and build a new village." With palms up, he turned to the younger Tulla warrior. "As a man of honor, I know you understand that our hunting party did not intend to take from your people."

Ta-kawa stepped between Casinca and the Tulla. "I speak for the hunting party," he shouted. "Hazaar is dead. I alone know of its intent and its misfortunes."

The people shifted. Manaha straightened. Casinca sat down.

"It was Hazaar," Ta-kawa continued, "who led our hunting party. He alone chose to cross the river."

Ta-kawa walked to the edge of the platform. "We did kill a few deer and found fresh signs of buffalo." He hung his head. "We were led to camp in a narrow valley on Tulla land." Ta-kawa swelled up and said, "Now men are dead, even Casinca's own son."

He let the murmurs grow and spread. "By the actions," he shouted, "and words of the *one* you see standing before you, the rest of the hunting party is alive. Your husbands and your sons were saved." Ta-kawa raised a clenched fist as people shouted and called his name.

"A fearless band of Tulla warriors surprised our guards and overwhelmed the hunting party. Every enemy of the Tulla nation knows and respects them as fierce fighters." Ta-kawa turned and bowed slightly to the two guests. "I have come to know them as giving friends."

The younger Tulla stood. He returned every glare with a sneer. "I am Hais," he said through their interpreter-slave. "I am a warrior, great among a nation of warriors. I fear no man nor have I any concern for a village of farmers. Your men were captured with so little effort. It should bring shame to all gathered here."

He let his words hang unchallenged. "I did not come to give you praise or hope. I am here to speak for the warriors of Tulla. Our way is to hunt upon our land and war against any who would come to take it. Our grandfathers fought the Spanish as did their grandfathers long before in our ancient homeland."

"The way of the Tulla warrior is not to offer peace to those who trod upon our land, but our leaders believe that for the good of the tribe, we must forgive your invasion. Should you prove the sacrifice misplaced, our revenge will be completed. I, Hais, speak the truth." He sat down.

The older emissary from Tulla rose. He stepped off the platform and walked around the sacred fire for all to see. Those who would allow, he looked them straight in the eyes. Manaha gazed past the shape and size of his head and saw his compassion.

"I, Xitude, offer my gratitude for the hospitality and gifts we have received from the good people of Hachia." He bowed. "I am not young like my Tulla brother, full of anger. I am old like your fallen Hazaar, full of regrets."

He circled the fire again. "I come to speak for the Tulla

High Order. Long ago, the Spanish drove our ancestors out of our ancient homeland far to the south. The ancestors settled into the valleys and plains on the other side of the Akamsa River. The land nurtured and healed our people. The streams flowed fast and clear, fruit and nut trees grew plentiful, and game roamed without concern.

"The people of Tulla grew to revere the land and swore to never again be chased out. To this day, our warriors take an oath to fight till death anyone who trespasses upon our land."

Xitude looked at Ta-kawa. "No man may enter the hunting grounds of Tulla without giving honor to the ancient ones and seeking their permission. The men of Hachia have broken this hallowed law."

His face hardened. "Many of my tribe wishes death upon them!" he shouted.

If horror had a form, had a hand, it touched all in the village-lodge at that moment.

"People of Hachia know this Tulla is a proud nation, proud to have survived wars and famines. We have fought, learned from and defeated our enemies. Two winters past, the coughing sickness took many of our bravest and wisest. Our young warriors are strong, but there are fewer than needed to hunt buffalo."

He stepped back upon the platform, nodded to Casinca, glared at Ta-kawa then looked into the faces of the Hachia. "I know that you had a small early crop and that winds ruined your summer corn. We all know that to survive the coming winter, the Hachia people need meat."

Xitude opened his arms. "Let us come together in peace;

two nations with one will to survive. Cross the river, join the Tulla tribe, and all will be forgiven. Save your men. Save your children."

The young Tulla stood and handed Xitude a bundle. Xitude carefully unwrapped the skin of an animal as black as night and exposed a long pipe. He held it high for all to see. A thin stem, as long as a forearm painted with stripes of red and yellow, pierced the back of a man down on one knee, and shouldering a large bowl of green jade.

"I hold the ancient Pipe of Tulla, which my people offer in peace," Xitude shouted. "Together we can grow stronger."

After a moment, he lowered the pipe. "Should you decide not to join our nation, the men of your hunting party will be killed or hobbled for use as slaves." He pointed to their interpreter who could hardly walk because the tendons on the back of his heels had been cut. "This is not good for either nation."

He handed the pipe to Hais, who returned it to the black pelt. "We are but guests in this House of Council. The discussion and the decision are not ours." Hais stepped off the platform as Xitude continued. "We will return tomorrow at midday to extend, one time only, the Pipe of Tulla."

The old man bowed and walked to the door. The younger warrior followed with less dignity and far more vanity. A breathless hush lingered until they had left the lodge.

Talk began and grew louder.

"Silence!" Ta-kawa shouted.

Casinca stood up behind him. "Everyone who wishes to speak must step before the council fire. All others hold your

tongue and listen to your kinsmen."

Many came forward. Every word was heard. After all the talk, the crying and pleading, there could only be one answer.

"The people of Hachia must make peace with the Tulla Nation," Casinca declared. "We must leave our village and become people of the buffalo."

Manaha stepped in front of the opening before anyone could leave.

"I speak for the last time before the tribe of Hachia." Manaha's voice rang with such authority, many did not recognize her. "I cannot disagree with the decision, though for myself, I will remain behind. I do not want for support, argument or companionship. I wish only to have my words heard."

A few grumbled, but she could not be denied.

"The Tulla path is different from that of our own," she said. "You will have to learn their ways to survive. But no one should forget what it means to be Hachia. Keep within your heart the old ways and when time will allow, tell the ancient stories to your children."

Manaha looked at those around her. She felt good about her decision to stay. "Children of Nine-Rivers," she said, "May good fortune guide your path." She stepped aside and studied the faces that passed, wanting to keep as many in her memory as she could.

That night, alone, with only a small story-fire, Manaha hoped for any listeners. It was well after dark before footsteps moved in behind her. She said nothing, stood, and circled the fire without a chant. When the three shavings of lightning wood had turned to black embers, she spoke. "For the only listener among all the people of Hachia, I will tell a story."

Chapter 25: Woman of the Falls

Nanza's Journey
Forty-nine years after "their" arrival

W hen I was young and called Nanza, I knew no other companion than the old man. Now he said the wild puppy sleeping next to me was my friend. I was not certain what "my friend" meant. I knew what I wanted it to mean, someone I could talk to. Someone I could trust. Taninto coughed as he rolled up his bedding. I knew, he was not that friend.

"Come on, Little Pup," I said. "You have wiggled and whimpered all night." I untied the rope Taninto had put on her the night before. "It is time to get up and run with the sun."

Patches of brown dotted the blanket of snow. The newly green forest now glistened white. The air smelled fresh and cold. Taninto hunched close to the fire. Little Pup bounded toward him, but he pushed her away and coughed again, deeper this time.

Little Pup raced across the field of snow as quickly as her long wobbly legs would allow. She stopped and waited for me. I chased after her. She chased me. We ran until I could run no more. I scooped her up and sat down on a rock jutting out of the snow. Little Pup found a comfortable spot on my lap and closed her eyes. I found an unexpected comfort, cradling a young life.

When we returned to the campsite, Taninto was leaning

over the fire, wrapped in his cloak. I said nothing as I took a bowl of the cold-meal porridge he had prepared. Little Pup and I shared.

"Wash the bowls," he said in a weak, raspy voice.

I tugged on the puppy's ear. "Do you know where we are going?" I asked.

"Use clean snow," he grumbled as he kicked some over the fire.

"We are going home . . . Going to my home," I sang while Little Pup jumped and bounced around me.

"It is time," Taninto said and walked away. I put the clean bowls in my back-bundle and followed, carrying my friend. The snow melted as the day wore on, except on the western slopes and in the hollow of the furrows that twisted and snaked down many of the hillsides.

"Who do you think cut those ridges?" I turned to ask Little Pup, who had stopped three or four paces behind to lick the snow. A trail ran from her to me—spots across the white snow. Red spots. Blood.

"Grandfather!" I screamed.

He ran toward me but stopped. "Raise your skirt," he said.

Blood ran down the inside of both my legs. "What is it? What is wrong?" I reached out.

He backed away.

"Nanza, do not worry," he said. "As you have wished, you are now a woman."

"No! Grandfather, help me."

He shook his head. "The bleeding is a most natural event for all women. When your time came, I had hoped you would be

among the women of Palisema." He took another step back. "A man must not be close to a woman during this time. It is our way. It has always been our way"

"What do I do?" Little Pup sniffed around my legs. I swatted at her. "Go away, dog. Leave me alone."

"Tell me what to do." I stared down at the bloodstained snow. "Help me, Grandfather."

Taninto turned away then back. "There is a place close by where you can rest." He spun around again. "Follow me," he said over his shoulder.

I took a few steps. My head began to spin. Snow swirled around me. I fell, face down into white-turned-black.

When I came to, Taninto carried me on his back. Little Pup ran alongside, yelping at both of us. I closed my eyes and let him carry me across the field, even though he struggled over each new furrow.

He sat me down on a boulder. Blood splotched his back. He squatted and leaned against a tree growing from the rock. No one said anything, even Little Pup. I wanted to lie down with the comfort of her in my arms and sleep.

"It is not far now," he said and stood. "Do you want me to carry you?"

"No, I can walk," I said, not certain I could.

He led us across a stream and followed it as it fell further into a deepening valley. Boulders shaped the bluff and filled the valley below. His path followed a ledge between the two.

Trickling and sparkling between the rock and boulders, the stream tumbled down through the valley. On the other side, snow still lay in a thick blanket, but on our path, most of it had melted. My guide stayed far ahead but never out of sight.

He stopped when I did, once venturing a few paces back to ask if I needed help. Little Pup remained always at my side. The trail turned steeper.

"I am going ahead to scout the valley," he shouted. "Stay on the path. I will be back."

"Do not worry, Little Pup," I said as she watched him over her shoulder. "We have each other."

Not far down the path, it turned to worn steps winding down to the valley floor. The narrow valley lay open and flat with more rocks and boulders than trees. Across it, I could see another stream. I followed the path to where they joined. Back up the other stream, Taninto gathered firewood. Behind him, the streambed circled to the left, following the curve of a long bluff formed from solid rock. A single boulder, as tall as any tree about, blocked the view of what lay upstream. I had seen large boulders along Tick Creek, but they seemed small compared to this giant.

A distant rumble mingled with the fast-flowing stream. With several pieces of firewood under his left arm, Taninto motioned to us. The sound grew louder. The bluff curved tighter, and the stream widened into a pool. Like the inside of a water bottle, the bluff hung out over the pool, curving up and back to form a lip. The rumble beckoned me on.

"Nanza, this way," he called, leading us around the huge boulder. Another stood just as large but still clutched within the hillside. Taninto climbed into the space between the two giants. I handed Little Pup to him and pulled myself up.

The rumble soared between the boulders up to the blue sky

stretched between their tops. To my left, water oozed out of cracks and trickled down toward an opening at the other end where Taninto waited.

He did not retreat as I walked toward him. The space between the boulders opened up to the pool I had seen from the other side. The bluff wrapped around it and folded into the hillside to form a natural shelter over the rocky shore that lay below me.

Above the pool, water rushed over the rim of the bluff in two streams, twisting back on each other to fall as one with a great unwavering roar. "Two-Falls-One," he said. "It is called Two-Falls-One."

The sight, the sounds, the wonder of it all emptied my thoughts and smothered my fears. I stood, captured. When I turned from the falls, Grandfather had climbed down to the pool and was building a fire on the shoreline. I carried Little Pup down.

"There is plenty of wood and food for you . . . and the dog," he said. "I will bring more tomorrow."

"Where are you going?" I asked.

"The bleeding will stop after a day or two." He climbed back up between the boulders.

I followed behind him. "What will I do? My stomach hurts."

"Stay here. Let Two-Falls-One renew you. Let its waters cleanse and heal you."

"It is too loud!" I shouted.

"Do not listen with your ears. Listen with your spirit. Feel the vibration that flows from the falls to the earth, around the bluff, and between the great boulders. Open yourself. Listen to the healing songs, feel the vibration of Two-Falls-One." He backed out and down the opening.

As I turned, I began to notice the bones, colored rocks, and bright feathers that filled the cracks and crevices around the two boulders. Little Pup jumped and tumbled down the path to the pool. She began barking. I looked up in time to see Taninto making his way around the top of the bluff and crossing the stream above the falls.

Little Pup paced the water's edge. "He is not leaving us." I waded a few steps out into the water. "Come on in, Little Pup. It feels good, not too cold." I tried to urge her in, but she dashed out of my reach.

Taninto set up a camp on the bluff across from us out of sight of the pool. I nibbled on the hard-bread that he had left soaking in a bowl and ate some of the cold-meal after it came to a boil. I gave Little Pup two big pieces of jerky, then we slept the rest of the day.

The freestanding boulder gave off warmth captured from the spring sun, and the mountain boulder blocked the chill of the north wind. That night, Two-Falls-One told the stories. I, Little Pup, and Grandmother Earth listened.

The next morning, I discovered that Taninto had brought more firewood and a cooked squirrel that Little Pup and I shared. When Father Sun was bright and hot, I swam out to the falls. As the water splashed over me, I watched Taninto build a small hut of willow branches on the edge of the bluff. He covered it with meadow grasses. On top, he spread his buffalo hide like his sweat lodge back home in our valley.

For the next two days, the only sign of him was the firewood he left in the morning and the gray haze rising above his sweat lodge. That evening, he appeared in the opening between the

boulders. Little Pup barked and I yelled, "Go away. Leave me alone."

"I did all I could," he said.

"We do not need you," I yelled back.

"It is forbidden for a man to be around a woman during those times." He reminded me. "It is the way of our people."

"And your presence is of no comfort now!" I shouted.

"Your bleeding has stopped?" He slowly climbed another step. "Nanza, has it stopped?"

I turned my back to him and nodded my head.

"It is safe for us to continue the journey," he said.

I had not thought of the journey in three days. "Leave us alone," I said, suddenly realizing I was not certain that I wanted to leave. The falls had filled my heart with joy and peace. I could stay in this valley. That would be enough.

"In the morning, you should be stronger," he said. "You will be ready to continue."

I spun around. "There is nothing wrong with my strength." I started to call him an *old man*, but I just glared at him.

"I have prepared a story-fire," he said as he climbed back down.

After waiting long enough for him to doubt my intent, I followed with Little Pup in my arms. On the rocky shoreline of the stream that flowed from Two-Falls-One, a fire was already burning. He knew I would come.

All manner of rocks, different shapes and colors, filled the streambed along with a few purple flowers. An old tree stood at the very edge with exposed roots dipping in and out of the swift, churning water. The twisted and bent trunks of the younger trees spoke of a determination and the struggle to survive among the rocks and rushing water.

Taninto sat on a large rounded stone half-buried in the dirt. I sat on the other side of the fire.

"I know how to make fire," he said. "I know how to raise a puppy." He ruffled her fur with his bad hand and poked at the fire with the other.

"I can fashion useless things from clay and plant corn. I know many things, having lived long, but I know little of what it is for a girl to become a young woman."

I nodded without looking up.

"I know how it is for a boy when he becomes a man." His voice faded. "I remember my time," he mumbled.

I waited. He waited. The fire burned on.

Finally, I asked, "Will you tell us a story?"

Taninto stood.

Chapter 26: Bridge to Pa-caha

Taninto's Journey
Four days after "their" arrival - June 26, 1541

I, Taninto, a man of only two days, had felt the power of the Cross of Casqui and witnessed it spread across the land. I watched the Spanish leave, and Father Sun slip away. Uncertain like myself, many remained on the plaza without direction, unsure which way to turn. The cross and stars beyond count filled the sky. It glowed as sap bleeding from the stripped cypress trunk glistened with the light of the four fires that surrounded it.

Across the Temple Mound, torches danced with light taken from one of the four fires. Down the mound steps and through the streets, torch-carriers hurried to ignite a new, purified fire at the center of their own lodges. It was in their lodges that most were gathered around those fires within the comfort of elders and kin.

I should have been in the lodge of my uncle even though I knew he was most likely in the Council House. Aunt Miluka and her two good daughters would be there, but I did not need her rambling. I needed to see Saswanna.

Hers was the largest of the seven lodges in the Red Fox clan south of the plaza. Unlike all the other lodges in Casqui with their doors facing the east, the clan of the Red Fox built their square lodges so that each corner pointed in a sacred direction and their doors faced southeast.

A clan fire burned brightly in the midst of the lodges. Several women moved about a large pot hanging from a tripod over the fire. The aroma of a bubbling stew filled the air. I crept around behind Saswanna's lodge. In the darkness next to the corn crib, I knelt down. I would be able to see her if she left the lodge and maybe catch her eye before she returned.

Saswanna bounced out of the lodge. Like a drowning man, I gasped. Standing tall, she gazed up at the cross, the curve of her face highlighted against the glow of the clan fire. One of the women around the fire called to her.

She turned away. I sank further into the shadows. Saswanna quickly returned, carrying a large bowl. My heart beat so loud, I feared someone would hear. A mist from the hot stew drifted up around her as she walked straight for the door. I slipped into the light. She stopped. I took another step toward her. She glanced back at the women then raced to me.

I pulled her behind the crib and set the bowl on top. Her eyes twinkled even in the darkness. All that I had experienced over the last two days lost its grandeur the moment she put her hand in mine.

"I saw you in the procession," she said softly.

I stammered, "Ah . . . ah . . ."

She smiled. My face flushed like I was standing too close to a flame. I turned away and looked back over my shoulder.

"What does it mean?" she asked, staring with me up at the cross. "I have seen you with their horses," she said. "You have

walked among the gods."

"No," I said, "the Spanish are not gods."

Saswanna dropped her head then glared back with her jaw set. "But look what they have done. Look at what they have given us."

"They are men of great accomplishments and greater ambitions. Even so, would gods need to wear armor?" I asked.

"What do you know—boy from down the river?"

I tugged at my hat. "I am not a boy."

She looked away, up to the cross. "I must go. My brothers would be angry if they saw me with you."

She disappeared into the lodge. I slumped over and grabbed my hat as it slid off my head. Somewhere deep inside, I ached. Like a young boy, wild-legged, wide-eyed, I ran away toward the wall and around to the north gate.

"The gate is closed!" a guard shouted from the tower.

I waved my hat. "I am a man of Casqui, who kissed the Spanish Cross."

The guard still did not show himself. "The gate is closed," he yelled.

"I must return to duty in the service to the Spanish warrior, Diego de Guzman."

"Today," the guard shouted back, "everyone is important."

From one of the small black openings in the tower, an arrow tip slid into the moonlight and pointed down. "And," he shouted, "I am more important than all those who come before my gate in darkness."

I slowly turned away. No amount of words would allow me to gain passage through his gate, but I knew another way. The first summer I came to visit my uncle. I met Saswanna. She took me to a tree she called the old wart tree, west of the gate close to the river. Shimmying up its thick trunk, she instructed me on which bulges to grab and which ones to step on. Even then, she always tried to be the best.

One of the lower limbs, straight and thick enough to be a tree itself, reached over the wall. Saswanna giggled that first night as she raced across the limb. I followed, but by the time I passed the wall, she had dropped to another tree and down onto the ground.

~~~

Taninto stopped. He stopped in the middle of a story. He had never done that before. I waited. He turned to me.

"Nanza, I carry more images from my youth than wit or spirit can bear most of the time. Even so, I tried to never forget Saswanna, but I could not remember her smile until this very moment."

The campfire flickered in his eyes. "Now, I remember," he said. "I remember her standing on the ground and smiling, smiling up at me."

I watched the wrinkles of pain fall from Grandfather's face. He smiled. I turned away and stared at the fire. After a moment, he took a deep breath, and continued his story.

~~~

I did not need Saswanna's help that night to climb up the

old wart tree and over the wall. Once outside, I tried to put thoughts of her aside. I made a promise, a promise to Master Diego. I crept along until I reached the grove then around the Spanish camp to the north side where I slipped in.

"Cooquyi," I called out as I approached the horse tenders' campfire, "it is your friend, Taninto."

Without even looking up, Cooquyi demanded, "Why are you here?"

"I come to serve my master, your master," I boasted. "If it would please you," I added, hoping he would offer me a place near the fire, "I could tell you of all the wondrous things I saw today."

"None of us want to hear about the fortunes of your people," he growled, "or any other good, except what might befall one of us."

He glared up at me. "Go back to your people. You are too small to be a horse tender, and no one wants to hear your stories."

I pointed at the ground. "I will just sit here and say nothing more."

"No!" Cooquyi shouted. "Leave! Go back to your world. Forget what you have seen. It is a false dream."

I turned one way and back the other but took a step in neither direction. Cooquyi stood. He said nothing, but his eyes spoke of intention.

I retreated before he could act, back out of the camp the same way I had slipped in. Outside, alone and between two worlds, I slept with my back against the only friend I could find, the mulberry tree.

The sounds of the Spanish breaking camp woke me. *Cooquyi knew. That is why he sent me away.* I stood and started running toward their camp. "I should go with the Spanish," I told myself before I remembered the anger in Cooquyi's voice.

I slowed to a trot, to a walk, a turnaround, and a slow amble back to Casqui. In the daylight, people moved in and out freely. The moment I stepped through the gate, my thoughts and gaze turned up to the Cross of Casqui. Above the crowds, above the grand plaza, above the temple, above all else that had once made Casqui great, it spoke to all who entered the sacred town. Simple in form and perfect in message, some believed endless in its power.

Those going through the gate before me knelt on one knee as they had seen the Spanish do and made the sign of the cross. I did the same, and ran for my uncle's lodge. I found him and the women on the summer patio. He stood. They did not.

"Son of my sister," Uncle Tecco growled.

The women hurried into the lodge.

"As is our way," my uncle said, "I have taken you into my home to teach you the skills needed to be a man." He paused as if he wanted me to say something. He continued when I did not. "You have not been in this lodge for two days."

I pushed back the hat that suddenly seemed too large. "Forgive my thoughtlessness. I have been in the Spanish camp learning to—"

"Say no more." Uncle Tecco sat down and motioned me to do the same. "Eat," he said.

I could feel his eyes on me, but I did not look up until I had

finished.

"The Spanish are leaving."

I jumped up. "I want to go with them."

"No, your place is with your own people."

"But I have sworn my service to one of the Spaniards while he is in our land."

"Forget your promise. They are marching out of the land of Casqui to battle our common enemy, the Pa-caha. Everyone is happy about what will happen to the Pa-caha Nation, but I am afraid of what will happen to us."

"I am not scared, Uncle Tecco. I can help. Let me go with them."

"No. Not with the Spaniards."

I slumped back to the ground as my uncle stood.

"But you can help," he said. "King Issqui promised guides for the Spanish and a safe passage across Chewauhla Creek. I have been given the task of building a bridge over its swamp."

His chest swelled as I bounced to my feet.

"I have already packed you a back bundle. Put your hat in it and come with me."

A party of workers gathered outside the north gate. Uncle Tecco talked to each one and inspected the tools and ropes they carried. When no others came forward, he motioned for all to follow at a quick pace but not a run.

"Why are you leaving?" someone called out from the gate.

"Where are you going?" they asked. No one answered.

I had never ventured in the direction of Pa-caha. Few did. Chewauhla Creek and the swamps surrounding it had always separated the lands of Casqui from its ancient enemy.

When the pace settled in, I moved next to my uncle. "Why do the Spanish wish to leave a land where they are worshiped and enter the land of our enemy?"

He kept his head forward. After a few paces, he said, "The Spanish seek more," and waved off my next question. "Save your strength."

We trotted on through the morning. Through villages and past farms, we heard the same questions. "Where are you going?" "What is the reason?"

"We go to serve the Son of the Sun." My uncle began to shout, "All who have rope, an axe, or a strong back, follow along."

We reached the swamps by midday. The party had swelled many times over, and still more came. While most in the party rested after the long run, I followed Uncle Tecco to the water's edge. Two canoes waited at the shoreline. They had been carried across land from the Tyronza River to Chewauhla Creek.

The creek flowed slow and wide with swampy shallows full of snakes and stubbed roots bulging up out of the muck. Crowded into the shallows, great bald cypresses stretched up straight and tall. With few limbs and thin needles, they cast forbidding shadows over the swamp. Out in the channel, the creek opened up. The water sparkled, and no trees grew.

My uncle and two others with long ropes pushed one of the canoes through the black water. Several paces out and no deeper than calf-high, they climbed in. Across the dark shallows into the light of the open channel, their canoe glided into the thick cypresses on the other side.

As Uncle Tecco approached Pa-caha territory, three men

appeared from behind a ridge. I glanced around at the others who had come to watch. No one stepped out to warn my uncle. I raised my arms, and started to yell.

Someone pulled them down. "Those are Casqui scouts," he said. "They crossed over before dawn."

I edged to the back of the crowd as my uncle stepped onto the land of our enemy. The scouts greeted him warmly. The four pointed and gestured as they walked the shoreline.

Uncle Tecco had the paddlers take him upstream to the narrowest gap of open water. He tied a rope to a tree at the chosen point and pulled it across the channel to a cypress he selected on our side. Picking his way through the trees and roots, he played out more rope as he went.

When he came ashore, he had a plan. My uncle selected a group of older men to work on the other side. They crossed a full canoe at a time. He sent parties up and down the creek to bring back recently fallen timbers. While I waited for my task, he ordered other men and boys to find cane, saplings, and firewood.

"Those of you, who remain," Uncle Tecco said to the women and old men, "set up camp and begin making as much rope as possible."

I followed his orders, but felt I could do more. I knew nothing of rope making. That night, as others worked in the darkness, I sat at a fire, tearing strips of bark from the saplings others had gathered while wrinkled, nimble fingers braided rope around me. I watched until I could mimic them then braided until I could hardly see. Sometime before the night's end, I lay down.

I woke to the sound of pounding hooves. Four horsemen charged into camp. In a panic, some yelled. Some ran. A few hurried to greet the Spaniards, boasting of their hard work.

"Casquis, hold your tongues," Uncle Tecco shouted from a walkway stretching out over the swamp. Almost like magic, the beginnings of a bridge had appeared overnight. A simple walkway of four and five logs lashed together wove through the cypress forest supported above the water by its trees.

"Silence!" Tecco yelled.

The Spaniards rode toward him. One dismounted as my uncle marched down the walkway. He stepped off onto the shore and bowed. The two conquistadors still on their horses argued, pointing at the creek and the incomplete bridge. Uncle Tecco said nothing but motioned for the one who had dismounted to follow him up the ramp.

The walkway reached to the open channel, but the cane handrails on either side did not. The Spaniard halted where the rails stopped. My uncle continued to the end. There, two tall timbers leaned out over the open water on a crossing timber, wedged and lashed to several cypress trees. Tecco pointed to the other side where they struggled to place their second timber out over the water.

The Spaniard shook the handrails and nodded to the other two.

"When all is ready on both sides," my uncle said with a great sweep of his arms, "long timbers will be laid between the two sides over the channel, and then cane poles lashed over them for a walkway."

Tecco Tassetti walked toward the workers gathered along

the shore. "Lord de Soto and his army will walk over the Chewauhla Swamp," he shouted, "and conquer our enemies."

Everyone threw their fists into the air and cheered. The Spaniard on the bridge returned to his horse. One of the Casqui scouts with the conquistadors stepped onto the bridge.

"Listen," the scout called. "Listen. Our prayers to the Spanish Cross have been answered." A few began to cheer.

"Hear me, people of Casqui!" he shouted. "Rain has fallen upon our land."

Everyone cheered and danced. One of the horses reared and snorted.

The scout raised his arms until the crowd fell silent. He bowed his head and said, "Amen."

The people of Casqui repeated in one voice, "Amen."

Uncle Tecco stepped up just as quickly and shouted, "The Son of the Sun will be here tomorrow. The bridge must be ready."

The camp flew apart like a disturbed beehive.

"Our prayers brought the rain," one of the old rope makers said.

"The Son of the Sun called down the rain," said another.

"No, no, the cross gave us the rain."

"The cross!" they all agreed.

No one around the fire spoke of the Great Creator, Father Sun, or Brothers Thunder and Lightning. They talked and wondered only about the Heavenly Father, Jesus Christ, and the Cross. The words stirred our blood and quickened our pace.

No one wanted to fail the Son of the Sun. Lord de Soto depended upon our labors and the wisdom of my uncle. As the day wore on, I could see his plan and watch his orders come together.

The bridge grew and improved until, by nightfall, only the center span remained unfinished and that would have to be done in the light. The campfires burned bright that night. Tired but proud men and their ancient stories gathered around each blaze. I listened and braided rope until I could no longer do either.

"Taninto." My uncle shook me at first light. "Go to the bridge," he said. "Help wherever needed."

Everyone laughed and smiled as they worked. Building the bridge would mark all our lives, young or old, man or woman. Our strength came from pride. Together, we lifted and pulled the last crossing timber into place. Those not needed to hold or lash the timber down rushed out to gather more cane poles to finish the walkway.

Juggling an armful of cane, I waited for my turn when I heard horses. Six conquistadors galloped out of the forest into the camp. Twenty or so slaves ran behind.

"Hurry! The Spanish are here!" the other workers shouted at me. I climbed up the incline and out over the open channel where they waited for my bundle of cane. There was no time to return to the Casqui side.

"Move on," the workers yelled as they tied the poles in place.

I crept on across the unfinished part of the walkway.

Behind me, the bridge filled with men carrying more cane. "Move on!" they continued to shout.

Casquis working on the Pa-caha side called out questions as I stepped off the bridge. I let the others behind me answer. I wanted to see the land of our enemy. I walked past the crowd, up

the gentle bank, straight to the top of the small ridge. Their land seemed no different from ours.

"Look," a Casqui worker yelled. "Something moves through the water."

I recognized the elegant head of a Spanish horse. The remarkable creature who could run like the wind with his master on his back could also swim. As those on the shore began to realize what I knew, I could feel their awe.

Following the first horse, swam three others. The last two horses remained on the Casqui side with their masters still mounted and yelling at the slaves. Some of the slaves and horse tenders hurried over the bridge, trying to keep pace with the horses in the water. They called to the beasts in Spanish, urging them along. After them, more Spanish slaves struggled across, loaded with blankets, saddles and horse armor.

The first tender over the bridge rushed out into the swamp to greet the lead horse. After wiping swamp muck off the horse's back, he walked it to the shore. The huge beast flicked its tail, stretched its neck and with an angry twist of the head let out a long, shrill neigh, terrifying the other Casqui workers.

None had been as close as I had to the marvelous beasts. The horse raised his head and gave out another loud cry. The last of the Casquis around me, backed away as two more horses came out of the swamp.

I waded out to one of the horses struggling in the black mud. His tender came from behind and pushed me aside with harsh Spanish words. The horse shook his head and snorted. The tender reached out and gently stroked its long, powerful neck. Fear faded from the big black eyes. The tender slipped a rope over the animal's head and offered the other end to me. Working together, we pulled the horse out.

When the tenders had dried-off and saddled all four of the horses, four conquistadors started across the bridge. Slaves carried their lances and shields, two in front of the Spaniards and two behind. Few of the Spanish could swim. They feared any body of water, no matter how shallow because of their heavy armor. Like frightened children, they squirmed across the bridge with both hands on the rails. Hardly setting a foot on Pa-caha soil, they mounted their horses. Grabbing up their shields and lances, they once again became mighty conquistadors, warriors to be feared.

They gathered along the top of the ridge, waved to the two conquistadors still on the other side and rode off in four different directions. I climbed the ridge as the other Casquis hurried back across the bridge before more Spaniards came.

Beyond the horizon stretched a land known only to those who had never returned. "Taninto of Togo," I mumbled. "Just a boy from down the river," I mocked. "No more. I walk proud from this day on, Taninto the Wanderer."

Chapter 27

Manaha's Journey
Ninety-four years after "their" arrival

Manaha slept well but woke with a heavy heart. She felt badly about how she had treated the old man who had raised her. Her grandfather had seen so much and had everything taken from him, yet he gave her all he had—his stories.

After her bath, she avoided the still, lifeless village as she walked to the growing fields. She found even less hope there. It swarmed with flapping wings, nodding heads, and bits of unwanted shuck flicked into the air. Birds screeched at Manaha as she wandered through the dried stalks. They fluttered up before her, screeching and cawing, only to land just behind her last step.

Manaha was the intruder now, the one to be chased away. It was their field until they had their fill. And soon the mice would come in search of their meager measure and, with that, snakes hunting their needs. And so it would go.

At the edge of the field, she laid out the few ears that she had not gathered two days before, not much to be proud of. She watched the birds feast and made plans for the beans if any survived.

"Leave the vines for me," she shouted at the flock.

Three or four flew away then just dropped down in a different place.

"A pot of beans will—" she stopped and listened to the distant shouting.

"The Lodge is open."

The call echoed around the village. Gasapa had pulled back the elk skin. The time had come, but no one hurried today. No one pushed. Manaha straggled in with the reluctant last.

Ta-kawa sat at the end of the elders' bench, proud and equal, with Casinca in the center, and Koyota, now the oldest of the elders, on the other end. The three remained motionless as the village-lodge filled and fell silent. All eyes turned toward the entrance.

Xitude stepped through first. He carried the Pipe of Tulla between his open hands. Hais followed, carrying nothing but arrogance. They walked around the fire to the Elders of Hachia. Hais stood back as Xitude bowed and spoke.

"From the people of Tulla, I offer to share the sacred smoke from the Pipe of Tulla in peace and agreement with the people of Hachia."

Casinca stood and bowed. "On behalf of our tribe, who hold no ill will for the people of Tulla or their emissaries, I receive this pipe given with promise and in peace."

Koyota disappeared behind the platform into the sacred inter-room as Casinca took the pipe with both hands. Koyota returned with a conch shell filled with bark of the red willow in his right hand and a tobacco pouch made from the hide of a white buffalo in his left. Casinca placed the tobacco and a small portion of the bark into the large jade bowl and returned the

pipe.

Xitude lit it with a flame taken from the council fire. He drew deeply, raised his head, and blew smoke up to the sky above him and down to the ground under him.

"Wise-ones of Hachia," he said as he handed the pipe to Hais, "with this smoke, the people of Tulla accept the friendship you gave so freely and the reason for your hunting party's desecration of our hallowed land."

After Hais had smoked the pipe, Xitude pinched two fingers of tobacco from his pouch and stirred it into the bowl with the Hachia tobacco. He extended the pipe to Casinca, stem first.

"Breathe in the mingled tobaccos," he said. "With this act, bind our two nations as one. Lives were lost. Let them always stand with honor and, from this time on, without revenge."

Before Casinca could reply, Hais added, "Smoke from this pipe with gladness and commitment, for there will be no change of heart."

"It is our way," Casinca responded, "that a pipe smoked in agreement must pass full circle around the council fire." Casinca carried the pipe of mingled tobaccos to the west side of the council fire. As he sat, he motioned the Tullas to his side: Xitude on his left and Hais to his right. Koyota took his proper place south of the fire.

Ta-kawa waited on the platform, beckoning to someone at the back. Behind the group of old men and boys, his son, Ichisi squirmed. As Ta-kawa walked to the north side of the council fire, he motioned again. The boy did not move.

Gasapa stepped out from the other side. He strutted around to the empty place on the east and squatted. Ta-kawa glared back at the platform. The son faced him straight on.

Casinca took a long draw, rose to his knees, and blew smoke in the four sacred directions. The last puff he blew into the fire. He held the pipe up and prayed.

"Great Spirit, receive the sacred smoke. Let it seal and harden the union of our two people," he said and passed the pipe to Xitude.

The Tulla drew and exhaled into the fire without words.

Ta-kawa took the pipe and stood. "I hold the people of Tulla and this wondrous pipe with great respect. I admire the bravery of Tulla's warriors and the cunning skill of its hunters. I breathe and exhale this smoke in honor of our union and the promise that I will, with all my wisdom and strength, lead the people of Hachia over a good path to our new homeland."

He sat down and relit the pipe. The flames of the council fire flickered as he blew a great chest full of smoke over them. He handed the pipe to Gasapa without looking at him.

Gasapa neither stood nor spoke before he took a shallow draw. The struggle not to cough stole his breath. He had none for the fire. Ta-kawa sneered at him. Another draw and, just as quickly, he blew the smoke over the fire and passed the pipe to his right. Koyota's hands shook as he took the ancient pipe. A thick haze rose around his long, slow puffs and fluttered over the flames.

Hais snatched the pipe from his old hands and stood like Ta-kawa. "People of Hachia," he said, "you are now a part of the Tulla Nation and as with all its people, you must follow the will of its leaders. You cannot just consider their words as you would *your* leaders. You must obey." He looked down at Ta-kawa.

"Listen all," he shouted, "you have today and tomorrow to gather your families and your belongings. On the second sunrise, we will march for Tulla." He took a short draw from the pipe and blew into the flames.

Where the circle began, the pipe returned, once again in Casinca's hands. He stood and looked about the lodge.

"All agreed," he said. "Words spoken and actions promised around this council fire by noble men shall be our common path." Casinca raised the Pipe of Tulla for all to see.

"Great Spirit, receive the sacred smoke.
Bless our people.
Great Spirit, receive our words.
Bless our union."

Manaha slipped out of the village-lodge and retreated to her island. She expected no one. Still she needed to tell a story. Sunset found her alone with her thoughts and a small fire. With the first rustle and a hope, she dropped the pieces of lightning wood onto the fire.

Chapter 28: Orb Stones

Nanza's Journey
Forty-nine years after "their" arrival

No longer a child, I looked upon the world with new eyes. The sun shone bright and warm. The many scents of spring sweetened the air. A butterfly fluttered about the edge of the pool that rippled out from Two-Falls-One. I saw all of it differently.

Anyone could hear water crashing over a rocky ledge, but I could feel the falls. It vibrated as Taninto said. It hummed with the insects, sang with the birds, brushed past in the wind. New life and rebirth vibrated all around me. For the first time in my life, I felt that I was a part of something more than an old man's dreary world.

A *woman* ready for change, I walked away from Two-Falls-One proud and strong. Taninto followed its stream through the valley. Little Pup bounced and dashed between our guide and the new woman.

The roar of the falls faded. The valley narrowed. Up its steep sides, huge boulders loomed. Our guide paused next to a fallen boulder that stood half-in and half-out of the stream. Pushing up from under the bottom edge bloomed a patch of white flowers with bright yellow centers. I started to bend down for a closer

look.

"Each is important, large and small," he said, "but none more so than the one who honors that importance."

I just stared at him

"Irorie. The flower is called an irorie." Taninto turned from the streambed toward the east mountain.

Following the curve of the mountainside, he climbed up then back in the direction of Two-Falls-One. He was more like an old man fighting against the mountainsides since losing his walking stick. With just one good hand, he pulled himself from tree trunk to branch up the steep incline. I needed both to keep up. Little Pup struggled behind, sliding in the dried leaves and loose rocks, but she never gave up.

Near the top, in a gentle gust, I heard the falls somewhere far below. Closing my eyes, I tried to feel the roar. Like the wind, it passed but with the hope that the vibration would flow over me again when the time came.

The forest opened to mountain meadows of tall brown grasses bent by the winter winds. Scattered about were large, thick briar patches with sprouts of new green. The early morning sun highlighted ridges in the grass like the furrows I had noticed in the snow.

Little Pup waited in my arms for our guide to weave a trail across the meadow. I followed, feeling the rise and fall of furrows under the newly stomped grass. The path led to the only boulder about, marking a high point in the field. So out of place, Taninto must have been drawn to it, as I was.

Sandy-smooth, like so many rocks I had picked up in the Buffalo River, it appeared completely round. A round stone like the one Taninto had sat on the night before but much larger and not half-buried. It lay on top of the ground, as tall as my shoulders.

Taninto pulled a handful of cornmeal from his bundle and laid it on top of the rock. He prayed, "Ancient spirits honor our meager offering. Grant easy passage through the land of your toils."

I followed him in silence through meadows spreading one into another. Here and there, the gray tops of other round rocks seemed to bob above swaying grasses. The once well-tended land offered a clear view in every direction. There were mountains rolling into mountains but no lodges, no gardens not even the wisp of a campfire. No one was around where many must have toiled for generations.

Behind those empty fields, the forest stretched out in a tangle of grays. Before us, off to the east, the ever dark greens of cedar and pine mixed with hazy yellows from post-oak shoots and white patches from cherry blossoms and the bare trunks of sycamore trees. Ranges of red varied from the dark first leaves of the water oak to the bright blossoms of the dogwood and hints of green glimmered off tender young leaves. Altogether it presented a sight more like autumn than the beginning of spring.

Taninto slowed his pace as we crossed the last open field. He turned back. "I found the land of Two-Falls-One," he said, "more than thirty winters ago."

I stepped closer.

"It has called me back many times. Each time, I found more round stones, various sizes in different places. I found more

furrows but no people, no villages, no lodges."

I held Little Pup while the old man studied the land.

"I have walked through this place of mystery for the last time." He squinted at the horizon. "Only now do I understand. The question is not where the Orb Stones came from, but where are the people who moved them about and cared for them?"

I dropped Little Pup and let her chase after Taninto while I lingered. In lifetimes to come, someone will discover Taninto's valley like this, empty and abandoned. I reached out and touched the branches of a young elm tree. I wondered, *Will they find anything to tell them I lived there or why I left?*

Like petals from a flower, shiny new leaves piled up in my fist as I pulled the limb through my hand. I pressed my nose into the soft scent. Few trees had leaves. I pulled off a handful of those that did and all smelled like spring. The season began as it always had; the difference came from within me.

I caught Little Pup and gave her a big hug. She wiggled free and ran down the steepening trail after Taninto. Glimpses of water shimmered below. Across the way, a mountainside of rock ledges stretched ever higher as we made our way down.

Close to the bottom, he said, "Wait here while I scout the creek crossing."

As he hobbled away, I thought about the many times he had left me alone. I pulled my friend in tightly as I sat down, but she spotted a rabbit and jumped out of my arms. Quick but inexperienced, she soon lost the chase only to have a grasshopper land near her.

Little Pup tilted her head to one side, watching for the slightest movement. I smiled at her seriousness. When the grasshopper jumped, she hopped just as high, again and again. I giggled until I heard Taninto walk up.

"Children," he grumbled, "come."

"I am a woman!" I shouted.

He whistled. Little Pup ran toward him, but I grabbed her. Taninto spun around and started down to the valley. I plodded along until we reached a wide ford in the creek with gentle, shallow ripples.

"A buffalo crossing," he said and waded in.

I sat Little Pup down at the edge of the creek. She backed away. Taninto stumbled across the channel. It reached no higher than his thigh. I stepped into the cold water, and Little Pup whimpered as she glanced from me to the old man.

"Come, Little Pup," I called as she ran up and down the shoreline.

Taninto whistled to her as he waded back toward us.

"Come on, puppy. Come on, come on," I called until she edged out into the water.

Coming up behind me, Taninto whistle again. His wake splashed over Little Pup's head. She turned around.

"I will carry her across." I said as he brushed past.

He jerked her up under his good arm and waded upstream from the crossing. I followed. Midstream he stopped, and pitched Little Pup into the air. She landed in the deepest part of the channel. Water splashed up and out. Little Pup went under. The rapids returned.

I held my breath until a black nose popped up between ripples. Her ears followed eyes wide. I lunged out into the channel. The water pushed back. I stumbled forward.

"Let the current carry her to you," Taninto said while he made his way to the other shore.

"She needs me!" I yelled.

"Do not pick her up," he barked. "She must learn to swim."

"She is going to drown."

"No," he shouted. "Stay close if you must but let her do it."

Little Pup looked more determined than frightened. She held her head high, and her feet moved faster than she could ever run. I eased my hand under her belly.

"Do not be afraid," I said, but she did not want my help.

As soon as she could reach the bottom, she scampered across the shallows. Once on the shore, Little Pup shook, rolled, and barked at both of us.

He walked off into the tree line without ever turning around.

"How far will he go without us?" I asked Little Pup. She did not wait to find out and ran after the one who had treated her so harshly. I followed the wide trail to the foot of a rock ledge slanting up from the valley. Ledges lined the steep mountainside one above the other, receding out of sight.

Little Pup climbed back down the ledge to show me the way. She scampered under the short, stout cedars and briars that slowed my climb.

"Follow the pup," he commanded from the ledge above me.

Little Pup sniffed out Taninto's trail but never got too far ahead. Another ledge and more cedars and flowers with long pink petals drooping from a large reddish-brown center edged the trail. Just steps away, a line of tiny flowers waved with the breeze on a thin, knee-high stem. The top bud, the only one open completely, had a yellow cone glowing at its center surrounded by five petals that changed from a faint pink to rich red at their tips.

On the next ledge, I found the largest spring flower I had ever seen. Morning had long passed, but drops of dew still lay among the folds of the bright yellow petals as wide as Grandfather's hand. Taninto grunted at me from the ledge above. I sat down to watch the sunlight ripple on the creek below and take in a deep breath of this, my season. Little Pup barked. I exhaled slowly.

The mountainside overtook the last ledge, rolling up to a forest of great sycamores and spruce with little underbrush. Here and there, the forest opened with small meadows but no furrows or Orb Stones. Taninto kept a good pace across the mountain plateau. It was almost dark when he turned downhill to a grove of cedars on the other side of a lazy stream. He stepped across its shallow pools and sat down his back-bundles. Little Pup waded in. I waited on the other side with her while she drank and explored.

Thick, flat rocks lay on both sides of the stream. An odd three-sided one caught my eye. Like the rest, it had a strange mix of brown and gray except for the blood-red that lined the oblong hollow on top, pooled with rainwater.

"Come away from there," the old man called from his side of the stream where he prepared a campfire.

Little Pup laid down next to him.

"Sit here," he said. "I will tell a story while we wait for this pot of hominy to boil."

Chapter 29: Revenge and War

Taninto's Journey
One week after "their" arrival - June 29, 1541

I stood upon the land of the ancient enemy of my people, watching a great party of strange men, stranger beasts, and their slaves cross Chewauhla Swamp over a bridge I helped build. One of the four horsemen from the advance scouting party galloped back toward the bridge.

"*Rápido*," he called to the Spaniard leading a party of foot soldiers. Creeping across the last section, they struggled to hold their weapons while keeping a grip on the handrails. A short leap to dry land and their confidence returned. Two lines quickly formed, and on command they marched to the top of the ridge. Spreading out in an arc, backs to the swamp, they stood ready to protect the crossing.

Behind the last soldier, horse tenders and slaves burdened with saddles and armor hurried off the bridge. From the shoreline, they searched for their horse among the herd swimming across the open channel. As the horses came into the shallows, slaves washed away the dark mud while others wiped them dry. As fast as a tender could saddle his horse, a conquistador mounted it and grabbed up his shield and lance from a waiting slave. Soon there were as many horsemen guarding the ridge as foot soldiers.

More soldiers and more slaves crossed the bridge as another group of horses swam into sight. First among them was Lord de Soto's black stallion, its noble head high above the sparkling waters of the channel. Just a few other Casquis remained on the Pa-caha side. We knelt and bowed when Lord de Soto stepped from the bridge. He mounted his black stallion and bounded up over the ridge.

Chewauhla Swamp filled with more horses, stretching back to the Casqui shore. I could not see Shadow Wind, but Cooquyi was among the crowd of tenders crossing the bridge. I shouted his name. He raced into the shallows without even a glance.

I ran toward him and Shadow Wind. "Cooquyi!" I shouted louder.

He ignored me and continued to wash the thick mud off Shadow Wind's front leg. I stepped to his side.

"I am here to serve, once again," I announced and started rubbing the horse's other leg.

"You fool, one leg at a time," he snapped. Shadow Wind shook his head as if he agreed.

I turned to brushing the water off as I had seen the other tenders do.

"Start at the top of his back," Cooquyi said, grabbing my hand. "Pull the water down his side then down the legs."

Wasse arrived with Shadow Wind's saddle and blanket. He smiled when he saw me. I think I smiled, too.

Master Diego slapped me on the back. "*Ardilla*," he said and laughed. After mounting Shadow Wind, he spoke to Cooquyi,

repeating the word *ardilla* when he glanced at me. He rode off after Lord de Soto.

I waited for Cooquyi to tell me what he had said.

"*Ardilla* is the Spanish name for 'chipmunk'."

"Chipmunk?" I questioned.

Cooquyi frowned. "Yes, my master named you 'chipmunk'." His face hardened. "He told me to watch over you."

More soldiers crossed the bridge, followed by a long line of the Spanish slaves carrying all manner of supplies, much of it gifts from the Casqui people. All four of the advance scouts returned, reporting no signs of Pa-caha people or their villages nearby. Lord de Soto ordered camp set up on the flat plain beyond the ridge but in sight of the bridge.

So much had happened since my uncle called me away from my village. Now, I lay in a camp of strangers in the land of my enemy. No one around me cared, but I fell asleep believing Saswanna would.

"You sleep like an old woman," Cooquyi said when he woke me.

"Forgive me. I have not had much rest for the last two days." I stretched. "Let me make amends for my laziness."

He stood with his back to me, brushing Shadow Wind. "You need to prepare," he said.

"For what?" I asked.

"For the path you have chosen." He threw a heavy woven blanket over the horse's back. "Today, you will see war the way the Spanish fight." He turned around. "Do not lose your life to the fury of war nor your soul to its glory."

"What do you mean? You know there will be war?"

"I may not know this land or its people, but I do know the Spanish," he said. "There will be death. There will be punishment."

"Punishment?"

"Yes," he said, "for the Pa-caha's attacks on the Spaniards when we first reached the Mizzissibizzibbippi River."

"Well," I boasted, "if twenty men are killed before me, I will not go back."

"There will be more, hundreds maybe."

He could see my doubt.

"Listen to me, seasons ago when you were but a child and Hernando de Soto was not yet a lord. As just a captain, he marched with a small army against the Incas, a nation far older and mightier than ten Pa-caha Nations. The Spanish asked to meet in peace.

"When the Inca king, Atahualpa, approached, Captain de Soto took him captive. In the battle that followed, the conquistadors killed more than a thousand Incas in one day."

Cooquyi turned back to the horse. "I am taking Shadow Wind to Master Diego," he said, and tightened the saddle. Shadow Wind danced with eagerness. "Come if you must."

I walked tall behind Cooquyi and Shadow Wind through the confusion of a Spanish camp preparing for battle. De Soto's black stallion waited outside his tent with several other horses and their tenders.

Lord de Soto stepped out of the tent with Master Diego and six other conquistadors. As quickly, slaves took down the tent while others packed away the rest of the camp. De Soto mounted his black stallion. Cooquyi steadied Shadow Wind for Master

Diego. Master and beast turned and trotted away.

"Stay close," Cooquyi shouted.

I fell in behind him as he ran after Shadow Wind. Spanish captains shouted commands. Lord de Soto waved his arm, and the march against the Pa-caha Nation began. Only a helper to a horse tender, I still held my head high and eagerly scanned the horizon.

"Cooquyi, why do you take so little notice of the land through which you pass?"

"Is this my homeland? Are its people my people?" he asked

I shook my head in silence.

"Then I care not."

Most of the morning, the surrounding Pa-caha land showed little difference between it and Casqui. Open forests of black willow, swamp cottonwood, and king-nut trees spread out across a flat terrain to a distant growing field off to the north. Lord de Soto dispatched a thundering charge of twenty horsemen toward it.

The sight of shining warriors riding beasts as fast as the wind frightened and scattered the women and boys working in the fields. They ran for a small village just over the ridge. The conquistadors chased the Pa-cahas like a coyote playing with an injured rabbit.

A Pa-caha fleet of two hundred boats had tried to stop the Son of the Sun from crossing the Mizzissibizzibbippi River and now the Spanish were having their revenge, poking and jabbing with their long lances. They gathered the prisoners and herded them back to the waiting Spanish army.

Two of the boys suddenly turned and ran from their captors.

A single horseman pursued them. He stowed his lance as he came up behind the smallest boy. The horse slowed. The rider pulled out his sword and swung it broad side down. The blow knocked the boy off his feet. He fell under the hind legs of the horse, bounced off the ground, and never moved again.

The other boy changed direction, as did the conquistador, one way and back the other. The Spaniard taunted him, waving the sword above his head. Then it came, sharp edge down. The boy jumped aside, but the sword caught his arm, slicing through the bone. I had never seen or heard of a blade so sharp. The boy dropped to his knees, cradling his dangling arm.

The Spaniard circled. He leaned over in his saddle and raised the sword high. The boy looked up but did not move otherwise. It took but one swing to cut through his neck. The head fell forward. His body crumpled to the ground.

A great cheer went up. At that moment, the might of the Spanish and their weapons overwhelmed me. This would not be the war my ancestors had fought for generations. The Spanish killed without concern or hesitation, without ritual or purpose. They fought to kill.

"Stay here with the other servants." Cooquyi ran after Master Diego as he joined the attack on the village.

The conquistadors killed the weak and chased down and captured those fit enough to be slaves. The few allowed to escape spread an epidemic of panic. Fear raced ahead of the Son of the Sun and his unstoppable army.

They found and killed only three Pa-cahas in the next village. The one after that was empty. Foot soldiers plundered the lodges and storage cribs, taking anything of value, then

burned the village. My chest swelled for a moment before I remembered Cooquyi's words: "Do not lose your life to the fury of war, nor your soul to its glory."

The governor ordered a halt to the march and then sent horsemen charging off to the rear. Everyone turned. Hundreds of warriors approached us from behind, too far away to tell much except that their number grew the closer they came. The Spaniards pointed and murmured among themselves but stood their ground.

"They say it is the Pa-cahas and we have marched into a trap," Cooquyi said with the hint of a smile.

"No, those are my people. Casquis . . . Casquis!" I shouted, relieved and somewhat disappointed. Now I would have to share the glory of the Pa-cahas' defeat.

Soon, two horsemen escorted Issqui and his Council to the front of the army. Lord de Soto looked down at them from his black stallion.

"Son of the Sun," King Issqui called out, "I come before you, escorted by honored members of the Red Council, to reaffirm my and my people's loyalty. I know that just as you, my generous Lord, gave Casqui the sacred cross and our prayers before that sign brought us rain."

King Issqui bowed deeply and said, "I commit the best warriors of my nation to your service, my Lord."

Lord de Soto accepted the praise and pledge with a simple nod while he also listened to a report from one of his forward scouts.

Through the interpreter, Lord de Soto asked, "What do you know of a large town with new walls off to the northeast?"

"It is a new main town of the Pa-caha," Issqui said. "I have heard rumors of its construction from traders. It is said it is surrounded by a great wall of cypress, and its plaza is as large as the entire main town of Casqui."

Lord de Soto studied the King of Casqui while he listened to the translation of his words.

"Issqui," Lord de Soto commanded, "select three young men from the captured Pa-caha prisoners who can convincingly carry my message to their king and repeat it three times."

"I, Hernando de Soto, emissary of the Emperor and King, Ruler of all Spain, come in the name of the one true God, seeking to enter your town in peace. Hear me, people of Pa-caha. Forgive your enemies, the Casquis, for they have accepted and prayed before the Cross of our Savior. Grant safe passage to all."

The messengers raced away as the army marched after them. Within sight of the town walls, a band of Pa-caha bowmen in a grove of trees off to the right released a spread of arrows. They fell short of the Spanish line. De Soto immediately sent two squads of horsemen after the hundred or so bowmen.

They took to their feet, running toward a smaller walled town away from the main town. Before the horsemen reached them, more Pa-cahas sprang from hiding places behind the squads. Their arrows found their mark among the Spanish, but bounced off their cloaks and hats of metal. A few horsemen turned back toward the second band of bowmen, who scattered like a flushed flock.

Lord de Soto signaled to King Issqui. Someone among his War Council let out a lone cry. And from behind the Spanish

army came a sound never before heard in that land—war cries of a thousand Casquis, swelling to a single voice.

The sound grew and spread as the warriors of Casqui chased the fleeing Pa-cahas. The Spanish army stood their ground as my people raced past. For the first time, the confidence of the Casqui people matched their hatred. Vengeance filled every heart.

Cooquyi grabbed my arm before I could follow. "Your place is here," he said.

I jerked back.

He gripped harder and said, "Honor your promise to Master Diego."

More Casquis ran by, young and old; some I knew by name and others by sight. I hung my head. Cooquyi let go. I dropped to the ground and hid my face. When the last of my people had passed, he offered his hand. I stood on my own.

From a distance, I watched my people charge after the second band of bowmen also running away from the main town. A handful of horsemen with their lances forced the Pa-cahas toward the charging Casquis. Caught between two never-envisioned forces, the Pa-cahas formed a circle. Back-to-back, they sent their arrows flying.

The conquistadors quickly galloped out of range while Casquis fell dead and wounded. However, their number was so great and their charge so swift, they overran the Pa-cahas before any one of them could release more than three arrows. A swarm of war clubs, axes, and fists rose and fell.

"*Prisioneros . . . prisioneros . . . prisioneros*," the Spanish horsemen yelled until the beatings and killing stopped. The

Casqui warriors then turned toward the first band of Pa-caha bowmen disappearing into the smaller town. The conquistadors held back as hundreds of Casquis broke through the gate. Behind the walls, there would be no Spaniards to stop their rage. Every Casqui wanted his due.

Horsemen gathered the Pa-cahas who survived the beatings and then pushed them toward the army. A thin, haggard conquistador riding Master Diego's brown horse led a group of captives, old men and boys, not a warrior among them.

"Juwne de Salvo," Cooquyi whispered. "He lost his horse in the battle of Mavila. Master Diego permits him to ride Old Brown as long as he shares most of his bounty with the master."

Juwne circled the huddled group as Master Diego rode up.

"Bounty includes slaves," Cooquyi said and ran to his master's side.

I followed. Master Diego pulled his sword from the scabbard and pointed at four of the Pa-cahas then at me. He spoke to Cooquyi.

"What did he say?" I asked.

Cooquyi hesitated.

"*Ya,*" Master Diego shouted. "*Cuatro.*" Again, he pointed at the Pa-cahas.

"What does he mean?" I demanded.

"Master has given you charge of those four prisoners," Cooquyi said.

I shook my head. "What can I do?"

"Make them understand your master's words."

"What words?"

"Listen." Cooquyi pointed to Master Diego.

He rose in his saddle and stared hard at the four Pa-caha prisoners. Grand-sounding Spanish words rolled out in an elegant and threatening speech. Cooquyi translated for me, and I to the Pa-cahas in my best Aquixo tongue, a version of their language.

"Cowards of Pa-caha, you are now prisoners of Spain," I said.

"Make the prisoners listen," Cooquyi barked. "Make them understand."

"Cowards of Pa-caha," I shouted at the four, an elder of high rank, and three boys not much older than myself. "You are all now prisoners of Spain. Your only escape from pain or death is through complete loyalty to your new masters, Diego de Guzman and Hernando de Soto."

I felt Shadow Wind's hot breath on my back.

Cooquyi shouted, "Tell them again!"

I stepped in front of the elder. "Listen to me," I shouted and repeated Master Diego's words.

The boys looked as though they might have understood. The old man did but refused to show it. From all of them, I felt disdain but no fear of me. I looked up at Master Diego. He nodded slightly and jerked back on Shadow Wind's rein with a snap.

The horse rose up on her hind legs, pawed at the prisoners, and let out her own war cry. The old man stood straight, but the rest fell on the ground and covered their heads. Shadow Wind's hooves came down just a step from one of the boys. Master waved his sword again. With a growl, he turned and rode back to Lord de Soto's side.

Juwne brought more captors as the Spanish army continued marching on the main town of Pa-caha. Master returned each time to choose the best of the lot.

I repeated his words with an ever-stronger voice and greater threats. "The Spanish beasts will run you down," or "The Spanish sword will cut you in half."

Naffja, Saswanna's oldest brother, came in behind a group of prisoners, supporting a frail, naked man. I never knew Naffja to help anyone. He caught me staring. I turned back to my charge of prisoners as though I had not seen him.

"Look here, look here!" He yelled until he had the attention of a growing crowd of Casquis. He wrapped his arms around the feeble man. "This is my uncle's son. This is my cousin."

"Pa-cahas took him two summers ago and sliced the back of his ankles. They crippled my cousin, our brother. He is as young as I but will never run again."

Naffja waited. The crowd closed in. He shouted, "My cousin says that inside the walls of the Pa-caha town, their Temple Mound is ringed with tall poles. And stuck atop each is the severed head of a Casqui."

The crowd began to kick and strike any Pa-caha prisoner they could reach. Foot soldiers rushed in between.

Naffja waved his war club in the air. "Hear me," he called. "Our people have given the Spanish many gifts: skins, fish, meat, and now many Pa-caha slaves."

The crowd cheered.

"Now it is time," Naffja shouted, "for the brave of Casqui to take what has long been ours—revenge."

"Revenge . . . revenge . . . revenge!" he yelled until all joined

in.

"I run for my cousin," Naffja shouted. "I run for revenge."

"Revenge . . . revenge," the young and brave chanted as they followed Naffja's lead.

Lord de Soto gave no commands to stop the forty or so Casqui warriors as they raced past the front line. He slowed the march and watched as the band crossed the cornfields toward the western wall of Pa-caha—higher, wider, and greater than all the walls of Casqui. A black mud-plaster covered most of it, but in some sections, bark could still be seen on the closely spaced upright timbers.

Arrows rained down from slots in the three towers that flanked either side of a narrow gateway. Young warriors around him fell, but Naffja did not slow down.

Spanish scouts raced around both sides of the town. De Soto ordered two squads of foot soldiers to the front. One group carried the Spanish crossbow: a small metal bow mounted across a piece of wood the length of a man's reach. The other soldiers carried a weapon called an *arcabuz* with a short staff, forked at the top, that they often used for a walking stick.

They advanced in two lines to a point just out of reach of the arrows coming from the towers. The front *arcabuz* soldiers knelt on one knee, laid their strange weapons on the forked rod, and rested the other end on their shoulder. The second line placed short arrows in their metal bows and put the weapon to their shoulders. Naffja and his braves came out of the cornfields and started across the open land toward the canal that surrounded the town.

Lord de Soto shouted, "*¡Arcabuceros listos, fuego!*"

A terrible roar followed. Not thunder, but more like thunder than any other sound I knew. Sparks spewed from the line of *arcabuceros*. Smoke rolled up and back over the Spanish. Wonder and fear mingled with the hushed voices of both Casqui warriors and Pa-caha prisoners.

The tower walls splintered. Chunks flew in all directions. Casquis began to cheer. Pa-cahas began to pray. I hung my head. *Saswanna tried to tell me about a weapon that killed with thunder.*

In the confusion, the Pa-caha arrows stopped. The Spanish bowmen released a wave of their own arrows. Naffja waded into the canal; his shrinking band of warriors followed. Over their heads, the Spanish arrows flew faster and further through the shattered holes and slots of the tower walls.

The *arcabuceros* thundered again. The Casquis scrambled out of the canal under a storm of arrows and splinters. Several more fell before they reached the safety of the wall. Against the wall, the bowmen on the other side could not see Naffja as he led his braves toward the main gate.

Like the one at Casqui, the gate had a narrow opening to a long passageway only wide enough to allow for two or three gatekeepers with bows at the other end. A Casqui brave jumped into and out of the opening.

An arrow hit the second brave who tried. He fell. The small band faltered until the Spanish weapons rumbled for the third time. The remaining braves charged the gate with war axes and clubs.

A scout came yelling and gesturing toward the right side of the town. His black stallion danced a circle as Lord de Soto

shouted commands to his captains. He led a band of his best horsemen, Master Diego among them, to the south around the wall.

A second band of horsemen rode off to the left while the army marched forward toward the main gate. Cooquyi ran after Master Diego. The twelve captors in my charge looked to me as Spanish soldiers passed by.

"Get up!" I shouted, waving my arms. "Get up and walk."

When we were close enough, Pa-caha arrows filled the air. Servants and prisoners fell but not one Spaniard. They marched on without concern. The closer we came, the fewer arrows flew. Word spread that the Pa-cahas had fled in boats down a canal running out the backside of the town into a swamp.

At the moat, all the prisoners, including my charges, were pushed across the bridge. Once before the Spanish had been tricked and attacked inside the walls of a town they had believed was deserted. They herded the prisoners toward the narrow entranceway.

"Into your conquered town," I shouted at my twelve prisoners. Two abreast, I shoved them into the passage behind the other prisoners. A Spanish swordsman pushed me in after my charges.

War cries then screams came from the front of the tight passage. The prisoners began to turn back, but swordsmen shoved us forward. Metal shield against my back, I tumbled into the main town of Pa-caha.

A wide road stretched before me onto a great plaza lying at the foot of a massive Temple Mound. My prisoners ran in every direction. Naffja's braves chased after them, shouting for revenge.

Two braves circled the elder Pa-caha. One kicked him in the back, knocking him to the ground. The other raised his war club. I ran in from behind and grabbed it.

"Stop!" I yelled. Pulling the club from his hands, I shouted my first Spanish command, "*Paren . . . paren.*"

Both Casquis and Pa-caha looked puzzled.

"This prisoner belongs to my Spanish master, Diego de Guzman," I said.

I stepped between him and the elder Pa-caha as other Casqui braves circled in behind. Naffja ran at me, his blood-soaked body shaking with rage. A war axe in one hand, he carried the head of one of my young prisoners in the other.

"Look around," he screamed. "This is the place of our enemy."

I stepped back as he waved the head in my face.

"Are you blind? Can you not see the Casqui heads impaled around their Temple Mound, left for the birds to peck clean?"

"Kill Pa-cahas if you must," I said, "but do not harm these prisoners of Master Diego."

Naffja dropped the head, threw down his war axe, and lunged at me. He grabbed the club. I wrestled him to the ground, but he came out on top with the club between us.

"*Alto,*" a Spanish swordsman shouted, pushing Naffja's shoulder back with the flat side of his double-edged sword.

Naffja jerked the club from my hands and stood. He handed it to the one I had taken it from. As more Spaniards came through the gate, he picked up his war axe and trophy, and led his braves in a run toward the Temple Mound.

"Revenge, revenge!" they chanted.

Spanish swordsmen and bowmen marched after them. I followed, pushing my remaining charge of prisoners in front of me. Every pole topped with a Casqui head came down and rose again with the head of a Pa-caha. The Spaniards laughed while the young braves danced and yelled, "Revenge!"

Naffja vanished into the most sacred building on the mound, the Temple of the Dead. Moments later, he reappeared carrying a carved wooden chest over his head. He strutted to the edge of the mound, shaking the box until its insides rattled.

Without a word, he grinned and cast the revered bones of a beloved Pa-caha ancestor down the mound to the plaza below. My elder prisoner broke away and ran across the plaza. He had gathered up a few of the scattered bones before a Spanish sword cut him down.

Soon, wild men screamed and danced about the mound, casting honored remains into an ever-growing pile. They stomped, smashed, spit on, cursed, and set fire to the Pa-cahas' ancestors. Rage boiled around the flames of the dead.

This is not honor, I thought.

"It is not a good day for the people of Casqui," I said, but no one heard.

Chapter 30

Manaha's Journey
Ninety-four years after "their" arrival

Father Sun welcomed the final morning for the Hachia village with a bright sky. The children would live on past this day, but their tribe would be lost as with the nations of the Nine-Rivers Valley. The youngest to the oldest of them rushed about with their own task. Manaha offered to help. In the harsh new reality, she found neither rejections nor any gratitude.

Overnight, Ta-kawa became the unchosen leader. As his sister had foretold, the village listened to his every word. He ordered the lodges emptied; bedding and skins stripped from the sleeping benches; mats and totems pulled from the walls; and, pots, baskets, and jars taken down from every shelf. If it could not be used or valued, he ordered it thrown onto a roaring blaze at the edge of the plaza.

The older boys collected the weapons, trophies, and ceremonial garments of those killed or captured in Tulla. Ta-kawa had them taken to the village-lodge. Each clan selected the most necessary items for the journey and their new life afterward. What remained would burn with the lodge.

Hazaar's lodge had already been emptied and pulled apart. On the plaza, women fashioned *travois*, drag-behinds with poles

taken from his lodge. Split-cane mats from the walls were woven together to make boxes. They were loaded with clothing and blankets packed around pots and cooking utensils. Spare skins were sewn into back-bundles. All the while, a few of the older women prepared food for the last feast and hard bread for the journey to come.

Boys ran as they must, carrying and fetching where needed. Manaha asked two to help her move the corn stored in the village crib to the plaza. There she worked to separate the ears. The best was for roasting that night or adding to the feasting stew. The driest ears would be ground into cornmeal.

Ta-kawa's sister stomped up and stood over Manaha. She called three girls to her side. "Two of you begin removing all the kernels from those cobs," she said, pointing at Manaha's work. "The other can start grinding."

Neither woman looked at the other. When she had gone, Manaha gathered up a small basket of the freshest corn from what she had harvested just days before. She carried it to the creek and washed the ears. Too moist for grinding, they would be Manaha's contribution to the village stew simmering in a large pot in the center of the square-ground. Many would add to it and all would enjoy.

With the light fading and most of the work done, the feast began. Manaha toiled with and for her people all day. Still no one had spoken to her. Waiting until the last, she took a small portion of the stew and returned to the island and her empty circle.

She sat watching smoke drift up from the burning lodges in the village and tried to imagine them as they once were, filled with happiness and laughter. Adding to her pain, Manaha suddenly remembered her own childhood lodge far away in Taninto's valley.

"Grandfather," she slowly mumbled. "The day he died—that is how I feel."

"I am too tired to tell a story," she announced to the night.

A branch shook, and leaves rustled behind her. A thin smile parted her grief. Without further hesitation, she prepared a fire and waited for other listeners.

"Is no one else coming?" she asked the shadows.

A voice, young and uncertain, called from the darkness. "Manaha, Nanza child, daughter of Palisema, may I come closer and sit in your circle?"

"All are welcome," Manaha said. "Come share the light of my fire."

Ichisi, the youngest son of Ta-kawa, the boy who had helped gather wood and corn, stepped out of the shadows. Burning lodges in the village lit the sky around him.

"I seek forgiveness," he said, "for the shameful act of listening to your stories but never respecting the teller."

"You listened to all of my stories?"

"From the first night, when my father doused your story-fire." Ichisi stepped in closer. "I knew he would not let me return, so I hid."

"Against the will of Ta-kawa, you came every night?"

Ichisi nodded as Manaha looked past him. "I have heard other footsteps. Are there more?"

"At first but since the storm, I am the only one."

Manaha tilted her head slightly and stared hard at the boy.

"If you thought you had only one listener," he said, "I was afraid you would stop telling your stories. I made all those noises."

"One, and only one, faithful listener," Manaha said and motioned the boy into the circle. "I am honored to have Ichisi, son of Ta-kawa, sit at my fire." She danced about the flames as best an old woman could. Tossing in the pieces of lightning wood, she chanted.

"I have a listener round about.
I have a listener round about.
I have a listener round about."

Chapter 31: The Swarm

Nanza's Journey
Forty-nine years after "their" arrival

I awoke under a canopy of swaying cedars with flashes of the story the old man had told the night before. "Could his tales be true?" I mumbled, not wanting Taninto to hear.

He sat with his back to me in a shallow pool downstream from the campsite. Little Pup lay behind him at the edge of the water.

"Little Pup, pup, pup, pup-pie-ee," I called.

She raced up to me, circled my legs, and headed back to the old man.

"Come on, Little Pup, we will find our own place to bathe," I said and turned upstream. I rounded the edge of the cedar thicket before she caught up with me.

The stream deepened up against a small bluff. I waded in, feeling as though I had never been naked before. The sun, the wind, and the water touched every part of my body. I felt proud but awkward. Confused, yet excited to be a woman.

"Come on in," I called to Little Pup.

She barked.

"It is just you and me," I said. "And I will not throw you in."

She edged toward the water.

"You can swim come on pup, pup, pup . . . pieee."

She bounced and barked. I slapped the water. She bounded in. We played and laughed until Taninto called. When we returned, he had put out the campfire and packed both back-bundles.

"Here," he grunted and handed me a strip of jerky.

Little Pup eyed the exchange.

"Do not give her much," he said.

I glared at him as I tore her off a big piece. He grabbed it from me, tore it in two, and tossed her the smaller piece.

"For a young dog an empty belly is a good teacher," he said and walked away.

"Nanza will always take care of you, Little Pup," I whispered and gave her more jerky.

I gathered my things and chased after our guide. Little Pup took her position between us. Taninto disappeared into the tree line. I imagined Little Pup as my guide, leading me, mostly downhill, over a land uneven and ragged. I hardly saw the old man all morning until I crested a steep ridge. Little Pup stood next to him while he studied the valley below.

"Little Pup, have you found the end of the mountains?" I asked as I picked her up.

Taninto shook his head. Below lay just another steep climb into another forested valley surrounded by more mountains.

Little Pup wiggled and jumped out of my arms. She barked at the sky. From over the trees, a thick black line slithered toward us.

"Grandfather," I said before I thought.

"River flies," he said as the first of them flew overhead.

"River flies?" I mumbled. I had seen them all my life, fluttering among the dry rocks along the Buffalo River: big eyes, long thin bodies, each with four wings but never this many.

Father Sun flickered behind their number as a haze spread across the sky. The flutter rose to a wind of wings—a sound few have heard, and none could repeat. Still they came over the tree line, flashing by like snowflakes in a black blizzard.

I dropped to the ground and pulled Little Pup under me. The sky darkened. Taninto stood in the midst, turning his back to the swarm as it stretched out over the valley. Against the white clouds, it moved through the sky like a giant black snake.

We watched in silence until it faded to a thin line that disappeared long before it reached the distant mountains. Gusts of moist wind followed, pushing against our backs. From where the swarm had come, the sky remained dark. Little Pup squirmed her way in between my legs.

Taninto rushed down the hill to a patch of red berry bushes. He smashed his way into the middle of the cluster and stomped out a small clearing. Little Pup barked and jumped around him.

"What are you doing?" I asked.

"A storm is coming," he said as he stripped the limbs from two of the tallest red berry trunks at the edge of his clearing.

"Take off your back bundle and get that dog," he shouted.

I wanted to resist even as I picked up Little Pup.

He swung the bundle off his back and untied his buffalo hide. "Get out your cloak."

The wind blew harder. Large raindrops splattered around us. A drop hit Little Pup. She tried to jump out of my arms, but I held on tightly. Taninto spread the buffalo cloak, tail down,

over the two bushes he had stripped. On the mesh of stomped limbs, he crossed the hind legs of the buffalo skin and pointed. "Sit here with the dog."

"Why should I?"

"You do not have four wings like a river fly," he said.

Trees swayed one direction then the other and I with them.

"Sit on the hide!" he yelled.

With the puppy squirming in my arms, I squatted.

He wrapped both bundles, his shirt, and his moccasins inside my cloak. "Keep these dry," he said and pulled the buffalo hide over the stripped trunks to form an arch, sheltering Little Pup and me. He tied a short piece of rope to the forelegs.

"Hold the rope," he shouted over the pounding of rain against the hide.

The wind pushed and pulled the cloak. I held on with both hands. He stood and walked up the hill. From under the cloak, I watched him stand with his back to the storm, water running off him like a rock, hard and unconcerned.

I squeezed Little Pup. "That old man is my grandfather."

She whimpered and tucked her head under a hind leg.

When the rain stopped, he stood in the same place. His head and back bent a little more. As the last of the storm clouds raced to the east, he climbed to the crest and faced west. Frail and naked against the sky, he chanted too softly for me to hear his words.

Before he came back down, I had wiped the rain off the buffalo hide. He untied it, shook it several times, and wrapped it around him. Without a word, we headed downhill. At the bottom, he kept the mountain to our left until it sprouted a line of bluffs. The bluffs turned back into a hollow as the sounds of running water flowed in from the right.

The forest opened to a wide field. Little Pup chased small butterflies swirling up from the moist sandy soil, some white, some black. I ran after her, spotting Big Creek before either of them.

More than a creek to my eyes, wider than the Buffalo River and much deeper, its banks were muddy and steep, lined with large trees leaning out over the water as if trying to reach their brothers on the other side. The late day sun sparkled off the creek as it rushed past a small, rocky island tangled with live trees and dead limbs piled one upon the other.

Taninto, with Little Pup bouncing about his heels, came up from behind. "We will cross tomorrow," he said as if he had heard my thoughts.

I said nothing.

"When you see these waters again," he said, "they will have joined with the Little Red River on their way to the villages of Palisema."

I tossed a stone into the creek and watched the ripples race away. "Roll on. Tell them Nanza will be home soon."

A small stream, more rocks than water, emptied into the creek. The gentle slope of its streambed and the well-worn path to the water's edge spoke of an old watering site shared by many, four-legged and two-legged.

Across the streambed, a towering bluff blocked the eastern sky. Not a bluff of large boulders but layers of flat rocks one upon the other, curving up and jutting out toward the creek. Tall oaks grew under the huge shelter that bore the signs of many

past campfires.

Standing under the ancient shelter, watching the light sparkle off Big Creek, filled me with a sense of calm, a fleeting closeness to those who had stood there before. The faint echoes of lost voices slipped past like cold, dark water through my fingers. I watched and listened until the day faded.

Taninto had built a fire in a stone-rimmed pit against a large rock near the back wall smudged black from past fires. Staring hard into the flames, he seemed not to notice me as I walked up.

"Did you feel the ancestors?" he asked.

Little Pup jumped from his side and ran to me. I nodded.

"In places like this, there are listening spirits and ancient stories." His gaze turned up to the overhang then caught my wandering eyes.

"Remember this," he said. "Once told, a story is never lost."

Chapter 32: Battle Won and Lost

Taninto's Journey
July 3, 1541

A man of Casqui, a servant of Spaniards, I stood on the grand plaza below the sacred Temple Mound of Pa-caha. Their nation once ruled over lands up, down, and both sides of the Mizzissibizzibbippi River. For generations upon generations, they killed and enslaved the people of Casqui. Now they fled from the sight of Casquis marching beside the Son of the Sun and his army.

Except for a few unfortunates, the main town of Pa-caha was abandoned by its people. Whether brave or foolish, their heads were now impaled on poles around the mound. I suddenly longed to see Saswanna to hold her to apologize for everything I had said. She told the truth. She was right about the power of the Spanish.

The Pa-cahas could not stop them from crossing the Mizzissibizzibbippi into the Nine-Rivers Valley. They learned the Spanish could not be frightened, even with two hundred longboats filled with warriors. They saw the Spanish cloaks of metal and their crossbows that could reach further than any Pa-caha bow.

The Pa-cahas saw the *arcabuz* weapons kill with thunder

and smoke and knew of their magnificent beasts. They knew the Casquis. They knew the Spanish. It was the Spanish not my people they ran from.

Atop their abandoned Temple Mound, flames from the bones of their honored ancestors danced with twenty or so young braves of Casqui. The braves chanted, Naffja the loudest.

"Pa-cahas run like rabbits . . . they run. They run like rabbits before Casqui warriors . . . Pa-cahas run like rabbits." The chant spread over the walls to the hundreds of Casquis gathered outside. Every Casqui warrior now believed the Pa-cahas feared them, but none more so than Naffja and the braves with him.

Of the prisoners in my charge, only seven remained. The Spanish had cut down the elder, and Naffja's band took the heads of the boys captured with him. Two others escaped during my struggle with Naffja and were surely dead. The survivors glared back at me.

"Sit here." I pointed to a place near the center of the plaza. None of them moved. I pointed again.

"I comman . . ." my words unfinished, they sat no longer staring at me but beyond. I turned to see what had bent their knees and taken their courage. A noble Spanish conquistador atop an even nobler beast emerged from the narrow west gate and raced onto the plaza with his sword drawn. The prisoners huddled together. The young Casqui braves on the mound cheered.

Two other horsemen burst through the gate and rushed to join the first. The horses pranced and pawed the hard plaza floor as their masters surveyed the town. I never tired of watching the Spanish horses and the bold men who commanded them. After the horsemen, Spanish foot soldiers flowed in, one on the heels of another.

Behind me, I heard shouting.

"Burn it all!" Naffja yelled from the mound as he waved a torch. "Burn it all!"

The soldiers quickly formed ranks and trotted across the plaza. To these Spaniards without horses, I had never given more than a glance. Their armor clanked, and their strange weapons gleamed as on that first day I saw them. As they passed by on either side, I noticed their tattered cloaks and leggings as worn as each face. Yet it seemed that whether a Spaniard walked in sandals or rode a horse. Each had a command of his given duty and a conviction of his own greatness.

The Casqui braves waved and called the Spaniards up the temple steps. Some knelt and bowed their heads, but Naffja and others ran for the king's lodge with torches high. The first swordsmen on the mound took positions between the lodge and the braves. The angry band turned on one of the smaller lodges and set it on fire before the will of the swordsmen pushed them back.

Naffja attacked the scattered remains of the Pa-caha ancestors. His braves chanted "Pa-cahas run like rabbits" as they tore open more chests of the dead and smashed their bones. They threw it all on the blazing fire along with the Pa-cahas' bodies from whom they had taken their heads. Against the smell, I covered my nose, but for the shame, I could do nothing.

Through the smoke of ancestors, the noblest of all Spaniards approached: Hernando de Soto, Son of the Sun, with the dogs at his side. He entered the town through an unfinished portion of

the eastern wall. He had led the chase after the last escaping Pacaha. They returned without any prisoners but had found an unfinished portion of the wall through which they could easily get the horses and all the soldiers.

I knelt and bowed to Lord de Soto. The prisoners pressed themselves to the dirt, trying to appear as insignificant as possible. Master Diego rode among the conquistadors who followed. Shadow Wind pranced as proud as any man.

Behind the horses, weary foot soldiers and horse tenders ran to keep up. I saw Cooquyi in the pack and started across the plaza. He waved for me to turn back. I had forgotten the prisoners. Even though they had no chance of escape, they were still my duty.

The black stallion carried Lord de Soto up the unfinished Temple Mound in a gallop. His guard of bowmen and *arcabuceros* charged up the steps behind him and circled the rim. More soldiers poured through the main gate and around the uncompleted wall.

Swordsmen encircled Naffja and the other warriors on the mound and pushed them to the edge. Some ran. Others tumbled down the slope. The fire consumed the ancestors' bones without further desecration.

Master Diego rode toward me; I bowed. He laughed, leaned over in his saddle, and pulled me up straight. Cooquyi stepped from behind Shadow Wind and studied the remaining prisoners.

"A swordsman killed the old man," I said. "My people killed four others. I tried to—"

Cooquyi shook his head and hands at me. Master Diego pointed at the prisoners and began giving Cooquyi instructions when loud chanting pulled everyone's attention toward the main gate.

Seven head warriors from the Red Council of Casqui sang the praises of King Issqui as they led his triumphant march into the conquered town of our enemy. Naffja and his braves ran toward the Council. Some danced, some boasted, but all tried to be seen.

Master Diego finished his orders and rode toward the mound, scattering the braves. Swordsmen escorted the Red Council onto the plaza and King Issqui to the bottom of the mound steps.

"Taninto!" Cooquyi shouted. "Master Diego commanded me to help you watch these prisoners, not to do it by myself."

"What did he say about me?" I asked.

Sweat and mud covered Cooquyi's body. His shoulders drooped. "Yes, Master said, 'You did good.' Little chipmunk."

I tried not to smile or notice the anger in Cooquyi's voice.

"What is your wish?" I asked. "I will follow your commands as though you were a Spanish noble."

Before he could answer, a clamor rattled up from every direction. The Spaniards clanged metal against metal and stomped. On top of the mound, Lord de Soto raised his arm and all fell silent. He stood in his saddle, thrust his sword to the sky, and shouted out across the plaza in Spanish.

"I do hereby claim this land, and all Pa-caha lands are now under the sovereignty of the Emperor and King of Spain, and henceforth governed by one Hernando de Soto."

Cooquyi sat with his back to the words. Facing the prisoners, he held his bare right foot in his hands.

"Where are your moccasins?" I asked.

"I lost them in the mud around the new canal." He snatched a pair from one of the prisoners. "That is how they fled in longboats out to a swamp by way of the channel they had recently dug."

"What did Lord de Soto proclaim?" I asked.

He loosened the moccasins to fit. "What Lord de Soto always says when he conquers another nation."

I waited for more.

"The Son of the Sun," he looked at me, "as you call him, has proclaimed all the lands of Pa-caha now under the rule of the Spanish king, who appointed him governor over all of it."

"That is his right. The Spanish will rule the Pa-caha lands wisely," I said.

"The true quest of these conquistadors is not to rule over this nation or any other they have conquered. Each time they conquer, they make speeches of honor and promises of good but seek one thing above all."

Cooquyi stood. He twisted and flexed one foot then the other, looking for comfort in the strange moccasins.

"What is it? What do they seek?"

He whispered, "*Oro et plata* . . . gold and silver."

My thought flashed to the brilliant sparkle of morning light reflecting off the king's polished breastplate as he prayed from the top of the Temple Mound to the first sun of the summer.

I said, "Our king has a breastplate made of —"

Cooquyi pulled me down as he squatted. "Say no more," he whispered. "Say nothing about the breastplate."

"But I know King Issqui would gladly give it to the Son of the Sun."

Cooquyi shook his head. "Taninto of Togo, you understand so little."

I looked away at the prisoners.

"Listen to me," he said. "Your king is a wise leader. He has not worn the breastplate in the presence of the Spanish, has he?"

"No."

Cooquyi stood and looked down at me. "And you should not speak of it."

"My uncle took out his silver ear-plugs," I remembered aloud.

"Do not speak of it!" Cooquyi shouted.

The rest of the day, I said nothing. I listened to Cooquyi's bidding, to the Spanish boasting and quarreling, and to the rumors. It was said Casqui scouts discovered a large island in the Mizzissibizzibbippi River where the people from the main town of Pa-caha had fled. I heard that King Issqui had promised Lord de Soto: more warriors, longboats and canoes with paddlers to ferry the Spanish to the island and help defeat our common enemy.

It would take at least two full days for boats to come from Casqui up the Tyronza River through the Wapanocca Swamp and out onto the Mizzissibizzibbippi River. Another day would be needed to travel upriver to Pa-caha. The Spanish settled into the town and moved all their slaves and animals inside the walls. The plaza filled with horses, tenders, servants, and new prisoners but no other Casquis.

In the hot summer night, victory fires burned outside the walls. Casqui warriors sang and danced. The master's horses took little notice of it all. Cooquyi slept. I could do neither.

Early the next morning, soldiers took my charge of Pa-caha prisoners.

"To be shackled," Cooquyi said as he saddled Shadow Wind. He led the prancing gray to Master Diego, who had gathered with a hundred or so horsemen and foot soldiers on the north side of the plaza.

Master mounted Shadow Wind without a word. Cooquyi trotted after him. I followed.

We marched until we reached a bank overlooking the Mizzissibizzibbippi River. The mighty river rushed by, ever worthy of its name: *old, big, deep, strong, turbulent, muddy, winding grandfather of all rivers.* Whole trees rushed by like sticks in a rain-swollen stream. I could not see the other bank, it was so wide.

We set up camp downriver from the island where the Pa-caha people had retreated. The following morning, Lord de Soto arrived with a hundred and fifty more foot soldiers. King Issqui followed with hundreds of warriors, all waiting for the boats to arrive from Casqui. Captain Antonio Osorio and four other Spaniards boarded the first canoe and headed upriver to scout the island.

Soon, more canoes rounded the bend, escorting twenty-two Casqui longboats, none of which had enough paddlers. They struggled against the swift current. King Issqui signaled them all to the shore.

The larger longboats were too heavy to reach the beach. The

Spanish did not trust the river or the small canoes. After much complaining, ten or so Spaniards boarded each longboat with their weapons and twenty fresh paddlers. Master Diego left Shadow Wind with Cooquyi and boarded one of the boats.

Without giving Cooquyi a chance to stop me, I ran into the river. I took a paddler's position on the next longboat. Once the Spaniards settled in the center, I and the other paddlers pushed the longboat out into the river and climbed aboard.

The loud, normally boastful Spaniards sat silent and rigid as we paddled away from the shore. Few even looked at the swirling brown water that raced by. I could see concern in the faces of the other paddlers as they watched the Spaniards.

King Issqui boarded his longboat while the fleet of canoes filled with eager Casqui warriors. The canoes held back as the slower Spanish-filled longboats led the strange fleet upriver. Lord de Soto, on his black stallion, marched the remaining foot soldiers along the rim above the riverbank.

The island came into view. Along the crest of its beach, driftwood piled up in a wall of tangled limbs surrounding the entire island. The size of the wall would have taken more driftwood than could be found on one island and much longer than two days to build.

Off the east side of the island, a hundred or more Pa-cahas scattered as we approached. Many of them waded into the river and swam for the distant shore or clung to rafts piled with belongings. Old women and mothers with their children scurried down the beach. Captain Osorio turned his canoe toward the Pa-cahas in the river. At the Spaniard's urging, all the paddlers pulled harder, trying to catch Osorio.

Above the sound of paddles slicing the river, a swoosh of arrows passed overhead. Like water dropping on hot coals, they hit the river, then the boats behind us with a thud or a scream. The Spaniards shouted, "Shields up, shields up."

A second flock of arrows flew up from behind the island's driftwood wall. Every paddler thought or shouted, "Turn downriver, turn downriver!"

Arrows fell like hail. The Spaniards suffered no harm, huddled under their shields, shiny hats, and cloaks of metal. They pushed our dead into the river without a word. The Casqui warriors in the canoes behind us were never within range of the arrows and drifted even further downriver.

Captain Osorio's canoe, missing three paddlers, glided among the scattered longboats. The captain stood in his canoe and shouted brave, proud-sounding words. The Spaniards in the longboats listened as the paddlers mumbled among themselves. Then Captain Osorio grabbed a paddle and turned his canoe around toward the west side of the island.

With little hesitation or discussion, the Casqui paddlers pulled the longboats about. We paddled close to the shore out of the stronger current and well away from Pa-caha arrows. Issqui and the Casqui-filled canoes followed but still at a distance.

Upriver from an open stretch of beach on the west side of the island, Captain Osorio began shouting orders and arranging the boats by what weapons were onboard. The crossbowmen in the boats closest to the island readied and raised their weapons.

"¡Carga, carga hasta matar!" he shouted and turned his canoe toward the island.

The crossbowmen released their weapons. Paddlers pulled

for the beach. Soldiers yelled. A second wave of Spanish arrows flew over our heads as Pa-caha arrows began to strike the longboats.

Two paddlers on my side dropped to the bottom of the boat. One had an arrow through his shoulder.

"Get up!" I yelled at the other. "Paddle or we will miss the beach."

A Spaniard kicked him out of the way and took his place. He helped turn the boat back toward the island.

We ran aground downriver from most of the boats. The river had the final say, pulling the back end around. The Spaniards leaped from the side of the boat into the oozing river sand. I slipped over the other side with the remaining paddlers. Using the boat as a shield, we pushed it onto the beach.

The Spanish quickly formed lines on the shore, shields and swords in front, bowmen and *arcabuceros* behind. Arrows flew in both directions. More Pa-caha than Spanish, still they advanced. As warriors, the conquistadors knew no fear. Blessed by the spirits, they marched ever closer to the driftwood wall that hid the enemy.

Their bravery became my people's bravery. Waves of Casqui canoes skidded onto the island with a roar of war cries. Just the sight of a hundred conquistadors followed by hundreds of Casquis would defeat any number of Pa-cahas hiding on the island. I grabbed a paddle for a weapon and ran after the Spanish line.

Soldiers carrying *arcabuceros* moved to the front; behind shields, they formed a double row. The front row knelt. Then the unnatural thunder rumbled across the island over the river.

Driftwood splintered; black smoke rose and drifted downriver, but the stench hung over the battle.

Arrows ceased to fly for a moment. The second line of *arcabuceros* fired. Thunder rolled anew. A row of soldiers rushed the splintered barricade carrying *halberdiers*: long poles with a metal point at the end, an axe on one side and hooked blade on the other. They hacked and pulled the barrier apart with their weapons.

Shielded swordsmen pushed through the break. The conquistadors spread out and advanced, slashing and jabbing. Pa-cahas fell. Their shorter weapons could inflict no harm against the Spanish *halberdier* and sword. The Spanish killed with skill, without hesitation. They forced the Pa-cahas back to a second driftwood barrier built inside the outer wall. Blood and bodies covered the brown sand.

Pa-caha arrows flew again, this time from behind the inner wall. Few were wasted on the Spanish; most found their mark among the Casquis. Yet my people charged on across the beach toward the opening, following the courage of the Spanish.

The Pa-caha ranks broke and split, fleeing in opposite directions between the outer and inner walls. Hundreds of Casquis flooded through the opening, chasing after them.

"Revenge!" they shouted.

With my paddle raised, I joined the assault, racing past the Spanish as they pulled back to the opening. I shouted as loud as anyone but ran a little slower.

Whoops, war cries, and the pounding of feet and bodies swirled with an ever-growing nameless sound, a great union from unseen voices. The shouts for "revenge" fell away. Courage faltered. Those in front slowed. I stopped. A growl of thousands filled the narrow land between the two walls.

The trap had fallen. The enemy rose up from their hiding places inside the second barrier, ten men for every one Casqui. Those we had been chasing turned back on us. The air filled with panic and arrows.

We ran in every direction, most back to the Spanish, and I the hardest. A boy stumbled in front of me. His head slammed into my right shin. We both fell. I dropped my paddle.

My leg throbbed as I tried to stand. An arrow through his heart, the boy would never stand again. I hobbled and rolled tightly against a log at the bottom of the inner wall.

Out of sight of the Pa-caha bowmen, I watched as they brought down my people one arrow at a time. Some tried to climb the outer barrier, but its limbs had been sharpened. Bodies hung in the tangle like frozen dancers.

I edged back toward the Spanish. Beyond the opening in the driftwood, I saw my people scurrying back to the river, taking any boat they could. Fallen Pa-cahas and Casquis lay side-by-side between me and the conquistadors holding the opening. They could not force another advance with the Casquis in retreat.

Soldiers with *arcabuceros* formed a line across the opening. Thunder rumbled on command. The Pa-cahas retreated behind their inner wall. As crossbowmen waited for them to rise up, I ran for the other side, trying not to step on the dead.

The *arcabuceros* flashed again. The crack rang in my ears. Smoke stung my eyes. I jumped over a body, stumbled on the next.

"*Venir, niño,*" a Spanish voice boomed. The large hand of Master Diego pulled me around behind the barricade. He stood me up. "*¡Correr!* Run, run! " he shouted and pushed me toward the beach, straight into another battle.

All the canoes had been taken, most only half-filled with panicked Casquis. Spanish guards fought to keep them from taking the remaining longboats. I turned back to Master Diego, but he and the other conquistadors were backing toward me.

Hundreds of Pa-caha warriors rushed through the gap in the driftwood, taunting and advancing on every step the Spanish took in retreat. With the river at our backs, more Pa-cahas came from around the ends of the island. Soon, thousands of the enemy filled the beach surrounding the small band of Spaniards and a few remaining Casquis.

The conquistadors formed lines at the water's edge and prepared to fight to the death. They began to shout and taunt back at the Pa-cahas. Then from atop the inner wall, a young man wearing a long red robe and a headdress of black crow feathers raised his arms and shouted.

The Pa-caha lowered their weapons. The Spanish taunts fell silent. No one moved. The river gently lapped against the longboats. One at a time, conquistadors began boarding their boats as the Pa-cahas stood back.

I saw Master Diego. He waved me past the guards to his boat. I helped push it off the beach. He pulled me in. The boat rocked. Everyone shouted and refused to let any more Casquis aboard. Grandfather River carried us peacefully away from the island.

The Casquis who had taken the canoes and abandoned the

battle now found the courage to fight over a bounty of Pa-caha rafts floating away from the island.

"*Cobardes*," the Spaniards shouted. "Cowards . . . cowards." They stood around me and shouted at my people.

Lord de Soto watched from the riverbank and Issqui from his longboat. When all the longboats filled with Spaniards reached the shore, the king of the Casqui Nation merely drifted out of sight.

Master Diego pulled me aside as Cooquyi brought Shadow Wind to him. I leaned on my injured leg like it was my favorite while he looked me over. He shook his head, mounted his horse, and spoke to Cooquyi.

"Master told me to keep you close," Cooquyi said before I had a chance to ask. "Your people are now the enemy of Governor de Soto and his conquistadors. "

"Where are we going?"

"Pa-caha."

Chapter 33

Manaha's Journey
Ninety-four years after "their" arrival

The last flame flickered and vanished, but the story lingered. Its words and images blurred the world around, holding teller and listener between the night and days past. An ember popped. Ichisi bounced to his feet.

"You must come with the tribe," he said.

"I am not wanted." Manaha circled the scar on her cheek. "The tribe does not need the burden of another old woman."

"You are not old. You harvested the corn when all the others had given up."

"No one needs me . . . or my stories."

"I do." Ichisi sat down next to her. "I want to hear them all."

"Now you speak," she said. "Before tonight, I told my stories to the shadows and stars. And when the tribe is gone, it will be no different but for one less shadow."

Ichisi tossed a twig onto the glowing embers. A flame sprouted and danced. Suddenly, he did the same. "I will stay with you," he said with a skip. "I will stay here until I have heard all of your stories."

"I have no time for childishness."

His face hardened. "I am not a child."

Manaha pointed her finger at him. "You must go with the tribe. I will not let you lose your family."

"I will not lose them." He sat down across the fire pit from her. "I am young. I can follow the tribe later."

"No." Manaha shook her head. "I will not be a part of it—not your family."

"I am staying or . . . you must come with the tribe."

"I am not prepared to leave." Manaha paced off into the shadows. Over her shoulder, she shouted, "I will not be a burden."

"You can pack your belongings in the morning," Ichisi called to her.

Manaha stepped back into the firelight. "I cannot walk with the tribe after what was said in the village-lodge."

"Then follow along out of sight." Ichisi smiled. "Our trail will be easy to find."

Manaha shook her head.

"Walk as far as you can," he said, "and I will come back to you every night."

She sat down and studied the scrawny, suddenly brash boy as he shifted from one foot to the other. "You have grown in the days since you first carried wood for me."

"I will gather wood, bring food, and water, whatever you need. Will you come?" Ichisi's smile grew as he waited.

"Return in the morning, you will have my answer."

~~~

The next morning, when the tribe was ready to leave, Ichisi ran to the island. Manaha stood on the far bank with her bedding and bundles over her shoulder. She raised her walking stick and waved it. Ichisi jumped and waved then leaped his way back to the tribe.

Manaha lingered, gazing over the island, another home she would never see again. She reached far into her pouch and rubbed the small, white arrowhead as she purposely avoided the burned village. Her grandfather taught her long ago that *painful sights tarnish cherished memories.*

Smoke from the smoldering fires hung over the creek, smelling of burned earth. The morning was strangely quiet with no one around but her. All of the Hachia canoes had left before the tribe in a race to meet them on the bank of the Akamsa River in three days.

Manaha gripped her walking stick and waded into the shallows of Long Creek for the last time. Ichisi was right. The tribe would be easy to follow. On the other side of the creek, a wide trail rolled through the thick undergrowth. The brush thinned, hillsides rose above the trees on both sides. The valley narrowed to a stream and its meadows, most of which would be wet but for the lack of rain. As the hills fell away and the forest opened, the meadows spread out. Manaha caught a glimpse of the tribe in the distance.

She pushed harder across the flat land. The only mountain ridges in sight were those just above the hills behind her. Unlike the steep drop-off at the *Edge of the Mountains* to the east, here they slowly faded away, each ridge smaller until there was no rise at all.

Late in the day, Manaha came to a stream muddied by the tribe's crossing. On the other side lay several mounds, not much higher than a knee. Manaha chose one just off the trail with little growth under the spread of a single red oak. In the fork of its split trunk, Manaha wedged her bundles and leaned her walking stick. The tree supported her back while she rested and listened to the stream flowing close by then off to the south.

The tribe would have already set up camp. How far ahead she had no way of knowing. She had not seen them again since that morning, but she believed Ichisi would do as he had promised.

After a time, Manaha stood and pulled down a dead branch. She used the thick end to clear a place for a fire. Under the leaves and dark-brown earth, a black layer crumbled as she scraped. Onto that, she piled dry grass, pine cones and twigs. She surrounded it with a good supply of wood, but decided to let Ichisi start the story-fire.

She took some jerky and a knife from her pouch, and sat down with the walking stick. She carved and waited. It was getting too dark to see in the moonless night when a faint light fluttered in the distance.

"Ichisi?" she called out.

The boy came running, carrying a fading torch. She pointed at the pit, and he laid it in among the kindling.

"Did you have to travel far?"

"No," he said, still trying to catch his breath. "We are camped on this same stream not much further south."

He knelt and blew on the kindling until flames crackled. She offered him some jerky. He took a piece and gave her a loaf of

hard bread he had brought from camp. Manaha cut a piece and dropped it in a pot of water to soften it.

"Toss some more wood on the fire," she said as she gathered the wood shavings.

Sparks swarmed up as the fire struggled then took hold. Dropping in pieces of lightning wood she had just carved from her walking stick, Manaha chanted louder than she had ever chanted.

"I have a listener round about.
I have a listener round about.
I have a listener round about."

Chapter 34: Edge of the Mountains

Nanza's Journey
Forty-nine years after "their" arrival

A new woman, but I giggled like a child when Little Pup licked my face that morning next to Big Creek.

"Stop it, I am awake," I said and rolled the pest over on her back. I rubbed her belly until she lost her fight. "Do not lick me when I am asleep," I scolded her.

She cocked her head and stared me down. I tried not to, but I laughed. With that, she twisted around to her feet and scampered after Taninto, hobbling down to the creek. The night before, he said if we kept moving all day we could reach the *Edge of the Mountains*. I wanted to believe, but as I hurried back from my time at the creek, I wondered.

Little Pup ran at me. "Are we going to see Nine-Rivers Valley today?" I asked. She hunched down, tail in the air, nipped at my toes, then ran back to camp without answering.

"There is a crossing, just up the creek," Taninto announced and started off in the direction of the dry streambed we had seen the day before.

Now, a day after the storm, it flowed with clear water and a song. I glanced back to where we had camped. The black jagged

bluff stretched up and out toward the horizon, waiting for the next wanderer.

We jumped the stream and I chased after Little Pup. She ran a short spurt and crouched down in the grass. As I came close, she barked and darted off again. I finally caught her at the creek bed. We sat together and watched Taninto trudge across. Rapids swirled around his legs up to his knees.

I took off my moccasins, put them in the back-bundle, and tied up my skirt. Little Pup hesitated but followed when I waded in. Eyes round and full of determination, she fought the current. Once her feet reached the bottom on the other side, she hopped across the shallows and onto the bank. She shook off the creek and looked to Taninto. He said nothing.

"Good puppy," I said and reached for her.

She sprang off toward Taninto so fast it seemed her hind legs would overtake the front two. Around him, back to me, and around again, she ran. I watched him as he watched her. For a moment, his face swelled and grinned, just a glimpse of the boy lost long ago, then it faded.

"Nanza, do not dawdle," he said.

Little Pup dropped down next to me while I put on my moccasins. I whispered, "We do not need him. We can find Nine-Rivers Valley . . . if we have to."

Taninto pushed the pace once we caught up. The land rose in a steady march up from the creek. The forest rose to a thick tangle overhead, but its floor was open except for the occasional spread of a towering cedar. On the surrounding hills, new shades of green stood out among the gray haze woven of countless branches.

I walked up next to Taninto when he stopped and squatted.

He jerked me to the ground and whispered, "Listen."

Far off to the left, I heard the rustling and snapping of something large moving through the forest. I shook my arm free of his grip. Little Pup lunged at a sudden, low rumble between a snort and a growl.

He grabbed her up and whispered, "Buffalo."

I squinted into the bright morning sun. Buffalo? I had never seen one. He hunted buffalo, but he always left me behind, alone in his valley. It seemed so small and far away, now.

"A mountain forest like this," he whispered, "is a good place for a hunting party to stalk a herd on their way to the lowlands. If there is a party following, we must cross in front of the herd to hide our tracks."

A great bull stepped into a pool of morning light streaking through the canopy. Huge black eyes sunk deep in a large head of thick wool stared straight into mine. For a time, no one moved.

"Hold her snout." Taninto handed Little Pup to me. He nodded to the east. "Palisema," he whispered, slowly stood, and pulled me up as two other buffalo ambled into view.

They stopped behind the first one. Taninto gripped my arm and headed straight across their path. The old bull shook his head and snorted.

Little Pup fought to wiggle free. Taninto paced on without a glance. I hid my fear but kept an eye on the growing herd.

Once the buffalo were out of sight, he hurried us away over unbroken land, dipping and rising only slightly. From the next ridge, I could see long, flat mountaintops standing far apart and dark blue against the light sky that spread from shoulder to shoulder in every direction.

Taninto walked on without resting or eating. We stayed with him, eating bits of jerky when we could. He kept going, long after we should have stopped to set up camp. Father Sun faded at our backs while the sky in front rippled in thin rows of red.

We crossed a stream. Darkness caught up with us, but he walked on. A half-moon cast a glow through the clouds, racing to fill the sky and block the stars. Together we crested the ridge.

The forest opened, and the mountain fell away. Before us spread a dark land of which I could see neither an end nor a mountain. Could it be? Did I stand at the *Edge of the Mountains*? Did the land of Taninto's stories, the Nine-Rivers Valley, lie below? I began to prance, ready to race across the field, down the slope, dodging trees, and leaping for joy.

"Too late to continue," he said as clouds covered the moon, its light and my hope.

I could hardly see his face. "We have to go on," I demanded.

"No! We will camp for the night back at the stream." He turned and walked away.

Little Pup followed. I stayed.

The flowers of yellow and purple, the leaves of green, the blue sky, and the earth had all faded to one color. I stared hard into that grayness, searching for the fires of Palisema. The only light anywhere came from the small campfire behind me.

Little Pup greeted me as I walked up. Taninto said nothing.

After a moment, he stood. "If you like, I will tell a story."

Chapter 35: *¡Oro!*

Taninto's Journey
July 4, 1541

I walked freely about the conquered main town of Pa-caha. The only Casqui inside of the walls while outside bands of Spaniards attacked the villages of my people for what they had done in the battle for the island. The Spanish had settled into the Pa-caha town as if it had been built for them. The king's lodge became Lord de Soto's. The Pa-caha Council House became a place of Spanish talk. Only a Spaniard could climb the Temple Mound without a guard.

The horsemen and captains took the finest lodges in the town; foot soldiers filled the rest. They herded the prisoners, Casqui and Pa-caha alike, into the center of the plaza. Horses and their tenders gathered south of the mound in the shade of three giant oaks. From there, they could easily get in and out through the unfinished section of the wall.

The day after the failed attack on the island, the brother of the King of Pa-caha, pretending to be the king, came with a large party of brightly feathered nobles to address Lord de Soto. The Spanish quickly unmasked the deception and took the brother prisoner.

Lord de Soto sent the party of false nobles back with a

message. If the king did not present himself before the governor, his brother would be tortured and killed. The next day, the true mico of Pa-caha, King Na-acha, marched through the gate with an even larger party.

"He comes to make peace with Lord de Soto," prisoners murmured.

"And join in the war on Casqui." Cooquyi added.

"Why would you say that?" I asked before I walked away.

Every Spaniard seemed to know I was a Casqui but none gave me reason for concern. I stood among them as King Na-acha strutted across the plaza. Much younger than King Issqui, he moved with ease and confidence.

When he reached the top step of the mound, I could see the weight of anguish fall on him. The desecrated and burned remains of his father, his father's father, their nation's grandfathers lay scattered around him. For all the power he had, all the lands he ruled, and all the battles he had won, at that moment he was a defeated, broken man. I felt shame for what a few Casquis had done.

Now King Na-acha moved as though he had grown as old as the few bones he could find. He placed the sacred remains into one scorched burial chest and carried it into the Temple of the Dead. The Pa-caha warriors in his party, not allowed on the mound, wailed and shouted curses against the people of Casqui. I hung my head.

When King Na-acha came out of the temple, he had changed. His face had hardened, his stride long and direct. He entered the Council House with no resistance from the Spanish guards posted outside the door. I wandered off with the crowd and through the town, lost in troubles that I alone knew or felt. I heard Cooquyi call my name.

"Come, quick!" he shouted. "Your master wants his favorite dog beside him."

I did not understand the anger in his voice. "What does Master Diego desire?"

"Taninto, your king is outside the gate, and he is requesting permission to enter."

"Enter Pa-caha? But . . ." I stammered, "why do you call for me?"

Cooquyi glared at me. "Master Diego wants you on the mound with him when Lord de Soto receives King Issqui. You are to listen to every word your king speaks then tell it to me and I to Master Diego." Cooquyi turned and shouted over his shoulder, "Go to the mound."

Master Diego slapped his thigh with the flat of his hand and called from the plaza, "Come, Chipmunk."

No one stopped me as we crossed the inner plaza and started up the steps of the Temple Mound of Pa-caha. I climbed a step behind Master Diego while studying the orderly town arranged around the plaza.

The largest lodges stood to the left of the mound with many of their thatched roofs still green while on the other side of the plaza stood two long mounds. The same shape and size, both had one lodge on top. Off the left corner of the plaza rose a spiral mound with no steps or lodges.

From the top of the mound, I could see over the walls of Pa-caha. Small villages surrounded it, except on the backside where the swamp with its thick forest of cypress spread north toward

the Mizzissibizzibbippi River. The newly-dug canal channeled the muddy swamp water around the town and had provided the means of escape for the people of Pa-caha.

Master Diego jerked me to his side and marched toward the Council House. I walked close as we passed the guards. Inside the lodge, a jester sent by King Issqui tumbled and hopped about, trying to entertain the Spaniards scattered around.

Seated on the raised platform built for the Pa-caha king, Lord de Soto looked on without expression. King Na-acha stood off to the left of his platform with his council of warriors. Between the Pa-cahas and the Spanish lay baskets of smoked fish and heaps of well-dressed skins, recent gifts sent by King Issqui and the people of Casqui.

A few of the Spaniards laughed when the jester staggered, fell then rolled out of the lodge. With every head turned toward the door, King Issqui stepped through.

"*Cobarde*," Spaniards mumbled, "Coward."

"*Death!*" the Pa-cahas shouted.

Issqui walked through the threats straight toward Lord de Soto. Na-acha rushed in between. He planted his feet and raised a Spanish knife.

"*¡Non!*" De Soto shouted and waved his hand. Issqui made no sign of retreat or effort to defend himself.

King Na-acha turned around. "Great Lord," he said, "I and my people could have done grave harm to your men who were abandoned on the island by these Casquis."

De Soto twitched and straightened but said nothing.

"Now, with your gift of the shining knife, allow me to slash the face of a coward who betrayed your trust."

"Do not harm him." The interrupter repeated Governor de Soto's command.

Issqui stepped around Na-acha and knelt before Hernando de Soto. He spoke, head down. "Son of the Sun, Lord of Lords, please accept these meager gifts as a sign of the great respect and honor that I and all of my people have for you, our Lord."

The governor nodded slightly as he listened to the translation. It pleased the Pa-cahas when he leaned forward and shouted. "Stand up, Casqui! I bear great anger for you and your people. Come before me and explain your deceit."

King Issqui spoke for all to hear, including the Pa-cahas at his back. "I and mine belong to you. My territory is yours. If you destroy it as is your own choice, it is your people you will slay. All that falls from your hand, I will receive as my Lord's gift. Know that the service you have done for me in leaving the cross has been a sign and more than I deserve. No sooner than we had thrown ourselves on our knees before the Cross—asking for the needed rain—He sent it. Your god has heard us by means of the Cross."

Lord de Soto listened to the translation of the eloquent words, and the hardness of his glare relaxed. The Pa-cahas began to mumble among themselves until de Soto raised his hand.

"When you fled without my permission," he said, "I thought that you held the teaching we had given to you of little account and with contempt."

De Soto clenched his fist. "I wanted to destroy you."

Issqui stepped in closer. "How is it possible, my Lord?" he asked. "After having given me the pledge of friendship, and

without my having done you any harm, you desire to destroy me, your friend and brother? You gave me the cross for a defense against our enemies."

Issqui pointed to the Pa-caha warriors, each one with a newly fashioned cross in his headdress. He raised his voice.

"Yet now, with the sign of the Cross," he said, "you seek to destroy me and the faith and confidence which my people, friends of the Cross, have in you."

"I wanted to destroy you," the Son of the Sun said as he stood. He took a deep breath. "Supposing that in pride, you had gone off. Pride is the sin which our God most abhors and for which He punishes us the most."

Lord de Soto glanced around the lodge and back, glaring at Issqui. "It is for us to do what our God commands, which is not to lie. Now that you have come in humility, I believe that you tell the truth, since to speak a lie is a very great sin amongst us. Be assured that I wish you greater good than you think."

King Issqui bowed deeply. The Pa-cahas grumbled loudly as their king, with his knife down at his side, stepped up next to Issqui. Face to ear, Na-acha spoke softly.

The governor demanded to know what had been said. The interpreter repeated Na-acha's words for all to hear.

"You must be exultant, Casqui, to have realized what you never dreamed or hoped to obtain with your own forces, revenge for your injuries and affronts. Be thankful to the power of the Spanish for this. Someday they will go away and we shall remain here as we once were."

Lord de Soto stepped to the edge of the platform and spoke down to the two leaders of nations as though scolding children.

"The Spanish people did not come into these lands to leave the Indians more inflamed in their wars and enemies than they had been before." He held out his open arms. "We came to bring peace and harmony."

The two chiefs remained rigid then hugged for a moment like long-lost friends. Their faces showed the truer and greater emotion, but de Soto seemed pleased.

"Come, King Issqui and King Na-acha, sit beside me and enjoy a meal and our friendship." He led the way to a long table outside the Council House set with all manner of food.

The governor sat at the head of the table. Both kings started for the position on his right side.

The Pa-caha pushed ahead. "You know well that I am a greater nobleman than you. I am of more honorable parents and grandparents. To me belongs the higher place."

"True," said King Issqui, "your forebears are greater than mine. Since Lord de Soto tells us that we must not lie, I will not deny the truth. But you know that I am older and mightier than you."

The King of the Casqui Nation swelled his chest and declared, "I have chased you from your walls, and you have never seen my country."

Lord de Soto motioned both kings to him as the interpreter explained their exchange. "In the eyes of God, all men are equal," he said.

The Pa-caha bowed. "I will not," he said, "in keeping with my people's beliefs, take a position that is less than what is rightfully mine. If that is your wish, my Lord, I will take my meal with my warriors rather than relinquish my rightful position."

Lord de Soto smiled, "I did not expect to find in men, so far removed from every good teaching and culture, such a refinement in the rules of honor." He motioned to the King of Pa-caha. "As it should be, at my right hand shall be King Na-acha because of his more ancient and noble ancestry."

King Issqui bowed and said, "I am your vassal and honored to receive any place at your table."

"Then to you belongs the honored position on my left," the governor proclaimed.

Master Diego stood back as the other Spaniards rushed for the remaining empty places. With the challenge of positions settled, eating came easy. De Soto's questions soon turned to the lands beyond the two nations.

Issqui responded first but with guarded answers. "The ridge that you saw to the west from the Temple Mound of Casqui," he said, "we call Little Brother Mountain. It is not a mountain, only a long ridge that runs through the Nine-Rivers Valley like a backbone." With his arm stretched toward the west, Issqui made a motion with his hand of crossing over Little Brother Mountain. "On the other side," he said, "are many swamps, and beyond those are the nations of Palisema and Calpista, both lying along the foot of the mountains."

Hernando de Soto stopped chewing.

Issqui hesitated then continued, "The springs of Calpista flow with the best salt found in Nine-Rivers Valley, and in the hills above Palisema is an abundance of bears, deer, buffalo, and cougar, from which their people make the finest leathers and dyed skins."

Lord de Soto waved his hand, "Tell me more about the

mountains."

Issqui glanced back at his Council of Elders. "We call them the Mountains of the Ozarks," he said. "They rise above Nine-Rivers Valley beyond Palisema, run north to south, and spread to the west. The town of Coligua sits on the White River where it flows out of the mountains down to Palisema and joins the Little Red River."

Lord de Soto reached under his cloak and pulled out a large gold crucifix hanging from a gold chain. "Is there any yellow metal like this in those mountains?" he demanded.

"My Lord," King Issqui said, "Coligua is the largest of the nations in the Ozarks. They are great hunters of buffalo and kind to guests, but I know of no yellow metal."

"My Lord, my Lord," Na-acha shouted as he reached toward the Cross.

De Soto quickly put it away.

Na-acha continued, "I know all who enter my territories on both sides of the Mizzissibizzibbippi River. And I know of traders who have traveled to a land with yellow metal."

Without any expression, de Soto eased back from the table. He said nothing as every other Spaniard twisted, squirmed, and whispered the same word, "*Oro, oro, oro.*"

I understood what Cooquyi had tried to explain. I could see it in their eyes, the power the yellow metal had over them. Issqui settled back as the Spaniards leaned in.

King Na-acha stood. "I know only what I have been told, for I have never seen this land."

The governor eyed his conquistadors as the king's next words were translated.

"I have heard that the land of yellow metal is in a small mountain range, four to five days journey to the north."

"What do they call this land?" de Soto asked quietly.

Na-acha began but paused. His thoughts frozen behind parted lips.

Hernando leaned in toward him and demanded, "Is it called 'Chisca'?"

"Chisca," King Issqui spoke up before Na-acha had a chance to recast his words. "I have heard of that land."

Lord de Soto turned to Issqui.

"Yes," Na-acha shouted to regain the attention, "it is called Chisca."

The Son of the Sun smiled. All the Spaniards smiled; some laughed and patted each other.

"Great Lord," King Na-acha said, "among those captured in your assault on Pa-caha are traders and outsiders. If you permit your loyal servant, I will determine the best of these for your guides to Chisca."

Two Spaniards on different sides of the feasting table stood at the same time. "I, Pedro Moreno, offer my services," began one.

"Hernando de Silvera," the other shouted over him, "I offer all of my abilities and courage to Governor de Soto as to his needs."

"Two trustworthy men from the same town," Governor de Soto said and spread his arms wide. "I accept both of your offers. I order you to gather twenty horsemen of your choosing, fifty foot soldiers, and go with my charge to find the mountains of Chisca."

Almost forgotten, King Issqui stood. "I offer six of my warriors to the service of this expedition. Also, for barter with the people on the way, I give more deerskins and a basket of pearls."

King Na-acha leaned over the table. "I pledge twelve of my best warriors, the finest skins of deer and elk, and more and larger pearls."

Master Diego slapped me on the back and laughed.

"¡Oro . . . Gold!"

Chapter 36: The Right Hand

Taninto's Journey
July 7, 1541

Early the next morning, an expedition assembled on the plaza. I waited next to Cooquyi and Shadow Wind for Master Diego. The six Casqui warriors promised by King Issqui and twelve Pa-cahas stood to either side of the fifty foot soldiers. Two captured salt traders from the north were conscripted to guide the odd party of three nations to a land unseen by my people: Chisca and the mountain of yellow metal.

The first day offered nothing that I had not seen in Pa-caha or Casqui. The allegiance remained strong and in good spirits. The Spaniards joked and laughed. Master Diego was often the loudest.

Three Pa-cahas ran ahead of the party while the rest escorted the two salt trader guides. Horsemen followed, and the soldiers marched behind them in lines by order of weapons. I, like the rest of the tenders and servants, trotted last, except for the six Casqui warriors and two horsemen guarding the rear.

The second day, the land fell barren and the air grew hotter, with hardly a tree in sight. The prairies filled with bluestem grass, taller than a man and so thick the horses began to balk. Some would go no further. The Spaniards ordered the tenders and servants to the front to beat down a trail.

Master Diego walked Shadow Wind on a tight rein most of the day. I learned from the first time I saw him that there is nothing these great beasts fear more than a snake. And I feared for him every time a tail slithered through the grass in front of me.

After a long day, the grasses thinned out. We set up camp for the night as Father Sun cast a golden spell across the jagged horizon of Little Brother Mountain. The Spanish built several fires. The horsemen stared at one. The soldiers complained and argued around the others. A troubled night for many, but I slept hard without alarm.

The next morning, the salt traders led us into another field of bluestems. The foot soldiers grumbled louder with every step. Pedro Moreno galloped to the front.

"*¡Alto! ¡Alto!*" he shouted and raised his sword.

"We have been deceived by these two liars and maybe others," Cooquyi repeated Pedro's words in a whisper.

Pedro pointed at the guides and Pa-caha warriors.

"They led us away from the mountains."

Hernando de Silvera mounted his horse and galloped up to Pedro. "Those are not mountains!" he shouted.

Pedro turned to the soldiers. "Do you trust your own eyes or the word of an Indian?"

"I trust the orders of my commander." Captain de Silvera rose up out of his saddle. "Turn your horse around and follow the guides as ordered."

Pedro shoved his sword into the scabbard and jerked his horse about. The soldiers followed, but their grumbling never

stopped. The grass grew thicker. Even with it stomped down before them, none of the horses would carry a rider.

Fearing for their lives, the salt traders pushed on until they broke onto an open plain of short prairie grasses and scattered trees. A village lay in the distance, on the bank above a stream: the first water seen since leaving Pa-caha territory.

The horsemen, so exhausted moments before, sprang to life. They galloped past everyone and charged toward the hamlet. Foot soldiers trotted after them along with Cooquyi. The sudden attack surprised the villagers. A few tried to escape, but they could not outrun the Spanish horses.

The small tribe called themselves Caluca, simple hunters who grew nothing. They fashioned huts from poles propped up around a circle over which they stretched sewn rush mats. When they had killed or frightened away all the game in the area, they rolled up their mats and dragged the poles to their next camp. They knew nothing of the lands to the north. They had no stores of corn or beans and very little meat. The Spanish took that and six large chunks of crystal rock salt.

After a night of questions and pain for the Caluca people, the Spanish had learned nothing more about Chisca or the yellow metal. Shouting soon surrounded every campfire. The Spanish reacted with anger and out of revenge quicker than any Casqui man. Swords were drawn against threats and cast Spaniard against Spaniard.

By early the next morning, the two salt traders forced to be our guides were dead. They were accused of misleading the Spanish, then tortured and killed. Cooquyi told me he had seen it all but refused to say more. He hardly spoke for several days after that.

We marched the next day to the northeast as the guides had indicated. Again, thick grasses slowed our pace. That night, a hush hung over the camp. In the darkness, secret planning took action and by day's light, Pedro Moreno had assumed command of the expedition.

On his orders, we retracted our path over tromped grasses, then turned west toward Little Brother Mountain. Casqui and Pa-caha warriors tried to speak to Captain Moreno, but he would not listen to "Indians," as he called anyone who was not Spanish. The pace was still slow and the journey hot, but the Spaniards could see a goal.

By the second day, some began to doubt. Captain Moreno sent horsemen ahead. By the time we stopped to set up camp, anyone could see that Little Brother was just a hill, long and narrow, but not a mountain. Only when the returning scouts reported the truth did Moreno accept it.

No secret plans, no complaining that night—merely the somber hush of failure filled the camp. Without quarrel or argument, the expedition turned back to Pa-caha with nothing more than six large chunks of rock salt and a copper breastplate taken from an elder of Caluca.

The closer we came to Pa-caha, the more Cooquyi began to talk. He seemed to enjoy the Spanish disappointment. Back on the plaza among the other horse tenders, Cooquyi gladly told his stories of Spanish foolishness.

As if they had heard his words, Spaniards suddenly appeared. A horseman shouted and pointed. *Halberdiers* with their long double-bladed pikes separated out Cooquyi, the other

tenders who had been on the expedition, and me. They pushed and shoved us to the top of the Temple Mound.

Captains and soldiers gathered around the small plaza next to the Temple of the Dead. They parted as the *halberdiers* pushed us onto the plaza. Lord de Soto sat at the far end. Captain de Silvera stood on his right, and just as proud, Pedro Moreno stood on the other side. Neither of the kings from Casqui nor Pa-caha stood with de Soto.

I searched for Master Diego among the Spaniards. Off to the left were the six Casqui warriors from the journey. King Na-acha was to our right, standing apart from his warriors. Of the twelve he sent with the expedition, the Spanish could find only six.

Lord de Soto stood. As he spoke, I watched Cooquyi's face. Before the translation began, I knew that I did not want to hear it.

"A mission of honorable men with honorable intent has failed. An expedition I commissioned returned with nothing, no report of Chisca or its mountains. As governor of all of these lands, I will know why!"

While the interpreter translated his words, de Soto studied one by one those kneeling before him. Cooquyi stared back. I looked away.

"A mission that must not fail—failed." The governor pointed a finger to either side. "Not because of Captain Silvera or Pedro Moreno." His hands shook in rhythm with his words. "I know the character and commitment of these men."

He turned both fingers toward himself and shouted, "I will know who plotted to deceive them and me, your lord and master!"

"Bring the Indian guides before me."

Guards pushed the Casqui and Pa-caha warriors to the center of the plaza. They all knelt, the Pa-cahas last.

"Stand and confess," Lord de Soto said as he sat down. "Tell me who misled my captains." He waited. None of the warriors moved. He turned to his right. "*Perros, vengan,*" he called.

"Dogs," Cooquyi whispered.

In the shade of the Temple wall, three angry dogs scrambled to their feet: two were black, but the largest was brown with black stripes that seemed painted on. They dashed to Lord de Soto's side as his interpreter shouted, "Who will point the finger of blame?"

Again, no one moved.

The governor swelled as he took in a long breath then pointed at one of the Pa-cahas. "Throw him to the dogs!" he shouted.

They grabbed the kneeling Pa-caha. He shook loose and stood on his own. Someone kicked him in the back.

As he fell, de Soto yelled, "*¡Ataquen!*"

Behind us, they yelled and shouted, "*Ataquen . . . ataquen.*"

The Pa-caha got upon his knees before the largest of the dogs jumped. Knocked back, his legs folded under as he fought off claws and teeth.

Two Pa-caha warriors rushed to help their friend. The guards killed one with a sword through the heart and slashed the other across the chest. Bleeding, he stumbled on with his flint knife raised.

All the dogs looked up. The one over the Pa-caha's bent right leg returned to tearing away the flesh. The largest dog

released a bloody arm and charged the knife.

With his free hand, the Pa-caha reached over the dog on top of him, grabbed his ear, and pulled. The dog rolled off. The warrior stood to his knees again.

The other Pa-caha dropped his knife and fell from a second sword slash across the back of his neck. His eyes fixed and wide, he could no longer fight or move. He could only watch as a black devil crushed his throat. The last three Pa-caha guides turned on their guards. The Spanish could have killed them all, but with malice and skill, they only crippled. The dogs did the killing.

With the dogs distracted, the first Pa-caha crawled to the flint knife. Tucking his mangled legs under him, he rose up ready to fight. He jabbed at the first black dog to charge him. He nicked it across the chest. That brought a yip and the other two dogs.

All three growled and circled the last Pa-caha warrior from the expedition. He could keep two at arm's length but not three. With his face ripped and bloody, he shouted words no one could understand. Then he held the knife to his heart and fell forward.

The dogs pounced in a fury of black, brown, and blood. The Spaniards stomped and cheered. Their roar stole my own screams, vanishing like tears in a raging river. Lord de Soto whistled. The dogs turned and trotted to his side.

He raised his hands, and the gathering grew quiet. "Now," he shouted as slaves dragged the Pa-caha bodies away, "who will speak?"

King Issqui pushed through the swarming Spaniards. "I will speak," he said, making his way to the six kneeling Casqui warriors. "I know nothing of a failed expedition, but I will speak for these brave and honorable men."

He took a position behind the first in line. "Each warrior here would gladly have given his life in battle rather than fail in his duty to so great a lord as you."

"I hear your grand words, but I do not hear an answer." Lord de Soto shouted, "Who is responsible?"

The dogs jumped to their feet.

"My Lord," King Issqui called out, "I do not know nor do these men." He placed his hands on the first man's shoulders as a father might do for his young son. He squeezed and reached to his side.

A Spanish knife gleamed. Casqui blood flowed. Issqui released his grip. The man swayed and grabbed his throat. Issqui stepped behind the second warrior.

"A testament of their loyalty are their lives," he said and slit the next throat.

The truth of their words and deeds belonged to their king. He alone stood in Lord de Soto's glare. "If you doubt these men," Issqui said, "you doubt me, your loyal servant." He stepped to next kneeling man.

"There has been too much death," Lord de Soto said. "Take your men and leave."

King Issqui raised the bloody knife, point down, and slowly turned it in front of his face. "Your gift has served this loyal servant well, but I no longer have a need for such a weapon." He handed the knife to a Spaniard behind him and walked away.

De Soto took a deep breath. "I will have an answer." Clenching his fist, he glared down at the servants and horse tenders. "I will take one hand at a time until someone speaks!"

he shouted.

As the interpreter translated his threat, two Spanish guards jerked Cooquyi to his feet.

"Who is your master?" de Soto demanded.

Cooquyi lifted his head like a proud son. "Master Diego de Guzman."

I searched the crowd again.

One of the Spanish guards called his name. "Diego . . . Diego de Guzman."

No one answered.

The two guards shoved Cooquyi across the plaza. He pushed back. They knocked him to the ground up against an old log that had been rolled onto the small plaza.

A large Spaniard stood on the other side. Unlike most Spaniards, he wore no shirt. Black hair covered his arms and chest as well as his face. Across his shoulder rested a double-bladed axe; the edges sparkled even on that dark day. One guard held Cooquyi down while the other tied his shoulder and left arm to the log.

Lord de Soto stepped off the platform and walked to where he could see Cooquyi's face. "Who among these servants misled my captains?" he asked softly. "Tell me and I will spare your hand."

Cooquyi twitched and twisted his arm. His lips quivered. His teeth clenched, but he said nothing.

The interpreter stepped between the two with his own plea, "Answer your governor and commander. Save your hand!"

Cooquyi's expression grew hard. His chest swelled. His eyes spread wild.

One of the guards grabbed Cooquyi's free right arm and twisted it back and up. Cooquyi bent and bowed his head out of pain, not out of respect. The hairy Spaniard raised his axe.

Lord de Soto strolled back to the platform and returned to his throne. Resting on one elbow, he studied the faces of the remaining servants in the breathless hush.

"¡Entregar!" he yelled.

A powerful swing buried the axe blade deep into the wood between Cooquyi and his left hand. He shuddered. The Spaniard wrestled his axe from the log and swept Cooquyi's lifeless hand aside. It fell to the plaza floor with a hollow thump.

They untied Cooquyi and stood him up. He swayed. One knee buckled, but the determination on his face did not change.

"All that are here know the compassion I have for lost souls," Lord de Soto called to the crowd. "In the eyes of God 'to lie' is among the greatest of sins, and great sins must be punished."

He turned back to Cooquyi. "Forego further punishment. Tell me who among these servants brought failure to my expedition?"

Cooquyi had humbled himself before the Spanish too many times. He had seen too many die, too many tortured, and been taken too far from his homeland. He raised his handless arm, wiped the blood across his chest, then began to dance and chant.

Lord de Soto shouted, "Off with his other hand! Cut off all of their hands!"

Most of the servants around me understood his commands. Some begged for mercy. The Spanish hooted and hollered. Cooquyi continued to dance. And I did nothing.

I did nothing—nothing when they beat him down, nothing when they strapped his other arm to the log. I did nothing but watch the blade crash down. His right hand flopped loose and slid onto the ground next to the left. They dragged Cooquyi out and threw him on the bloody pile of mangled Pa-caha bodies.

Then I stood. I stood and shouted, "He is not dead!"

De Soto pointed, "Take him."

The other servants retreated as the guards came for me. They forced me toward the cutting stump with a tight hold on each arm and a sword at my back. I moved without senses or struggle. A strange calm spread over me. My spirit, like my voice, floated above the commotion.

The guards strapped down my left arm. The axe man stepped in close. My fingers stretched and strained. The Spaniard raised his axe. The fingers closed one at a time and my thumb folded over them.

"*¡Entregar!*" Lord de Soto shouted.

"*¡Alto! ¡Alto!*" someone yelled even louder.

The guards eased their hold on me.

"Master Diego," I called out.

The axe man wavered for a moment. I heard his blade split the air. I jerked back. I saw the ugly Spaniard pull his blade from the log. I heard him grunt. I smelled the blood. But I felt nothing.

When my senses found me, I gasped for breath. He had missed my wrist, but my hand, across the heel to the bottom of the thumb, was gone.

Diego de Guzman pushed his way across the plaza. He untied my arm without looking at me. Still, I could see the pain in his eyes.

Lord de Soto jumped to his feet and demanded, "Follow my orders. Cut off both hands."

Master Diego struggled with the guards as they held down my right arm. The axe man raised his blade. I had no struggle left. Master shoved him aside and put his right hand over mine.

"Take my hand," he shouted, "before you take another from this boy."

The axe man lowered his weapon. De Soto sat down. The two guards loosened their hold and Master Diego helped me to my feet.

"Walk tall, Chipmunk," he whispered.

I stumbled alongside Master Diego to the center of the plaza.

"Governor de Soto," he said, "I am a man of some wealth and great heritage, yet with all that, I have no right to interfere with your given commands. For that trespass, I humbly ask your forgiveness."

De Soto waved Master Diego away with the flick of his hand. "I will hear no more talk of Chisca or failed expeditions," he commanded.

Master pushed me toward the mound steps. I stumbled through the crowd.

Behind me, I heard the Son of the Sun shout. "Men and servants, return to your duty. Remember what you saw here today."

I will always remember. I could never forget that day and the darkness I fell into.

Chapter 37

Manaha's Journey
Ninety-four years after "their" arrival

When Manaha woke, the story-fire had died and Father Sun was well into the morning. *What would Ichisi think of her sleeping so late? The tribe must be far ahead by now.*

She sat up with a grunt. A glimpse of last night's dream came to her. It was Grandfather waving to her with his good hand. A brief warmth filled her chest, then it was gone, and she was alone again.

"No sense in wasting any more time," she told herself and began rolling up the bedding. With her walking stick leading the way and haste in her stride, Manaha left the knoll and the stream behind.

She walked the rest of the morning before coming on the tribe's campsite, abandoned since early dawn. She picked up the pace. The land remained flat and open with few trees for shade. Looking back, she realized that she had been slowly climbing out of a shallow valley up to a low ridge. The distant mountains called to her with a tug she could feel. She listened a moment before she turned away.

From the ridge, a path made by the tribe flowed down the gentle slope. Manaha searched the open forest and meadows in front of her. No one was in sight. Further south across the horizon stretched the rim of Lone Mountain, hazy blue against the bright sky. Unlike the mountains she knew to the north, this one stood alone—untouched by any other mountain. The land of the Tulla was across the Akamsa River among the rolling hills on the far side of Lone Mountain.

Ichisi said there would be two ridges to cross before reaching the river, Manaha thought as she trotted down the first. The heat and distance proved greater than her will. She stopped long before day's end and set up camp in a field of small furrows like she had seen snaking across the land of the Orb Stones.

It was well after dark before Ichisi found her fire. "Greetings, Storyteller," he called out.

She smiled, as she looked up from her carvings on the walking stick.

"The tribe is camped on the bank of the Akamsa River," he announced.

She set her work aside.

"What are you making?" he asked.

She said nothing.

"Akamsa River is much wider than I imagined," he said.

"And the Mizzissibizzibbippi is greater than three such rivers," boasted Manaha, feeling the need.

"Well . . . the canoes that left from our old village were waiting at the river's edge. The tribe will cross tomorrow."

Manaha put away her knife and began gathering the shavings she had carved from the walking stick.

"That next ridge overlooks the river . . . It is not far," he said

while he studied the old woman hunched over her work. "You can camp there until you are ready to cross the river, and I will come back every day."

"Once, you carried wood from the lightning struck tree for my first story-fire," she said as if she had not been listening.

Ichisi lifted his shoulders and rocked his head.

"To every story-fire after that, I have offered three pieces from the center of that tree, with a prayer to the ancestors to guide my path and the stories I tell."

She handed her basket of shavings to Ichisi. "One by one, drop three pieces onto the flames."

After long, silent moments, Manaha said, "I will tell a story."

Chapter 38: My First Sunrise

Nanza's Journey
Forty-nine years after "their" arrival

On my last night in the Ozark Mountains, a half-moon slid with its following of clouds across a sky—black and speckled with countless pricks of light. I found no comfort in my insignificance. My sleeping guide grunted a snore. Even Taninto had been a part of something—had friends, and a family with names. He had a story.

I will find my people. I will know their names, I told myself until dreams overtook hope. In the battle between the two, I rolled from side to side while the heavens faded from black to blue. Exhausted from the struggle to rest, I sat up.

Few stars remained. I could have counted them all, but I wanted to see Nine-Rivers Valley in the day's first light. I stood and pulled my cloak up around me. Neither Little Pup nor my guide stirred. To the west, I could make out a few trees against a forest of shapeless grays. To the east, the horizon glowed.

I turned toward the coming light. Little Pup stretched front legs out and tail up. The old man breathed softly, the weight of time gone from his face.

"Come on," I whispered. She stretched again, back to front. Then with the suddenness of an attack, the lazy puppy jumped

to one side, twisted in the dirt, and bolted after me. She jumped and bounced off my leg. I pushed back, too late. Snorting and hopping backwards just in front of my next step, she challenged me.

"I am not going to chase you," I said, "not today."

The sky was clear but for a few stubborn clouds just above the horizon, the last blackness in a deepening blue. My thoughts turned to last night's story.

"This is my day," I announced to Little Pup and the world. "I am not going to think about hands, dogs, the axe man, or gold."

Little Pup and I hurried across the field to where I had stood the night before. Among patches of briars lay two large boulders. Side by side, they seemed as out of place as the Orb Stones I had seen in the fields above Two-Falls-One. Neither of these boulders was at all round. One of them leaned forward as if ready to tumble down at any moment. The other one nested firmly into the hillside.

Little Pup ran off to explore a rustle in the briars. I climbed atop the leaning boulder and hung my legs over the side. Nine-Rivers Valley, the land of my future, the homeland of my ancestors, lay below, a mystery—still dark. As I waited for Father Sun, I remembered a morning prayer that Grandfather had taught me.

"Great Spirit, Father of all that I have received.
Creator of all that is known and all that is unknown
grant me this day and time to understand your greatness
to walk in harmony with all your creation."

Birds began to chatter. Soon there were so many songs, I could not tell one from another. A gray fog crept in from behind and spread down the hill. An owl gave her last hoot of the night. Little Pup yelped and came running. She leaped onto the boulder and lay next to me. I watched her paw at her nose and whimper.

"Did you stick your nose in the briars where it did not belong?" I asked and rubbed her head. In the moments Little Pup had my attention, a sliver of burning red appeared above the distant flat horizon.

Father Sun's first rays broke through and flew over Nine-Rivers Valley to paint the mountainside about me with golden light. Suddenly everything vibrated with life. Even the brown winter grasses waved their bent stems with pride. The trunks of trees stood apart from their leaves and leaves from their branches. Each color vibrated with separation. Morning dew twinkled on the new leaves as they swayed in the gentle breeze rolling up from the lowlands.

"This day is mine!" I shouted into the sweet, moist air. I had dreamed of this, and now the time had come. "What will I find?" I lifted Little Pup's head and turned her curious face toward mine.

"What will I say?" I asked. "Will my people accept me?"

I looked into her eyes and shook my head. "You do not know, do you?"

"He would know," I mumbled.

Little Pup stood and turned around, tail wagging. I pulled her to me. Taninto was behind us. I hoped he had not heard my doubts.

The last two clouds in the sky burned purple as the red disk took full form. Once again, I looked down on Father Sun as I had done at the start of our journey. Not a setting sun this time, but a rising sun marking the coming of my day.

The life-giving light rolled slowly down the hillside, and into the valley as lazy whiffs of fog drifted up. Father Sun changed from red to bright yellow as I strained to see a village, growing fields, or even the smoke from a campfire. The sunlight exposed nothing but forest, green, vast, and unbroken. Soon, all that remained of the morning fog rose in a thin line weaving a path along the edge of the valley and off to the southeast.

"That last bit of fog," Taninto said as he climbed on the other boulder, "drifts up the White River." He motioned with his bad hand.

I turned away. He dropped it and pointed with the other hand.

"There," he said. "This side of the White River is the Little Red River. Just above where the two merge, you will find the villages of Palisema along the banks of the Little Red."

I stood up and declared, "I am ready."

Little Pup leaped off the back of our boulder and ran to the front, but Grandfather did not even move.

"You promised to take me there," I said.

He reached across the gap between the boulders. I stepped back and glared down at him.

"This is your journey," he said. "You must face the sun and travel your own path. It is time for you to leave me and the mountains."

"You promised to take me."

"I can go no further," he said.

"What do you mean?"

"You can find it from here. I will tell you the way."

"What do you mean, you can go no further? Is your strength lacking or is it courage?"

He looked away. I sat back down and stared over the valley.

"Long ago, I vowed never again to enter Nine-Rivers Valley."

"I will not go without you," I said.

"You have to go, and I have to stay in the mountains." He reached across the boulders again. "Nanza . . . my child."

I did not pull away.

He squeezed my hand. "It is my hope," he said, "that you will forgive and forget my lies, but that you will remember the stories. They are the truth, and all that I had to give to you."

"You have to tell me why," I shouted and scooted out of his reach.

We both stared out across the land of our ancestors.

He glanced around. "The morning is glorious and young. I will tell you my reason. I will tell you what happened after I lost my hand."

Chapter 39: All Things Lost

Taninto's Journey
August 5, 1541

Wrapped in a smothering dark dream, I woke to a confusion of murmurs. Sounds tumbling through the blur like a mountain stream, too rapid to grasp. My body ached. I had no memories of where I lay or how I got there.

Afraid to move, I eased one eye open. It was still dark, but I could see that I lay on a pallet. The sounds I heard were two men mumbling in Spanish words a few paces away. The tattered bottoms of their long, brown robes told me they were Spanish priests. I had nothing to fear from these gentle men.

I opened both eyes and raised my head.

In two quick steps, the tallest of the priests stood next to me and stammered, "This is Cleric Francisco Del Pozo from Cordola, and I am Friar Luis de Soto."

"De Soto?" my dry throat crackled.

"Yes, I am a cousin of Governor de Soto."

"Where am I?"

Instead of an answer, he offered me a drink. I rose up and reached for the water bottle. Then it all came back: Lord de Soto, the dogs, the axe man. I fell back and closed my eyes.

I told myself, *just a bad dream*. With eyes still shut, I raised my left hand and wiggled my fingers. I felt them all. "Just a bad dream," I said and opened my eyes.

They were gone. "I feel my fingers!" I yelled at the priest. "How can I feel my fingers? I have no fingers. I have no left hand!"

I held my right hand next to the bandaged stump. "I have only one hand," I mumbled over and over, as I watched my remaining fingers dance. The second finger had a sore on the inside. I turned my hand and saw more: black boils on my arms, on my chest, everywhere I looked.

"Yes, my son," the friar said. "You suffer from smallpox. Your people call it the *Black Sleep*."

I reached to comfort as one hand often does for the other. "What can I do now? I have only one hand."

The priest raised the water bottle to my lips.

I grabbed it and snapped, "I can hold it."

He pulled the water away before I had my fill then placed a soft hand on my forehead. "The fever is gone," he said. "Tomorrow you should be fit enough to walk."

"Walk? Walk to where?"

"Quiguate. I am told that it is the main town in this province." The friar spoke in an unsettling union of Casqui and Pa-caha words. "We are two days south of the last Casqui village," he said.

I cleared my throat. "How did I get here?"

"Slaves of your master have carried you for four days, delirious with fever."

"How is it that you speak my language?"

"I and my five brothers are here to tend to the souls of all men. Learning some of the languages is my contribution in our mission to teach the word of Our Savior, Jesus Christ."

I tried to sit up, but he easily pushed me back down.

"Rest, my son. Diego de Guzman will not be pleased with me if you are not better tomorrow."

"Master Diego?" I pushed up. "Where is Cooquyi?"

Cleric Francisco bowed his head and began to mumble a strange chant.

"Where is he?" I demanded, "I must see him."

"Your friend is dead," Friar de Soto said.

"He is not dead," I told them. "He is not dead!"

"Yes, my son, he has passed. Cleric Francisco and I bandaged Cooquyi's arms and cared for him. But the next day when you were so ill, he walked out into the swamp." The friar placed his hands on my shoulders. "With no will to live or hands for fighting, Cooquyi perished in the murky swamp."

I rolled over and covered my head with my only hand.

Morning light spread across the camp when Friar Luis woke me. "I think it is time that you tried to walk," he said and helped me to my feet.

I felt unsteady, off balance.

Around us, slaves packed away the camp while the Spanish assumed their marching positions. I followed the six priests with my arm flopping, uncertain without a hand to guide its purpose.

Late in the day, I heard Master Diego's laugh. "*Ardilla*," he called out as he rode up on Shadow Wind. He laughed again.

I bowed my head and smiled.

"Why does he call you 'chipmunk'?" Friar Luis asked.

I shrugged my shoulders.

"Bless you, my son." The friar greeted my master as an old friend.

While they talked, he studied me. I stood straight, both arms behind my back. Master Diego galloped off.

The friar turned to me, "Your master says you are to return to your duties tending Shadow Wind as soon as you are stronger."

"Friar Luis, how would the Spanish say, *I am ready?*"

He frowned at me.

"I am ready?" I asked again.

"*Yo estoy listo . . . Yo . . . estoy . . . listo,*" he said.

I mimicked him as best as I could. He listened, repeated and nodded on my third attempt. Without another word for the friar or the other priests who had cared for me, I tucked my bandaged hand under my right arm and ran after the dark-gray horse.

"*Yo estoy listo, Master Diego,*" I called until I caught up with him. He waved me to Shadow Wind's side as he took his place at the front of the expedition. The main town of Quiguate lay in the distance. It had no walls or canal around it, yet appeared much larger than Casqui or even Pa-caha.

The first day the expedition entered his territory, the King of Quiguate sent gifts of smoked meat. Today, no one came out to greet Lord de Soto. He called a halt to the march. We waited while horses danced, riders studied the town, and foot soldiers readied their weapons.

The Spanish priests moved to the front of the army. Most passed by me by with little more than a nod. Friar de Soto stopped.

"Bless you, my son," he said while the other priests arranged themselves behind Lord de Soto's black stallion. "It is important to my brothers that men of God are present at these events of first encounter."

The friar paused to watch a band of horsemen charge toward the town with swords drawn. Then he whispered, "But the governor has yet to ask for counsel."

The disciplined stampede of horses and men disappeared into the thick cluster of lodges and sheds.

"*How can a main town not have walls around it?*" I wondered.

"This may be the largest town we have seen in our two years of travel," the friar said.

A horseman galloped back from Quiguate, shouting as he approached.

Friar Luis translated for me, "It is empty. The people are gone. The Temple Mound, the plaza, all the lodges are empty."

The friar listened as the report continued then said, "The town is divided by a small river. The horsemen spotted women and children on the other side, but they could find no means to cross over."

Lord de Soto dismissed the scout and motioned the expedition forward.

"Why would they run away?" I asked.

"Some nations run from Spanish conquistadors. Some fight to the death, but none have welcomed us like the people of Casqui." Friar Luis de Soto patted my proud shoulders before hurrying off to march with the other priests.

The path into Quiguate was wide and without gates. Large,

round lodges spread out on both sides. Standing poles with carved faces lined the road through the town to the largest plaza I had ever seen. At the far edge, a Temple Mound stretched almost as wide and stood higher than the tallest tree around.

The Little Muddy, the river of my homeland, flowed behind the mound, a little wider but no less muddy. Across the river, smaller lodges in the other half of the town spread up and down the far bank. A bridge over the river had recently been torn down. Two support timbers were all that remained standing on our side.

Lord de Soto charged up the Temple Mound on his black stallion. From the top he could see all of Quiguate both sides of the river and beyond. He raised his sword and stood in his saddle.

Hernando de Soto proclaimed himself Governor of Quiguate and all its territories, using the same words he had shouted from the Temple Mound of Pa-caha. As if they had never heard the speech before, the Spaniards shouted and clanged their weapons.

Master Diego turned Shadow Wind away from the plaza, toward the river, and I followed. His two new horse tenders which he won in a game of chance had already set up camp. Both the new tenders spoke Spanish, but neither understood me nor I them. They knew how to care for Shadow Wind as well as Cooquyi and left little for a one-handed horse tender to do.

The next day, I explored the town. I found Friar Luis and the other friars north of the plaza on a low mound. They worked to rebuild a large clan lodge. A portion of its walls were knocked down by soldiers the day before.

After greetings, Friar Luis asked, "Would you like to help?"

I held out my arm and pointed where my hand had once been.

"We are going to be in Quiguate for a while," he said.

I had heard the same rumors and nodded.

"Could you teach me more of your language?" the friar asked.

I nodded again. The rest of that day and several to follow, we traded work and words: Casqui for Spanish and Spanish for Casqui. Working with the gentle priests gave me the time to learn new and different ways to survive with only one hand.

When they finished work on the lodge, the holy men painted a white cross next to the door. They cleansed the old clan lodge with sacred smoke, blessed it with prayers, and named it, *Iglesia de Santo Francis*, Church of St Francis.

After the ceremony, Friar Rodrigo remarked, "We should have done this for the people of Casqui."

They all agreed.

"A proper church," he said, "should stand where we raised the Cross of Our Lord and Savior."

"True," Friar Luis said. "Of all the nations and people we have encountered, we have found no greater friends or more passionate believers than in Casqui."

A young solider raced up from the river. "Friar Luis," he shouted, "they are burning the town!" Behind him, a spread of dark smoke rose above the trees. The soldier gasped for breath and said, "The governor gave orders to burn the town across the river."

"Why?" Several of the priests asked at once.

"Last night, Governor de Soto spotted a large party of Indians moving in among the lodges on the other side."

Luis looked away. "There were women and children in some of those lodges," he mumbled. "What have they done? What are we to do? "

"We will do as the Scripture teaches." Friar Juan Gallegos raised both hands to the sky. "We will pray to our Heavenly Father for his blessings of mercy on those lost heathens."

"We should do more," Luis grumbled.

Friar Gallegos placed a hand on his shoulder. "Kneel, Friar Luis de Soto. You cannot control the actions of the governor, even though he is your kin, but you can pray for the strength to understand and to obey."

The lodges burned all night. The next day, a party of warriors in bright headdresses and elders in cloaks of fine-colored cloth appeared at the edge of the forest. Governor de Soto ordered their safe passage to the Temple Mound.

When the King of Quiguate arrived, Lord de Soto accepted his gifts then took him prisoner. De Soto's guards quickly surrounded the rest of the party and escorted them away.

The king was kept confined to the top of the Temple Mound while Governor de Soto questioned him about the surrounding territories. The Quiguate people had no gold or silver. To satisfy the ransom payments demanded by the governor, they brought copper plates, vessels, and jewelry along with food and treated skins. The king appeared reverent and obedient, arranging for new and larger offerings every day. Even so, Lord de Soto grew distrustful.

One morning while he walked with Lord de Soto toward the

Council House, the king of Quiguate suddenly turned and ran. He out-paced the guards, jumped into the river, and swam to the other side. The far bank filled with warriors shouting and sending arrows after any Spaniard in range.

By the time the conquistadors crossed the river, the Quiguate warriors had fled. Horsemen and foot soldiers chased them through the forest to the edge of a swamp. The warriors waded in and escaped. None of the horses or any of the soldiers would enter the mucky black water.

That night, Governor de Soto learned that a captain who had once talked of mutiny refused to stand his watch. The whole town heard the governor's call.

"Soldiers and captains! Soldiers and captains!" He shouted until every Spaniard not on duty had gathered in the plaza and looked to him. In the moonless night, de Soto stood on the balcony of the king's lodge with a torch in one hand and his sword in the other.

"What is this that I hear?" he asked. "Do those conspiracies of returning to Spain or proceeding to Mexico still prevail? So that now, on the pretext of being an officer of the Royal Guard, you refuse to take the watch which has fallen to your lot."

He pointed his sword at the crowd below and shouted louder, "What honor do you think they will pay to you when they have learned as much? Be ashamed of yourselves. We all must serve his majesty."

Lord de Soto raised his sword to the sky, "None shall presume to absent himself." He slashed the air and yelled, "I will strike off his head!"

Thrusting the sword forward as if poking someone in the

chest, he proclaimed, "All under my command be not deceived, for as long as I live, no one is to leave this land before we have conquered and settled it or all have died in the attempt."

The next morning, I heard Friar Luis talking to Master Diego. I had learned enough Spanish from the priests to understand most of the words.

"What are you saying?" Master Diego asked. "Is it the soul of a man such as me that causes you such concern?"

I moved in closer.

"No, my friend," the friar said, "your reasons are confused, but your intent is good." He lowered his voice. "It is for the soul and mind of my cousin, our Governor Hernando de Soto that I worry."

Master Diego stepped back and shook his head.

"You know," Luis continued, "that Hernando left behind our greatest friend and ally since we landed in Florida. The gentle people of Casqui welcomed us into their land, freely fed and clothed our battered bodies. They gathered in the thousands to witness the raising of the Cross of Our Lord and Savior. The governor abandoned them without a church to grow their faith or a force to withstand the revenge of Pa-caha."

The holy man leaned in closer. "The governor is battling the devil and losing. The conversion and commitment of the Casqui people are the only acts Hernando and even the rest of us can hold up as Christian. There is no gold, no silver, or riches. There is nothing else which we can carry back to Spain for our own glory and the glorification of Our Lord Jesus Christ."

Diego took another step back. "Too many good men have died for our mission to fail."

"And there have been too many acts committed for which both of us are ashamed. I see it in your eyes. You know, if Hernando loses the battle for his soul and his mind, we will all be damned."

"What has this to do with me, Father?" Diego asked.

"You have in your service one who is loyal to you, yet is a son of Casqui and can carry a message to them of Christian faith."

"I will obtain permission from the governor," he said. "By this act, Hernando de Soto can begin the redemption of his wayward soul."

Later that day, Friar Luis sent for me. He removed a small wooden cross that hung around his neck. "Take this crucifix to your King Issqui," he said, "with a message from Lord de Soto."

He spoke slowly and waited for me to repeat each phase. "Our sincerest prayers and thoughts are with the Nation of Casqui. It is my hope that this message finds you and your people in good and bountiful times. Be diligent in your faith. Pray each day to the cross for guidance and for your needs. Believe and know that the men of Spain are your friends and will return in time."

"Can you remember all of that?" Friar Luis asked.

"It will be as though you spoke it."

"Good, my son," he said. "But know that Governor de Soto is determined to march northwest for the mountains in hopes of finding gold or silver. Tomorrow, preparations will begin. It will be a day or so before we leave Quiguate. You have at most three days to reach Casqui and return. After that, you will have to find us on the trail to Coligua."

With the message in my head and a cross on my chest, I ran. I ran for Casqui. I ran for Saswanna. I ran until balance found my stride. Hand, no hand, my arms swung once again in rhythm.

After sunset, I came upon a burned village at the edge of Quiguate territory. My strength had long ago given way. Determination alone carried me through the darkness to the base of a great hickory tree where I spent the night.

Well after the cool of the morning, I passed the first and second villages in Casqui territory. No one was working in the growing fields. I saw no movement and no reason to stop until I reached my village of Togo.

Its fields were empty too. As I trotted into the stillness, an uneasiness grew. My pace slowed. In the distance, I heard drumming and raced into the village past bare lodges and cold fire pits.

The home of my mother's family for three generations stood lifeless, beckoning to no one. Its door seemed so small and my fears so large. I backed away, then I saw the burial mounds, two of them next to the lodge.

I stumbled over another as I turned toward the slow drumbeat. Quohaka, a village elder—too elder some said—sat at the edge of the plaza, beating the weeping drum.

"Quohaka," I asked, "where are my mother and father?"

Without ever looking up, he struck the drum again.

"Where is my family? Where is everyone?"

He swung, and I grabbed the beater.

"What happened?" I shouted at the madness in his eyes.

"Gone . . . most have gone," he said. "All are gone, except for

the sick. It is for them that I beat the drum." He pulled loose and struck it hard.

"Where did they go?" I grabbed his arm. "Answer me, now."

"Those that could," he said, "left for Casqui."

I released him.

He struck the drum again and began to chant, "Take away the curse, all who are mighty. Take away the curse."

He would probably die where he sat. I turned my back to him and my face toward Casqui, with hope for my family and a painful longing for Saswanna. I ran hard past the next village and down onto the dried shoreline of the Little Muddy River just below Casqui. The river had narrowed since I had walked along its bank with Saswanna.

My heart ached, and questions whirled like the brown muddy water. *Where is my family? Is Saswanna well? What about my brothers? Who is buried next to our lodge?*

Rays of golden light streaked through the tops of the trees on the far bank. I rounded a bend of the barren riverbank. There stood the answer, the hope, rising above all—the Cross of Casqui. I knelt. I had learned the motions. I could even recite the Spanish words.

I prayed as they would and believed all would be well inside the walls of Casqui. The power of the cross would make it so. But I could not remember a time when there were no boats or canoes pulled onto the riverbank below the south gate. When I approached the gate, a guard stepped into the opening and pulled his bowstring taut.

"It is Taninto of Togo, nephew of Tecco Tassetti, Wise-One of Casqui," I called out.

"In honor of your uncle," he said, "you may enter, but you will not find him here."

I stopped. He looked away. I waited.

"Your uncle is dead," he said.

"Uncle Tecco? He is dead?" I stumbled.

The guard grabbed me.

"Do you know my mother and father?" I asked.

He shrugged. I pushed past and ran for my uncle's lodge. I kept hearing myself ask, *Uncle Tecco? He is dead?* I slowed to a walk then stopped all together. "He is dead."

"Saswanna!" I shouted, turned around and ran.

She was working in the garden next to her lodge and looked up as if she sensed my approach. She ran toward me, calling my name, "Taninto, Taninto."

We embraced. I held my left arm behind my back. She hugged me with both of hers and squeezed ever harder. With her face pressed against my chest, she cried. I smiled.

She noticed the gift the friar had placed around my neck. We both turned toward the cross, standing so exalted atop the Temple Mound. For a moment, I experienced the same warmth I had felt the first time Father Sun set behind the Cross of Casqui.

"So much has happened since you left," Saswanna said softly.

"Do you know anything about my family—my mother, father, and my two brothers?"

"No, I know nothing. So many people have died from the Black Sleep. It is terrible. I prayed for your safe return every morning in the manner that the Spaniards taught us, no matter

what my father said." She held my one hand in both of hers.

"And here you are," she said and tugged at my left arm. "What do you have behind your back?"

"Saswanna . . ." I stammered and let her pull it free.

Her face twisted. I stepped back, but she held onto my arm. She lifted my mutilated hand to her perfect face. Gently she pressed it to her cheek. Tears rolled down onto my stub, uniting our spirits. Death and sickness on all sides, we knew nothing but peace in that moment.

Suddenly, Saswanna was ripped from my grasp. Azaha, her father, wrapped her in his arms.

"You Spanish devil," he shouted. "You dare to return after what your masters have done to Casqui?"

"There is no greater friend of Casqui than Lord de Soto," I said and waved the small cross. "The Son of the Sun sent this lowly servant with a gift and a message for King Issqui."

"King Issqui is dead!" Azaha yelled as others began to gather around me.

A woman cried out, "Black Sleep took my sons."

Another screamed, "A Pa-caha war party killed all of my family."

"Look at his back!" someone shouted. "He carries the mark of the Spanish curse, the sickness!"

"Taninto!" Saswanna screamed.

Her father clamped his long, thin hand over her mouth and pulled her back. I lived with that last image of Saswanna for the rest of my life.

Her call was a warning and a good-bye. Naffja grabbed me from behind. My arm without a hand slipped through both of his. I could feel and hear things being thrown at me.

I ran toward the wall and away from the lodges of the Red Fox clan. Both of Saswanna's brothers chased me to the old wart tree that she had shown me summers before. I climbed the tree faster with one hand than I ever had done with two.

Across the limb and over the wall, I dropped to the small elm below. I had done it many times and did not hesitate. The brothers did, and that gave me time to get to the river before they reached the ground.

I raced across the cracked riverbed and waded in. Without looking back, I swam for the other side where the river deepened and pushed up against a wall of crumbling, dried mud. I tried to crawl up the bank but slid down and back into the river.

An arrow splashed into the water somewhere behind me. A growing crowd at the river's edge cheered, but no one came in after me.

"Death to the Spanish!" they shouted.

Grabbing onto a root growing out of the bank, I pulled myself up. Another arrow splashed against the water. I wrapped my arm around the root and reached for the top of the bank.

Almost without a sound, an arrow appeared next to me, sunk to its feathers in the dark brown mud. I lunged up. The necklace snagged on the root. The small wooden cross silently, slowly slid down into the river. I wiggled onto the bank and rolled out of sight.

"Death to the Spanish! Death to the Spanish!" they shouted.

Above all the shouting and whooping, I heard someone calling, "Hear me. Hear me."

I could see him backing up the embankment. The crowd

turned to him. Even at that distance, I recognized Saswanna's father and remember his words.

"The Spanish took our gifts and left us with war and Black Sleep," Azaha shouted at the crowd. "They took our pride, dignity, and honor, and in return, gave us a cross."

He pointed up at it. "It may be holy and honorable to the Spanish, but for the people of Casqui, it is the sign of sickness and deceit."

The crowd chanted, "Death to the Spanish. Death to the Spanish."

"Burn it before it destroys us all!" Azaha shouted back.

With the Spanish Cross flaming like a giant torch behind me, I ran from my homeland, carrying nothing but a curse. My people, save Saswanna, hated me, and all feared my curse. I had nowhere to go but back to the Spanish. I swore then never to return to the land of my ancestors.

Chapter 40:One Circle Ends

Nanza's Journey
Forty-nine years after "their" arrival

The teller became the story. The great chasm between past and present faded. What once *was* now *is*. Manaha is Nanza, and Nanza shouted, "Finish the story! I want to hear it all."

Taninto hung his head and said nothing. I glanced over the lowlands, trying to grasp all that I had heard in his many stories.

"Nanza, the stories I told you were to help you understand Nine-Rivers Valley," he said. "What happened to me between leaving Casqui and finding you as a child is of little importance where you are going."

"Then there is more," I said as I glared across the boulder. "Tell me the rest."

"I returned to the Spanish," he said, closing his lips and puffing his cheeks in and out. "I returned to the service of my master as I had promised."

I studied the gap between our boulders and waited.

"I . . . I followed Master Diego de Guzman through four seasons, traveling from Quiguate north to Coligua, back south through Calpista to Palisema and onto the province of Cayas.

"We crossed Akamsa River into the land of Tulla. There the people tattooed their lips black and spoke a language unknown to any of the interpreters. Both men and women fought the conquistadors with a rage that seemed generations in the making. Using long poles, they stood against the Spanish horsemen, knocking many riders to the ground and killing some of the horses.

"Friar Luis began to avoid me, and Master Diego grew more troubled every day. After the attack on the town of Anilco, where the Spanish massacred every male from young boys to old men, he lost his laugh.

"Not long after, a scouting party captured the daughter of the King of the Chuguate Nation. Master Diego was taken by the beauty of the young woman. Over the next two days, he wagered and lost two of his horses in a Spanish game of cards to win the woman of his desire.

"Diego de Guzman renounced his loyalty to Governor de Soto and his service to the King of Spain. That night, riding Shadow Wind with the king's daughter, he left the people of Spain forever, and I followed."

"Where did you go?" I asked to break the silence.

"We took shelter in Chuguate in the king's own lodge. Lord de Soto sent soldiers, assuming my master had been taken against his will. They brought with them parchment and paint so that if Diego did not return, he could explain his actions and intent in symbols that only the Spanish understood.

"Master Diego took the parchment, then threatened an attack if the Spanish did not leave Chuguate territory. After the expedition marched east toward the Mizzissibizzibbippi River, Master Diego released me from service."

Little Pup wiggled in my lap. Taninto looked at me. Years of pain and loneliness filled his eyes.

"I could not return to Nine-Rivers Valley carrying the Spanish curse," he said, and looked away. "So I climbed into these mountains and wandered the Ozarks without hope or purpose until I found the Hiding Cave. In that dark place, I hid from the world and the ones upon whom I would bring the sickness.

"Seasons passed, and finally, the madness. I crawled out of the cave to live in the valley below, believing I would never talk to another person. Then I found you. It is there that my story ends, and yours begins."

"You never returned to Nine-Rivers Valley?" I asked.

"No!" he said. "From this day on, Nanza, the journey is yours."

"You cannot send me down there alone. How will I find my way?"

"It is not far from here—less than a half day's walk. Straight down the mountain, you will come to a creek. Follow it until you can cross over. On the far side is a road which leads to the villages of Palisema."

"How can you know this?"

"I walked that road all the way from Coligua to Cayas with the Spanish."

"Did they harm my people, the people of Palisema?"

"I remember your proud people well. They were known to be generous and good hunters. Wearing garments of cougar skins, they built lodges using buffalo and bear hides and covered the floors with deerskins. They welcomed Lord de Soto with many gifts. The Spanish took the salt, hides, corn, and more

than offered, but left in peace."

"Will Palisema welcome me?"

"Nanza, I do not know."

"If all that you have told me is true," I said, "I would be just as wise not to enter Nine-Rivers Valley."

"No!" he said. "The time has come. Find your people or live with an emptiness you can never fill."

He turned. I looked away.

"The past and the future are on the same path," he said, "differing only in which direction you choose."

I had heard enough and jumped off the boulder.

"Here, take your back-bundle," he said as Little Pup dashed to my side.

Down the mountain we bounded, never intending to look back. But I did. He stood on my boulder, waving his good hand. How long would he have stood waiting to wave if I had never turned around?

I ran, leaping with one great stride to the next, almost flying over rocks and bushes. I felt more alive than all the trees glistening in their new leaves, more than all the birds in their branches. The bright sun lit a day well made.

It did not take long to reach the valley floor. Its soil felt moist and soft. The breeze was gentle and rich with the smell of everything that bloomed. The trees grew to great heights and stood far apart. Little Pup quickly found the creek. A road lay along the other side, not as well traveled as I had hoped, but flat and wide.

As I stepped onto the road, I thought, *I know no faces other than his and mine. Will the people of Palisema look like me?* I looked down at Little Pup in wonder, "I have seen fawns, cubs, and puppies, but I have never seen a baby or even a girl my own age."

I rubbed my face. Would they have scars? Would it matter to the faces I had never seen? Women and men, young and old, boys and girls—would they smile at me like Grandfather did when I was young, before he told that first story?

My stride shortened as the road turned alongside the Little Red River. It appeared as he had described it, a deep channel with steep banks of sandy, red soil. Not much wider than the Buffalo River, but its slow waters suggested it was much deeper.

"On the banks of the Little Red River," I had heard him say so many times.

"It cannot be far now," I told Little Pup. I wanted to run. Run the other way, but I stepped forward, caution without haste. I saw a lodge with plastered walls then another and even more.

I began a shout "Pali . . . sema" that ended in a whimper. A dark silence swallowed my voice. No one called back or rushed out to greet me. Little Pup tucked her tail and retreated.

I summoned my courage. "Is this Palisema?" I yelled.

As I got closer, I could see some of the lodges had burned. Most of them still stood, but all had been abandoned. Little Pup remained behind. I made my way past the empty lodges to the center of the village. The large plaza would hold more people than I could imagine. Where were they?

I knew I had found Palisema, not because of the remnants of skins on the walls or because it stood where he said it would be. I knew in my heart. I knew they had gone, left without me.

I sat down in the center of the abandoned village. I tried to

imagine it full of my people with children running and shouting, with young women my age gathering at the river's edge. One of the grander lodges could have been my grandmother's. My childhood hopes withered in the bleak surroundings.

Little Pup eased across the plaza and slid her nose under my arm.

"Come on, puppy, there is nothing here for us. This may be Palisema, but it is not my home."

As we walked away, I kicked the wall of one of the empty lodges. Several rotten posts snapped. I grabbed one, yanked it down, pulling away part of the roof. I attacked the lodge, tearing at the walls, smashing benches until the whole thing collapsed. Hunched over the post still in my hand, I gasped for breath while Little Pup waited at a distance.

I walked away from my dreams with my heart heavy. Why had he brought me this far? Did he know that they would be gone? There is no one left, no one but the old man.

Once we crossed the creek, Little Pup led the way up the mountain. I paid little attention to the world around me or to her when she ran out of sight. When I saw her next, she lay at Taninto's side. He sat where I had seen him last, on my boulder.

As he stroked Little Pup, I saw the gentleness in his spirit, the sadness and concern in his eyes. I knew then, no matter how far I searched. I could find no greater love. Here was my family.

"They are all gone," I said. "Everyone is gone, many seasons ago."

"As I feared," he mumbled.

"No, listen to me, there is no one down there to fear anymore. No one to hope for."

He hung his head.

"You said my time has come." I reached up and touched his handless stub. "This is my journey, you told me. Climb down off that boulder. I am the guide, now."

He looked puzzled. I stepped back.

"Do not dawdle," I said. "I know a place on the Little Red River where we can camp."

He smiled like I had not seen since we left our home.

"Come, Grandfather, walk beside me."

Chapter 41: One Circle Begins

Ichisi's Journey
Forgotten generations after "their" departure

The fire died long before the story ended. What was Nanza slumped into Manaha, battered and aged. The sky glowed from pale to dark in the west where a few stars still twinkled.

I stood, "You only need to follow our trail to the last ridge before the river. You can rest there until you are ready to cross over."

Manaha said nothing.

Squatting so I could see her eyes, I said, "No matter what happens, I will return tonight."

"Ichisi," she said, "take this," thrusting her walking stick at me.

I stepped back. "I must return to camp before I am missed."

"It is for you," she said.

"I cannot take your walking stick." I turned to leave as she used it to stand.

"Ichisi, this is more than a splinter from the lightning tree."

I walked around to the other side of the fire, stirring the ashes in search of a flame.

"No," she mumbled, "it is too hot. Let it go."

She eased back onto her bedding. "If you will not take the

stick," she said, "you must promise to tell me a story when you return." She closed her eyes.

I promised and slipped into the mist of a beginning day. A day filled with new experiences, places, and people. I witnessed every detail: joy to sorrow, hope to despair. I committed to memory every word I heard from the quiet whispers of fear to the grand speeches of pride. All in all, and part, it made for another story of my people that should not be lost.

I rehearsed the story as I ran to the top of the ridge where I hoped to find Manaha's camp. I saw her resting against the trunk of a great oak, so old it had lost most of its limbs and some of its bark. From where she sat, she could see the mountains she loved to the north and the Lone Mountain that took her tribe to the south.

She held the stick across her knees in the hand that had once been lifeless. I called to her, "Manaha." At the same moment, I knew she would not answer.

I sat down next to my friend and took the gift she offered. I rubbed the smooth sides of the white arrowhead lashed to the top and caressed the delicate carvings. Each different with no pattern, then I made out a turtle and next to it a bird and on around a dog, a child.

I understood then. The stout wood from the heart of the lightning tree had become more than a walking stick.

"It is a story-stick," I said quietly.

She had carved symbols for each story she had told and ones she could not. Here was Manaha's life, Taninto's life, and so the lives of their people. All to be forgotten but for the stick I held in my hand and the stories I carried in my heart.

And here lay my life, to walk a path that would keep the stick safe, its stories sharp and deep in my heart until they could be told once again. I stood and called to the spirits.

"Know that a good and wise woman passes your way.
Greet her with kindness and honor.
Know that she is Manaha, the storyteller."

Then I lifted my head and proudly chanted.

"For I am her listener.
For I am her listener.
For I am her listener, Ichisi the Storykeeper."

The De Soto Map, as it is often called, is located in the "General Archive of the Indies" in Seville, Spain, originally found among the papers of the Spanish Royal Cartographer, Alonso de Santa Cruz. It is the earliest known map (ca. 1544) to illustrate the Interior of North America, based on or drawn by a member of the Hernando de Soto expedition.

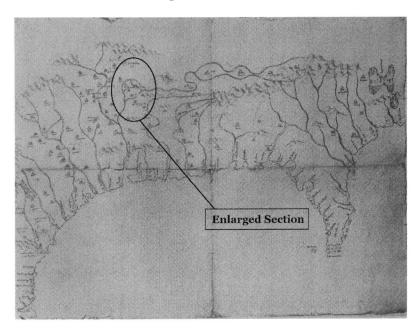

The enlargement show the town of Casqui described in three different journals from the de Soto expedition. It had an estimated population in the thousands in 1541, the year it was discovered by the Spanish. The generally accepted location for the capital city of the lost nation of Casqui is along the east bank of the St. Francis River near the present-day town of Parkin, Arkansas.

To learn more about the De Soto expedition and the town of Casqui, visit the mounds and museum located at the Parkin Archeological State Park, 60 Highway 184 Parkin, Arkansas, online at www.arkansasstateparks.com/parkinarcheological/ or visit www.DanielASmith.org.

References

Bierer, Bert W.
   1977 *Indians and Artifacts in the Southeast*, Bierer Publishing Company. Columbia, SC.

Brown, Joseph Epes, Recorder and Editor
   1953 *The Sacred Pipe*. University of Oklahoma Press. Norman,OK.

Catlin, George
>1844 *North American Indians*, Volume II. David Bogue. London, England.

Clayton, Lawrence A., Vernon James Knight Jr., and Edward C. Moore, Editors
>1993 *The De Soto Chronicles The Expedition of Hernando de Soto to North America in 1539-1543* Volumes I and II. University of Alabama Press. Tuscaloosa, AL, and London England.

Covey, Cylcone Translator and Editor
>1986 *Cabeza de Vaca's Adventure in the Unknown Interior of America.* University of New Mexico, NM.

Crosby, Alfred W.
>1973 *The Columbia Exchange: Biological and Cultural Consequences 1492.* Greenwood Press. Westport, CT.

Eastman, Charles A.
>1971 *Indian Boyhood.* Dover Publications, Inc. New York, NY.

Davis, Hester A., Editor
>1991 *Arkansas Before the Americans*, Contributions by Morris S. Arnold, Samuel D. Dickinson, Patricia Galloway, Michael P. Hoffman, John H. House, Dan F. Morse, and George Sabo III. Arkansas Archeological Survey. Fayetteville, AR.

Fundaburk, Emma Lila, Editor
1958 *Southeastern Indians Life Portraits*. American Bicentennial Museum. Fairhope, AL.

Fundaburk, Emma Lila and Mary Foreman, Editors
1955 *Sun Circles and Human Hands*. American Bicentennial Museum. Fairhope, AL.

Green, Rayna
1992 *Women in American Indian Society*. Chelsea House Publishers. New York, NY.

Harrington, Donald
1986 *Let Us Build Us a City*. Harcourt Brace & Company. Orlando, FL.

Hudson, Charles
1997 *Knights of Spain, Warriors of the Sun*. The University of Georgia Press. Athens, GA.
1997 *The Southeastern Indians*. The University of Tennessee Press. Knoxville, TN.

Lumb, Lisa Cutts and Charles H. Mc Nutt
1988 *Chucalissa: Excavatio in Units 2 and 6, 1957-67* Memphis State University Anthropological Research Center. Memphis, TN.

Mainfort, Robert C., Jr. and Marvin D. Jeter
1999 *Arkansas Archaeology*. University of Arkansas. Fayetteville, AR.

Milanich, Jerald T. and Susan Milbrath

    1898 *First Encounters: Spanish Exploration in the Caribbean and the United States, 1492-1570.* Florida Museum of Natral History and University of Florida Press. Gainesville, FL.

Montgomery, David

    2000 *Native American Craft & Skills.* The Lyons Press. New York, NY.

Neihardt, John G., Recorder

    1932 *Black Elk Speaks, Being the Life Story of a Holy Man of the Ogalala Sioux.* MJF Books. New York.

Palmer, Edward. Edited by Marvin D. Jeter.

    1990 *Arkansaw Mounds.* The University of Arkansas Press. Fayetteville, AR.

Rolingson, Martha Ann, Editor

    1981 *Emerging Patters of Plum Bayou Culture.* Arkansas Archeological Survey. Fayetteville, AR.

Schambach, Frank and Leslie Newell

    1990 *Crossroads of the Past: 12,000 Years of Indian Life in Arkansas.* Arkansas Humanities Council. Little Rock, AR.

Sabo, George III

1992 *Paths of Our Children.* Arkansas Archeological
Survey. Fayetteville, AR.

Shaffer, Lynda Norene

1992 *Native Americas Before 1492.* M.E. Sharpe.
Armonk, N Y, London, England.

Sherrod, Clay P. and Martha Ann Rolingson

1987 *Surveyors of the Ancient Mississippi Valley.*
Arkansas Archeological Survey Research.
Fayetteville, AR.

Swanton, John R.

1929 *Myths and Tales of the Southeastern Indians.*
Bureau of American Ethnology/Smithsonian
Institution Washington, D.C.

1942 *Source Material on the History and Ethnology
of the Caddo Indians.* University of Oklahoma Press.
Norman, OK.

Terrell, John Upton

1994 *American Indian Almanac.* Barnes and Noble
Books. New York, NY.

Thornton, Russell

1987 *American Indian Holocaust and Survival, A
Population History Since 1492.* University of
Oklahoma Press. Norman, OK.

332

Whayne, Jeannie, Compiler

    1995 *Cultural Encounters in the Early South, Indians and Europeans in Arkansas.* The University of Arkansas Press. Fayetteville, AR.

Wright, J. Leitch, Jr.

    1990 *Creeks and Seminoles.* University of Nebraska Press. Lincoln, NE.

The
Great Turtle
and the
White Bird

A Short Story by
Daniel A. Smith

The
Great Turtle
and the
White Bird

A Short Tale

By

Daniel A. Smith

~~~

The Great Turtle and the White Bird is a short story
written while researching and drafting the historical novel
Storykeeper.

Once long ago, there was a great flood, and all the land was covered. The only survivors were ones who could swim the endless waters or fly above them. Those who had walked upon the land were no more.

The creatures of the water were pleased that the flood had come, all except for the Great Turtle.

"I am tired of swimming all day and night," he said. "I wish for a small piece of earth where I could rest if only for a short while.

"When my children come to me and ask, 'Where can we rest?' What will I say? The lands are gone and so are the ones who once walked upon them."

Once in the ancient times before the flood, all the creatures of the world lived in harmony. The Great Turtle missed the oneness that all had shared. "What will happen to my children's children?" he asked.

A white bird flying high above the water heard the cries. She flew down closer to hear the Great Turtle's words.

"There is no place to rest or lay the eggs of my children's children," he shouted.

"Oh, Great Turtle," the White Bird called down. "I have heard your words, and know them, well. I am also tired, tired from flying all day and night. I wish for a land where plants and trees grow. In all the endless skies above or in the endless waters below, I have found no place to build a nest and raise my

young."

This made the Great Turtle even sadder, "We must do something for the children." He asked those around him. "Who will help?"

The creatures of the water all swam away saying, "We have no use for any land in our boundless seas."

Only the White Bird offered to help. "What can I do?"

The Great Turtle thought a moment and then said, "I will swim to where the water is shallow and stand as tall as I can on my four strong legs. I will stretch until my shell reaches above the water. Then upon my back, my children's children shall come to rest, and upon my back, you may build your nest."

"Oh, Great Turtle, if you can do that, I will do more than build my nest. I will fly as far as I can in all directions and return with every bit of dry earth I find. Together, we will make an island. On that island, the children of your children can gather to raise their children, and at the top, I will build a nest for my young."

The Great Turtle did as he said he would. He stood tall and strong so that others might have what he could never have. The White Bird did as she promised. She flew every direction, but the gathering was slow. As soon as she placed her newest find on the turtle's back, she flew off in search of more, day and night, back and forth. She did not want to disappoint the Great Turtle who was giving so much.

The exhausted bird flew so hard that soon other birds became curious. "Why are you flying so fast and so far?" they asked.

When she explained her mission, each of the winged-ones

asked if they could help. White Bird told them she must first seek permission from the Great Turtle.

"Oh, White Bird, friend of my children's children, tell the other winged-ones to bring what they have." The Great Turtle said without hesitation, "I will give them each a place to rest and raise their young."

The White Bird had already found most of the bits of earth, so the other birds brought grains of sand, shells and bones of sea creatures. The new land grew quickly. Some of these gifts were used in raising the land, and some in building a grand nest. It was large enough for the eggs of all the winged-ones. The land under the nest became a place for the children of the Great Turtle to deposit the eggs of their children.

Many winged-ones were hatched and raised in the grand nest. When they could fly, the young would search for more gifts to place on the Great Turtle's back. They brought seeds, twigs and bark found floating in the endless waters. These were scattered about the island, each becoming a new plant or tree. The island and everything on it grew.

The nest grew so large that some bird's eggs slipped down through it. So many of the Great Turtle's children came to lay their eggs on the land under the nest that some turtle eggs were pushed up into the nest. In this way, the eggs became mixed.

The bird eggs hatched under the nest became not turtles that could swim under the water nor birds that could fly above it. Instead, they hatched out as four-legged creatures who could walk only on the land that the White Bird, and the Great Turtle had created.

The turtle eggs hatched by the birds became neither birds

nor turtles. They hatched as two-legged creatures who could not fly above nor live under the water. These were the ancient people of the Great Turtle Island. They were pleased to live on such a beautiful land.

The people honored and respected their scared gift from the Great Turtle. And as it should be, the two-legged and the four-legged creatures of the Great Turtle Island walked in harmony once again.

Made in the USA
Middletown, DE
02 February 2020